To Theresa, my sister –
in Christ.

Love,
Dini

Though
the Waters
Be Troubled

Guin Calnon

WESTBOW°
PRESS
A DIVISION OF THOMAS NELSON
& ZONDERVAN

WestBow Press books may be ordered through booksellers or by contacting:

WestBow Press
A Division of Thomas Nelson & Zondervan
1663 Liberty Drive
Bloomington, IN 47403
www.westbowpress.com
1 (866) 928-1240

ISBN: 978-1-4908-6829-5 (sc)
ISBN: 978-1-4908-6830-1 (hc)
ISBN: 978-1-4908-6828-8 (e)

Library of Congress Control Number: 2015901852

Print information available on the last page.

WestBow Press rev. date: 3/31/2015

Scripture taken from the King James Version of the Bible.

The Netherlands
Early 1900s

Chapter

⌒〰〰〰〰〰⌒

1

A somber tone from the church belfry rang the hour of one and echoed throughout the town of Kollumdijk. Anneke Haanstra raced through the gateway. *It couldn't be closing time already.* She glanced at the clock in the tower. The black hands stared back at her, confirming her fear.

She tore through the square, dodged a horse-drawn cart, and almost tripped on the cobblestones. Anneke flew by the vacant meat stand and past the old wooden barrels where only the stench of herring remained. On she ran and nearly upset a fruit stand jutting into her path. Rounding a corner, she hurried toward the cheese booth up ahead. There had to be a wedge left for her to buy.

When she drew near, something white whizzed through the air and plunged at her feet. Her shoe landed in raw egg oozing from the broken shell. With a slosh, her foot twisted and slid out from under her. She struggled to regain her balance but fell to the ground, scraping her hand on the rough stones. Blood oozed from the cuts on her hand. She tried to get up, but her ankle gave way, and she slumped back down. Anneke squeezed her eyes shut against the throbbing pain in her ankle and her bleeding palm.

Wooden shoes pounding over the cobblestones forced her eyes open. A dark-haired young man, his black cap leaning to the right, rushed to her side.

"Are you badly hurt?" His accent told her he was from another province.

"I sprained my ankle. And my hand . . ." She turned her right palm face up. "It's bleeding pretty bad." Anneke tried again to stand, winced, and fell back.

"Here, let me help you." He dropped to one knee. The double row of silver buttons on his black shirt glistened in the sun. He drew a large, fresh handkerchief from his pocket, reached for her hand, and wrapped it securely. "There, that should stop the bleeding."

"Thank you so much."

"You're more than welcome. Do you need assistance to stand?"

"Yes, please. I can't put weight on my right foot."

With one hand supporting her back and his other hand gripping her elbow, he helped her to her feet. "Do you have far to go?"

She held her breath at the feel of his arm around her—the arm of a stranger. "Three kilometers." She took a step and tensed with pain, moaning as her leg buckled under her.

Instantly the young man caught her. "That's too far for you to walk." He paused. "I'm Romke Veenhuizen. I'd be glad to take you home in my cart."

Anneke hesitated. She didn't even know him. She looked around for a familiar face, but only a few strangers remained in the square. She was at the mercy of this man—but if she refused, how else would she get home? "You're right. I could never make it."

"It's only a few steps to that tree stump over there." Romke pointed up ahead. "I think you can get there if you hop on your good foot. Lean on my shoulder and hold tight to my arm. I'll walk slowly."

Gritting her teeth, she hopped her way along and sighed with relief when she reached her goal. "I could never have done it without your help." She slipped her hand from his arm and sat down on the stump.

"I'm glad I was here to help you. May I ask your name?"

Her cheeks grew warm. "Anneke Haanstra." A June breeze fluttered her long skirts and played with her cap, loosening wisps of blond, wavy hair. She pushed back the loose strands escaping from her lace cap.

"Wait here, Anneke. I'll bring my horse and cart around."

She watched him leave. His trousers, made of cavalry twill, were suede-like, and his jacket flapped as he hurried along. His clothes differed from those worn by the men of her village, but she had to admit she liked them, especially his cap. The way it perched to one side of his head intrigued her.

Startled by a tap on her arm, she looked up. "Lambertus, you're still here?"

Her ten-year-old cousin stood before her, scuffing his shoe against a broken cobblestone. He hung his head, stealing glances at her from half-shut eyelids. "I'm sorry I made you fall. I wanted to see how far I could throw an egg. I never saw you coming." He lifted his head and pushed his glasses up on his nose. "Please don't tell my moeder." He wrinkled his forehead, and the freckles scattered across it grew larger.

She should have guessed Lambertus had thrown the egg. "Don't worry, I won't give your secret away." Anneke watched his forehead relax. "Would you like a ride home?"

"No, thanks." He pushed his glasses up once more and ran toward the town gates, then stopped and called over his shoulder. "Remember your promise."

Anneke nodded, then sighed. She had almost made it to the cheese stand. Now, because of Lambertus, her family would have to get along without cheese for a whole week. If only she had left for market earlier.

Her thoughts faded when Romke brought his cart to a stop alongside the stump. A large cheese lay on his lap, cartwheel-shaped like those of her village, but deep gold instead of cream-colored. He stepped from the wagon and retrieved a wicker basket from the tall grass. "Could this be yours?"

"Oh, you found it. *Dank u!*"

Romke placed it in her hand. "You can't go home with it empty." He sliced off a generous piece of cheese and handed it to her. "Here, take this with you. It's farmer's cheese from Lijdendorp."

"Lijdendorp?"

"It's a village in the province of Overijssel."

So that's where he was from, but what a strange name for a village. A chill shot through her heart. She unclasped her purse secured around her sash and pulled out a guilder.

"*Dank U well.*" She held out the coin.

"No, don't pay me."

"Oh, but I must."

"No, the cheese is yours."

"Are you sure?"

"More than sure."

She broke into a smile. "Thank you. I can't wait to try it."

He took her arm and helped her into the cart, then stepped around and climbed up beside her. As they jostled along, a lilting waltz from a street organ floated through the air. The tune lingered in her mind while they rode through the countryside. She turned and studied his face. The sun had blessed his skin with a golden tone, his nose was prominent but finely chiseled, and the warmth in his dark eyes touched her heart. Yet she sensed sorrow in them. *Sorrow.*

Icy tingles ran up her spine. *Lijdendorp—where he was from. The very name meant "Village of Sorrows."*

She pushed the troubling thought from her mind and shifted her focus to the cheese in the basket at her feet. *She wouldn't have to go home empty-handed after all. But what would her parents say if they saw her riding home in a stranger's cart?* Anneke glanced up at him.

He turned to her. "Are you feeling any better?"

"Yes, much. I really appreciate your help."

"I wouldn't dream of leaving you stranded in a pool of raw egg." He winked at her.

She laughed. "I found the culprit. It was none other than my cousin Lambertus. He came over and apologized while you were bringing the cart around."

"Boys can be quite a trial, sometimes."

"My cousin's a constant trial, especially to my younger sister."

Romke chuckled, then fixed his gaze on the road and grew silent.

Anneke hardly noticed the winding road edged with poplars or the homes they passed. They rounded a bend, and the family windmill waved to them in greeting. Anneke reached for the basket and placed it in her lap. "We're in Zevendorp now. That's my house on the right." Here and there the sun glistened on its white exterior, while sycamore maples, red oaks, and sweet cherry trees shaded other portions of the house. Flowers danced along the pathway that led to the door, sending a message of warmth and welcome.

Romke turned up the lane to her house, jumped from the wagon, and tethered his horse to the apple tree. Supporting her arm, he helped her down and waited while she took a tentative step.

"I think I can walk now. My ankle feels a little better."

"I'm glad, but this time I'm not taking any chances." With her arm through his, he walked her to the house.

Anneke opened the door. Her mother sat at the kitchen table shelling peas. "*Moeder,* I have a surprise for you. A new kind of cheese."

While Anneke introduced Romke and told her mother what had happened in the marketplace, Kea, her ten-year-old sister, peered into the kitchen. She stared at Romke, a scowl darkening her face, turned and slipped away.

Moeder dropped several shelled peas into a bowl and extended her hand. "Welcome to our home, Romke. Thank you for helping our daughter."

He shook her hand. "Thank you, *mevrouw.* I'm glad I could be of help to her."

A curious smile played on her mother's lips when she noticed the cheese Anneke held. "Where did you find that?"

"In the marketplace. Romke sells it." Anneke laid it on the table. "Can we try a piece now?"

"Yes, let's." Moeder took a knife from the table and cut off a small wedge for both of them.

Anneke took a bite. "Mmm, delicious."

"This really is good cheese," said Moeder, her eyes sparkling.

Something rustled in the doorway, and everyone turned to look.

"Come try some new cheese, Kea," said Moeder. She cut off a piece for Anneke's sister.

Kea glared at Romke, shook her head, and again disappeared from the room.

Moeder dropped the cheese into her own mouth. "Can you stay long enough to join us for dinner, Romke?" she asked a moment later.

"Thank you, mevrouw, but I need to be heading home." He walked toward the door, opened it, and caught his breath. "My horse . . . he's gone!"

"What?" Anneke looked out. The horse and cart were nowhere in sight. "How could he have gotten loose?"

Romke shook his head and shrugged. "I have no idea, but he can't be too far away." He stepped out into the midday sun.

Shading her eyes, Anneke followed. "I don't see your horse anywhere, but I'm sure we'll find him."

"Wait." Romke cupped a hand to his ear, listening. "I think I hear the cart rumbling." He darted across the field.

Her ankle throbbing, Anneke struggled to keep up. She blinked. Had someone slipped behind the barn? Romke must have seen it, too. He hurried in hot pursuit, but the pain in her ankle slowed her down. Romke approached the barn from the left. She would go to the right, so they could corner the person. Limping, Anneke finally reached the tall mass of bushes beyond the barn, but no one was there.

Something moved in the thicket. She stepped up closer and peered through the shrubbery, when a sudden impact knocked her off her feet. Her head swirling, she looked up into Romke's face, only inches away from hers.

"Oh, Anneke, I'm so sorry. I didn't even see you there."

"Don't worry, I'll be fine." She leaned toward him and whispered. "Someone's in the bushes."

"I saw it, too." He stood and brushed off his clothes. "Wait here. I'll take a look." He reached into the foliage. "Aha, and who could this be?" From the cluster of bushes, he brought out Kea.

Kea wriggled to free herself. "Let go of me, or I'll tell Moeder."

Anneke scowled at her. "Why were you hiding?"

Her sister turned away, ignoring the question.

Romke placed a hand on Kea's shoulder. "Do you know anything about the disappearance of a horse and cart?"

"If I did, I wouldn't tell you!"

Anneke's mouth dropped open. "Kea, that's no way to talk to a friend. Tell us the truth, or I'll tell Moeder."

With a stubborn shake of her head, Kea worked her arm free and tore across the fields.

Romke stepped over to Anneke. "I'm not sure what to do. You shouldn't be walking anymore with your bad ankle. Why don't you wait here while I see if I can find my horse?"

Before she could answer, hooves clopping on the dirt path caught her attention. Her father drove up in Romke's cart and pulled on the reins.

"*Vader,* where did you find him?"

"Trotting across the field, headed straight toward the flax. Do you know who he belongs to?"

"Yes, *meneer,* he's mine." With a smile, Romke extended his hand to Anneke's father and introduced himself. "I'll have to teach that horse a thing or two. He has a real mind of his own."

Vader's eyes twinkled. "Pleased to meet you, Romke. What brings you here?"

"Anneke fell in the marketplace and sprained her ankle. I brought her home." He hesitated; "And now that I have my horse again, I need to be heading off."

Vader stepped down from the cart. "Thank you for your help, Romke. You'll take Anneke back to the house now?"

"Yes, meneer."

"If I can ever be of assistance to you in any way, Romke, please let me know." With a parting handshake, Vader left for the fields.

Romke turned to Anneke. "It's time to get you back to the house." He drew her to her feet and helped her into the cart.

Tucking another stray lock of hair under her cap, Anneke looked up at him. "Thank you so much for the cheese and for bringing me home. I feel bad, though, for the trouble you went through to find your horse and cart."

"It was nothing."

"Do you suppose Kea loosed them?"

Romke grinned. "It's likely. Kids will be kids, you know. But the real trouble I had was running into some rocks near shore this morning and damaging the hull of my boat."

Anneke looked at him, perplexed. "Boat? But you came by horse and cart."

7

Romke chuckled. "I actually came by both. With my horse and cart on deck, I sailed down the Zuider Zee from my home to the seaport of Kollumdijk and left my boat there to be repaired. Then I came by horse and cart to the marketplace. I hope they can have my boat repaired by the time I return this afternoon, but it's not likely they'll have it done that fast. It'll be a much longer trip home, by horse and cart."

Anneke sighed. "I'm so sorry that happened."

"I'll take extra precaution, next time."

When they reached the house, he stepped from the cart, took Anneke's arm, and helped her down. "I hate going off and leaving you like this. Are you sure you'll be all right?"

"I'm positive. Thank you for your concern." Her ankle throbbed, but she determined not to let him know how bad it hurt.

Romke climbed back in the cart and took the reins. He sat holding them, looking down at her. His eyes held hers with a tenderness that struck a new chord in her heart, a chord she'd never heard before but one that stirred her very soul.

"Goodbye, Anneke." He lingered a moment longer, keeping his gaze on her.

Heat rushed up her neck and over her face. "Thank you, Romke. Thanks for everything."

"It was my pleasure." He paused. "By the way, the handkerchief is yours to keep. I want you to have it."

She looked at her hand—almost hidden in his large handkerchief, and remembered how tenderly he had wrapped her bleeding palm—as though he really cared. She brought her bandaged hand to her lips and gently kissed the handkerchief. She would keep it forever. She looked up at him.

A big grin had spread across his face. He started down the path, looked back at her and waved. "Promise me, you'll take good care of your hand and ankle?"

"I promise." Anneke watched until he disappeared from sight. She leaned against the door and thought back over the day's happenings: Romke's gentleness and concern for her, his tender smile, how when he fixed his gaze on her she couldn't pull her eyes away. Nor had she wanted to. She brought her bandaged hand to her lips again and held it there. Yes, she would keep his handkerchief forever, no matter how badly it was stained.

If only she could see him again. But why had he come to their harbor town? He didn't even live in their province. Would he be back next market day? Did he hope to see her again, too?

Chapter

2

Her mind on Romke, Anneke opened the door and stepped inside. Without thinking, she put her weight on her injured foot and let out a cry.

Moeder dumped the last of the peas into the bowl and ran to steady her. "No more walking by yourself until your ankle is healed." She guided Anneke to the sitting room and eased her into a stuffed chair, then grabbed the footstool and propped up Anneke's foot on several cushions. "Just rest, dear. Dinner's almost ready. I'll bring in your food, and you can eat it here. If you need anything, just call me."

Moeder frowned as she checked Anneke's ankle. "It's swelling quite a bit. We've got to get ice on it and wrap it securely. I'll be right back with a towel and stocking."

Anneke settled into the cozy chair. She shut her eyes and drifted off to sleep.

"What's wrong with you?"

Anneke woke with a start.

Kea stood in the doorway, staring at her. "Ohhh, look at your ankle—it's all purple and puffed up! What happened?"

"I fell in the marketplace."

"How?"

After Anneke relayed the incident to her sister, Kea threw her hands on her hips. "Well, I'm sure it was no accident. I know Lambertus all too well. He did it deliberately. He's nothing but a troublemaker."

Moeder returned and gripped Kea's shoulder. "We'll not accuse anyone without knowing what actually happened. Right now, I need you to go to the cellar and bring back some ice for Anneke's ankle. Take the pail with you."

Kea continued to stare at her sister's foot.

Moeder sighed. "Go now. We need to apply it before it swells any more."

Kea sauntered out to the kitchen. The clank of the pail hitting the doorknob and the sound of the door closing with a bang brought relief to Moeder's face. "I hope she hurries. I probably should have gotten it myself."

Sooner than Anneke expected, Kea returned with a full pail. Her eyes softened when she saw Anneke's ankle again.

Moeder stuffed the stocking full of ice, wrapped it around the swollen ankle, and secured it with the towel.

"Ohhh, thank you." Anneke sighed. " That feels so good."

Moeder gently hugged Anneke and returned to the kitchen.

Kea moved closer and laid her head against Anneke's shoulder. "I'm sorry you fell. I hope your ankle heals soon."

Anneke put her arm around her sister and drew her closer. "Thank you. I'm sure it will."

Kea stood up. "Whenever you need me to fill the pail again, just let me know."

Left to herself, Anneke leaned back in the chair and closed her eyes. How dear her family was to her. Soon her thoughts turned back to Romke. Already she missed him. Would her ankle be strong enough to walk to market next Thursday? If not, how could she wait two long weeks before seeing him again? Yet, he may not even come back. She had almost drifted off to sleep once more, when Moeder arrived with her dinner.

"Go ahead and start eating, dear, while I tend to your ankle."

The hours dragged for Anneke. By evening, boredom and restlessness plagued her. She longed to get up from the chair and walk around the house, but she knew that would only make her ankle worse. Patience— she had to learn patience. How could she take her mind off her situation? Then she remembered the books that filled the shelves in her bedroom.

Never had there been a better time to read than now. She'd ask the first person who came in the room to bring her some books.

It wasn't long before Kea came back with another full pail of ice. "How does your ankle feel?"

"I try not to think about it. What I need is something to take my mind off the pain. Would you bring me some books to read? I haven't read the ones on my top shelf yet."

Kea plopped the pail down and stamped her foot. "Oh, so now I'm your slave. Why, of course, Queen Anneke. What else can your humble servant do for you?"

Moeder appeared in the doorway. "We'll have none of that kind of talk, young lady. It was a reasonable request. If you were the one with the sprained ankle, you know as well as I do, that your sister would do everything she could to help you."

Kea hung her head and slunk from the room. An hour passed before she returned—empty-handed.

Anneke stared at her. "Didn't you bring me any books?"

"You have too many. I didn't know which ones you'd want."

"I told you which ones I hadn't read yet. Remember?"

"I couldn't reach that high. What'd you expect me to do, climb up all seven shelves to get them?"

"There's a step-ladder right by the bookcase."

"Well, I didn't see it."

"Never mind, then." Anneke tried not to let her frustration show. But it hurt that her sister didn't care enough to bring her a few books.

Kea left the room without apology.

A tear slid from Anneke's eye. She lowered her head and brushed it away. She might as well try to sleep.

The next morning, she awoke to find a pile of books on the table next to her. So, Kea must have brought them, after all. Now the days would fly by, and she wouldn't even have to feel guilty about not doing her chores. She took the top book off the pile and began to read.

By Monday, she needed a break. Every day lasted an eternity and she still had half a week to go before market day. What was left for her to do?

Embroider! She'd start working on that set of pillowcases she bought last year. Remembering the pretty water lilies printed on the material, she could hardly wait to begin, but that meant asking Kea to get them for her. As if her sister had heard her thoughts, she walked into the sitting room. From the expression on her face, she appeared to be in a better mood. Even so, Anneke weighed her words. "Good morning."

Kea stood silent, waiting.

"Remember that set of pillowcases I bought last year?" Before she could finish, Kea interrupted.

"Oh, you mean you're tired of reading already, after I risked my life getting those books for you? I might have guessed this would happen. Now, I suppose you want me to search your room for pillowcases. Where are they, anyway?"

"They're in my hope chest, lying right on top. You'll find the embroidery floss, scissors, and needles in the top chest drawer in a tin box. Do you mind doing that for me?"

Kea glared at her sister, then bowed low to the floor. "Not at all. I'm here to serve you, Your Majesty. I'll have plenty of time left to do that after I've finished my own chores and Queen Anneke's."

Kea's words stabbed deeply. What was the matter with her sister? Kea had never responded this way to her before. "If it's going to be that much trouble, don't bother. I shouldn't have asked you." Anneke paused for a long, awkward moment. "I'm sorry you have to do my chores besides your own. I promise I'll make it up to you."

Kea left the room without a word.

Anneke picked up her book and tried to read, but she couldn't keep her mind on the story. Kea's hurtful words kept coming back to her. What had she done to her sister to make her so antagonistic? This wasn't like her. Yes, her sister was spunky and opinionated and never hesitated to speak her mind, yet the two of them had always been so close. Now, she acted like a different person. When her sister brings the pillowcases, she would get to the bottom of this—but the pillowcases never came.

Tuesday morning arrived. How could she stand it, sitting in this chair for two more days? She didn't even think she could take it for another minute. She adjusted her position, stretched her arms and wiggled a bit, but that didn't chase away her boredom.

After finishing the breakfast Moeder had brought her, she leaned back in the chair and gazed across the room. Something dangling from the fireplace caught her eye. Colorful threads looped from the mantel and stretched across the stones. More strands draped over tables and lamps, backs and arms of chairs. She stifled a laugh. So, this was Kea's latest attempt to upset her, but she wouldn't give her sister the satisfaction of seeing her frustration. The embroidery floss was here, but how could she reach it? Nor were there any pillowcases in sight.

Footsteps made Anneke turn toward the stairs. Down came Kea, appearing as innocent as an infant. To Anneke's surprise, her sister burst out laughing.

"I couldn't resist it. It was the most fun I've had in a long time. I thought you'd wake up any minute while I was hanging the embroidery floss last night, but you slept the whole time I was doing it."

Anneke studied her sister's face, then glanced at the colorful strands of floss scattered over the room. "So, do you intend to leave them there?"

"No, I'll take them down. I just had to do something crazy to break the monotony of the chores." Her lip quivered and her eyes filled. She suddenly burst out crying. "You don't know how lonely and hard it's been. I've had to do double the amount of chores, and every time I turned around, someone was giving me another job to do." Kea brushed the tears from her face and wiped her eyes on her sleeves. "Nothing was fun anymore, so I had to think of something I could do to make me laugh again." She paused, blinked the tears from her eyes, and glanced up at Anneke. "You must hate me. I know I've been obnoxious." Her voice escalated. "But I couldn't take it another day."

Anneke had never seen her sister in such a state. Now she could understand Kea's point of view. It must have been harder for Kea than for herself. Anneke broke into a giggle. "Seeing your side of it puts a whole new dimension on our situation. No, I don't hate you. I could never hate you. I'll admit I was hurt, and I couldn't figure out why you were acting the way you were, but I forgive you.

"You know, Kea, I never asked for a sprained ankle. Sometimes things happen beyond our control. But we have to make the best of it. It doesn't help a bit if we take it out on others. It only makes things worse. I must say, I've missed the real Kea, but I'm sure glad to have you back again."

Kea went over to Anneke and wrapped her arms around her. "I love you. I'm sorry for the way I've acted." She buried her head in Anneke's lap. Moments later she stood. "I'll go get the pillowcases." She ran up the stairs, two steps at a time. When Kea returned with the pillowcases, she set to work pulling down the strands of floss from around the room.

Alone once more, Anneke gazed at the printed design of water lilies resting in a quiet pond. A thought crossed her mind. When the set was completed, who would lay his head on the other pillowcase? Could it possibly be Romke? "No," she chided herself. It was ridiculous to think such a thing. She couldn't let her thoughts dwell on that. She might not ever see him again. But as she laid out the embroidery floss, she wondered which colors would please him most.

Chapter

3

Since yesterday's market day, Romke could think of nothing else but Anneke. She had become a permanent fixture in his thoughts. Several times, while weeding out the long rows of vegetables, he paused, rested his hands, and thought back to the beautiful girl he had rescued. How he longed to see her again.

He gazed across the field. Something wasn't right. His father had stopped working. With his mouth stretched taut and his hands grasping the hoe, his father stood as stiff as a windmill's blades on a calm day. Moments later, his father relaxed and continued to weed.

From time to time, Romke glanced back at him, but his father appeared to be all right. It must have been another kidney stone. Again, Romke's thoughts drifted back to Anneke, while his garden tool lay idle in his hand.

Clutching his hoe, his father marched over to Romke. "Whatever is the matter with you? Are you here to work or dream?" His father scowled at him as if waiting for an explanation.

Startled out of his reverie, Romke could think of no excuse. "I'm sorry. I'll get back to work."

"Isn't that what the day is for? Why do you think the Lord gave us sunlight? It's a gift and not to be wasted on dreams."

Even his father's words of disapproval couldn't keep thoughts of Anneke at bay. Her lovely smile, her graceful figure, the endearing way she tilted her head rose before his mind's eye. Her gentle voice lingered in the air. *Anneke.* Even her name was like a caress. And when he whispered it, he could feel a gentle brush of sweet air on his lips. How could he wait a whole week to see her again when even today seemed as though it would never end?

The days dragged by, but Wednesday finally arrived. It was a half-day's trip by boat to Anneke's marketplace in Kollumdijk. Like last week, he'd set sail at eight this evening in order to arrive when her market opened the following morning. Thrilled that he would see her tomorrow, he began weeding his portion of the garden with new vigor.

Stopping to shoo away a fly, he saw his father across the field, doubled over, his hand pressing his back. Romke dropped his hoe and ran to him. "What's wrong? Here, let me help you to the house."

His father's face turned ashen, and he struggled to stand up straight. "Don't worry about me. I'll finish this last row of turnips and quit for the day." He'd barely finished speaking when he grimaced, deep lines etching his face. Again, he crumpled while he clung to his wooden tool.

"No!" Romke reached for his father's hoe. "You've got to get back to the house. Mother can take care of you and call for the doctor."

His father shook Romke's hand off his back. "I don't need anyone's help. I can take care of myself. It's just another kidney stone."

"Here." His father thrust his garden tool at Romke. "Since you have so much time on your hands to dream, you'll do my work tomorrow as well as yours. And another thing, there's absolutely no need for you to be selling our cheese in other towns. Mother makes a fine profit selling it in our own marketplace. Now, get back to work." He turned abruptly, clutched his stomach, and stumbled back to the house.

Gripping the handle of his father's hoe, Romke stared after him, hardly believing he'd heard right. His hands slid down the length of the shaft as he sank to his knees. All that waiting for nothing. How could he bear another week without seeing Anneke? Reality hit him. He might never see her again. Would his father really deny him the right to return to Kollumdijk? His head buried in his hands, he poured out his heart to God.

"Oh, Lord, You know my dilemma. I sought Your will when I set out last week. I felt Your presence and approval when I sailed down the Oostelijk River, and Your guiding hand leading me out to the Zuider Zee. I didn't know what marketplace to go to, but when I reached Kollumdijk,

You filled me with such peace, I knew this was Your destination for me." He paused to gain control of himself. "And when I saw her. . ." A deep sigh escaped his lips. "When I saw her, Father, I knew beyond a doubt You had brought our paths together. Lord, if Anneke is really the woman You've chosen for me, I know You will bring us together once more." He raised his eyes toward Heaven. "God, I beg of You to bring us together again . . . and keep us together, forever." He stood, drew his sleeve across his moist eyes, and clutched the handle of the hoe.

Romke's emotions left him drained. Silence permeated the air, but it was a calming stillness. No audible words had answered his cry, but a sense of peace filled his heart. Surely the Lord had heard him. He had no idea how God would answer, but he would trust in His goodness.

✿

A chorus of birds woke Anneke and set her heart soaring. Market day! Last week's scenes flashed through her mind. Would she see Romke today? Would he come back this soon? He lived so far away. Again, she wondered what would bring him to Kollumdijk, but it didn't matter what brought him, as long as he came. And she'd make sure she looked her best. She inched her way to the edge of her bed and stopped. Minor pains shot through her ankle, leaving her uncertain. Holding her breath, she eased her foot to the floor. That wasn't too bad. If she were careful, surely she could make it to the market.

After freshening up, Anneke loosened the strips of cloth and re-bound her ankle securely. She exhaled, feeling more confident already. Next, she overlapped a white muslin cloth around her neck, fastened it with a large coral pin, and slipped on her black blouse. Its scooped neckline framed the brooch, and the flowers printed on the dark blouse matched the pin's coral hue. Her black woolen skirt brushed the floor as she stepped to the mirror.

Satisfied, she gathered her hair into a bun, pinned it, then covered it with a black skullcap. Over this, she placed her *oorijzer*, a casque of gold metal, and covered it with her white lace cap with its trailing soft-blue material. Pearl-headed pins secured her cap on both sides. She turned this way and that before the mirror. Yes, she was ready to meet Romke.

Forgetting all else but him, she left her room, but before she could reach the kitchen, a sharper pain shot through her ankle, stopping her in her tracks. She squeezed her eyes shut, dabbed at a tear that had escaped, and gingerly made her way to the kitchen. Anneke could feel her mother watching her as she entered the room with measured steps and took her place at the table.

Moeder walked over and laid her arm across Anneke's shoulder. "Are you sure you're up to walking that distance? Why don't you wait until next week before going to market?"

"I'll be fine, Moeder. I'll walk slowly and take extra precaution."

"I think it'd be wise to stay home today. There's nothing we really have to buy anyway."

"But I've been sitting and resting all week. There must be something you need. I don't think I could stay put for another hour."

A knowing grin spread across Moeder's face. "Well, if you really want to go, I'm sure we could use some blueberries and lettuce. But do be careful, dear."

"Don't worry, I will."

Moeder laid some coins on the table. "This should be plenty to cover the cost."

Anneke was thrilled, but misgivings began to haunt her. What if Romke didn't come this week? It could have been just a one-time visit to her marketplace. Maybe this week he would choose a different place to sell his cheese. And if Romke didn't show up in Kollumdijk, it'd be a long, painful trip for nothing. Then, too, she'd have to walk all the way back home. Would her ankle hold up that long? And what would she do if it grew worse? How would she get home then? Maybe she shouldn't go, after all.

When she finished her porridge, she decided to walk around outside as a test. Then she would make her decision. She gathered the coins on the table and dropped them into her purse. Anneke shoved back her chair. As she rose, nagging thoughts troubled her. Could she really do this? Or was she making a drastic mistake?

She stepped outside, breathed in the fresh air, and decided on the spot. Yes, this was what she needed: to be out and about. Her spirits lifted higher with each step she took. Soon she would see Romke.

By the time Anneke arrived, exhaustion consumed her and her ankle throbbed, but she had made it, even if she was limping. First she would purchase the produce, then she'd be free to spend the rest of the time with Romke. After paying the vendor, she placed the lettuce and blueberries in her basket. She left the stand, the tantalizing aroma of fresh strawberries following her.

She picked up her pace, but soon slowed down. The additional stress on her ankle only made matters worse. Protecting her foot must take top priority. Her anticipation grew as she wound her way through the marketplace. Soon she came to her own village cheese stand. Romke's was right behind it—but his stand was empty. No customers were queued up waiting to be served. No cheese covered the counter. Romke was nowhere in sight.

This couldn't be. It wasn't even near closing time, and she was actually early today. Surely he's around here somewhere. Disappointment tore at her heart. A tear ran down her cheek, but she quickly brushed it away.

Maybe he was at a different booth. She took her time walking through the aisles, looking to the left and right, hardly noticing the people she passed. The extra walking around the huge marketplace began to take a greater toll on her ankle. When she reached the last booth without finding Romke, she felt like sinking to the ground, burying her head in her arms, and letting her tears run free, but no place offered her a refuge. Her eyes clouding, she limped through the town gates and headed for home.

ᏳᎠᏯᏳ

The scorching sun beat down on Romke as he labored in the field alone the following day. Thursday, Anneke's market day, and he wasn't even there to see her.

Hot and tired after the long, grueling hours, Romke trudged back to the house. Somehow, he had managed to do both his own and his father's work in the field. But just the thought that he might never be able to return to Kollumdijk made him feel as though he were in a deep well with no way of getting out. Again, he prayed that God would intervene and make it possible for him to see Anneke.

He entered the house, more tired than hungry. One glance at his mother's taut lips and the escalating clatter of pots and pans told him she was in no mood for conversation. He made his way to the sitting room, plopped into his favorite easy chair, and began to read the newspaper.

When the commotion in the kitchen ceased, and the family had seated themselves at the table, Romke joined them, and they all bowed their heads for prayer. No sooner had his father pronounced the Amen, than his mother's fist landed on the table with a thud.

"Don't expect me to ever go to market again and waste a whole day. It wasn't worth the time and effort." She glared at her husband until he looked away. "Not one of our cheeses sold today." She pounded her fist on the table again. "Did you hear me? Not one!"

Romke's father finished chewing his food before replying. "I can't imagine why."

His mother's eyes burned with anger. "It was a hot, miserable day and we have nothing to show for it. I'll never set foot in that noisy, stuffy marketplace again." She turned to Romke. "You sold a ton of cheese at that new place you went to last week. From now on, selling our cheese is your job, Romke, not mine. I have plenty to keep me busy right here at home."

Romke glanced at his father to see his reaction.

Mr. Veenhuizen jammed a forkful of ham into his mouth, chewed it with vigor, and let out a grunt. The scowl on his forehead deepened.

Romke held his breath.

Mr. Veenhuizen clenched his fist. "Not so fast, *vrouw*. I'm the one who makes the decisions in this household, not you. If you can't draw a crowd to your stand, Romke will go in your place . . . to *our* market, not to some unknown village that's a day's journey away. They don't need our cheese. They make their own."

Again, Mrs. Veenhuizen slammed her fist on the table. "Did you even hear what I just said? Last week, Romke sold more cheese in Kollumdijk, than we've sold in a month, here in Lijdendorp. It appears to me that they do need our cheese."

Mr. Veenhuizen shoved back his chair, stood to his feet, and faced his vrouw. "What I've said, stands, and that's final."

Romke sank back in his chair. All hope of ever seeing Anneke again died at his father's words.

Chapter

⬷⬶⬷

4

Wednesday, the following week, finally arrived. Throughout the day, while Romke worked in the field, all he could think about was Anneke. Was there really no future with her? What could possibly happen to change his father's command? Ever since Romke was a child, his father had stuck to his decisions, whether they were for the good of the family, or the bad. Once he set the law, it was a closed subject.

How Romke longed to see Anneke. When he finally completed his duties on the farm, he had no desire to return to the house. Dragging his feet, he wandered over his land. Two weeks ago, he had set sail after supper on Wednesday, to arrive at Anneke's marketplace the following morning, but there was no chance of that ever happening again.

He headed for the pier where they docked the family boat. But the boat was gone, of course. Why hadn't he told his father earlier that the hull of their boat had suffered damage? But he already knew the answer. His father would have been furious and never would have trusted him again to sail the family boat alone. Then, any chance of him sailing to Kollumdijk by himself would have been out of the question—and that meant he'd never see Anneke again. But, still, he should have told his father.

He collapsed on the bank. With his elbows resting on his knees, and his hands pressed against his head, he struggled to think of the best way to approach his father with the news. Romke was the only one who could pick up the boat. His father would never be able to make the trip there and back while suffering from his painful kidney stones, though he just might be stubborn enough to try it. His mother had never managed the boat by herself, nor did she have any desire to do so.

He would just have to face his father and let him know the situation. Since the repairmen had assured Romke that his boat would be waiting for him this week, there was no alternative but to state the facts to his father, regardless of the consequences. And if his father approved of him bringing the boat back, that would be his ticket to see Anneke. But if he didn't approve . . .? Romke raised his eyes toward Heaven. "Oh, God, show me mercy. Only You can move Father's heart."

Romke headed for the house. He wasn't sure what his father's reaction would be when he heard the news, but their boat had to be picked up. Romke would need to leave this evening to arrive in Kollumdijk in the morning to open his booth.

He entered the kitchen and sat down at the table.

The Veenhuizens' Kitchen

His father scowled at him. "Where have you been, Romke? We've been waiting for you."

"I'm sorry, Father. I was just finishing up a few things."

"What kind of answer is that? You've had all day to get things done."

Romke nodded, but said nothing. Being the last to arrive at the dinner table was not a good beginning to ask for favors. He waited until dinner was finished, then silently begged God to give him the right words. "Father, I had to leave our boat in Kollumdijk last week to have a few repairs done on it. They told me it would be ready this Thursday. I'll leave tonight, and pick it up tomorrow."

Mr. Veenhuizen's scowl grew deeper. "Why didn't you tell me this earlier?"

"I really didn't have much of a chance, since we were working opposite ends of the field."

His father continued to stare at him. "Well, you could have told me earlier this week while we were at the table. I don't believe our table is quite as wide as our fields."

Not knowing how to answer, Romke remained silent.

Mr. Veenhuizen speared a large piece of fish on his plate and crammed it into his mouth. After chewing for a moment, he turned back to Romke. "So I suppose you want to sell our cheese while you're there, is that right?"

"If it's fine with you, I might as well."

A big grin spread across Mrs. Veenhuizen's face. "Why, of course, he should. It'd be foolish not to. We might as well make a profit when we can."

Mr. Veenhuizen slammed his fist on the table. "I didn't ask for your advice, Vrouw. This is between me and our son." He turned back to Romke. "You had better come back with a good profit, to make this extra trip worthwhile. Is that understood?"

"Yes, I'll do my very best."

"You'd better do better than your very best. Do you hear me?"

"Yes, Father."

"In fact, I want to see that every single one of those cheeses you take with you are sold when you return home, is that clear?"

Romke swallowed hard. "Yes sir." He left the table and stepped outdoors. No sooner had he brought the horse and cart around, than his mother began loading the wheel-shaped cheeses into the cart. The two of them worked together, his mother stacking them as high as she dared. The more she piled up, the uneasier Romke grew. How cold he ever sell *this* many?

When they were nearly finished, Mr. Veenhuizen came outside. "What in the world are you doing, vrouw?"

A smirk spread across his wife's face. "Well, as long as Romke's making the trip to Kollumdijk, we might just as well try to sell all the cheese that's ready to go."

"But this is ludicrous, you've loaded it to the gills. He'll never sell all those."

Mrs. Veenhuizen continued to place the last few cheeses into the cart. "We won't know until we try."

"Don't be ridiculous. That would never happen. Trust me, Romke will return with half of the cheeses still packed in the cart. Just see if he doesn't." Mr. Veenhuizen grunted, turned, and left for the fields.

Chapter

―――――――――― ⟨✿⟩ ――――――――――

5

Market day finally arrived, but Anneke had overslept. To make matters worse, she'd taken far too long getting ready. She wondered if Romke would even be at her marketplace. Maybe his visit two weeks ago was a one-time event. But just in case he did come, she would be there.

Sitting on the edge of her chair, she finished her boiled egg in two mouthfuls, and gulped down her coffee between large bites of almond bread.

Moeder stacked the dirty dishes and placed them in the sink. "How does your ankle feel today, dear?"

"It's doing better. The elastic bandage you sewed for me gives good support. It's made a big difference."

"I'm so glad." Moeder paused. "Even though it's late, before going to market, you'll need to take a loaf of bread to Cobie's mother. She's not doing well again." Moeder shook her head. "Sometimes I wonder what will become of those two."

"Why can't Cobie make their bread? She's not helpless."

"Her mother's never been well enough to teach her. I don't know how Cobie will manage when she's on her own. Maybe we could invite her over, and you could show her how to make bread, as well as sew and spin."

Anneke reached for the basket. "I'll take the bread to her mother, but please don't invite Cobie over. She's impossible to work with. I know. I've tried."

"We ought to do what we can, dear. Before leaving her house, ask Mrs. Tasman if there's something more we can help her with."

"All right, Moeder." A sigh escaped Anneke's lips. Dragging her feet, Anneke set off for the Tasmans' home. She had hoped to arrive at the marketplace earlier to spend more time with Romke—if he came. She was already late. This would set her back even more, since the Tasmans lived in the opposite direction. Anneke groaned. She didn't like going to their place, but probably Cobie wouldn't be there. She would have already left for market. On the other hand, it'd be almost as bad if she weren't there. Anneke felt sorry for Mrs. Tasman, but being alone with her made Anneke uneasy. Weird things always happened when she went to their home. She grew tense just thinking of Cobie's mother. What would she do this time?

Anneke finally arrived at their house. She'd get this over with quick, and be on her way. She knocked at the door. No one answered. She knocked again, listening for a stirring in their house, but all was still. Maybe Mrs. Tasman wasn't home. She'd leave the bread on the bench by the door. Cobie would see it there. She reached into her basket, and then froze at the sound of rustling in the grass.

Cobie's mother, draped in a long, white gown, appeared from the side of the house. Her straggly, gray hair fell over her forehead and down her shoulders, half shrouding her face, but her sunken eyes pierced through the tangled strands and held Anneke's gaze.

Anneke opened her mouth to speak, but no words came.

Silently, the figure drew nearer. The hem of her gown brushed the grass, hiding her feet. Or. . . could Mrs. Tasman really be floating? A breeze blew her wispy hair away from her face, fully exposing the haunted eyes.

Shivers crawled up Anneke's spine. She stood for a moment, paralyzed. Then she grabbed the loaf from her basket and thrust it toward the creature. Forgetting her injured ankle, she turned to run, but cold, clammy fingers clasped her wrist.

"Why are you leaving so soon, my dear? Stay with me a while."

The hollow voice chilled Anneke, and her hand cried out for mercy as the bony fingers held it fast. Sweat broke out on Anneke's face and neck. She almost wished Cobie were here—anything to divert this woman's attention. "I'm on my way to market, Mrs. Tasman, so I won't be able to stay today." Anneke's voice didn't sound like her own.

"Surely, you can keep me company for an hour or two. My Cobie never talks to me. Come, let's sit beneath this tree."

"It's late, Mrs. Tasman. If I don't leave now, the market will be closed when I get there."

As though she hadn't heard Anneke's plea, Mrs. Tasman pulled her to the ground, her firm grip cutting off all hope of Anneke's escape. Leaning close to Anneke, Mrs. Tasman whispered in raspy tones. "Have you seen my husband in the marketplace or in the village church?" The wind tossed her disheveled hair while her piercing eyes searched Anneke's face.

"N-no," said Anneke, her answer barely audible. The pressure from the claw increased, making the pain in Anneke's wrist unbearable. Her eyes smarted and her hand tingled. A tinge of blue had spread across her fingers.

Without acknowledging Anneke's reply, Mrs. Tasman continued. "Night and day, I search for him in my dreams, but I never find him." She paused. "He's somewhere—I know he's somewhere out at sea, tossing with the restless waves. But he'll return—one day he'll return."

She shifted her gaze from Anneke and stared across the grassy meadow to the rippling waterway that bordered her land. "The waters whisper to me, morning and evening, that he'll return. Listen! You can hear them speaking." Her eyes grew wild, and her body, rigid. "Dionysius, Dionysius . . . oh, Dion, come back. Come back!" Her voice crescendoed, then gradually faded away. Her lips moved in silence for what seemed like eons. At last her body grew limp. Mrs. Tasman's bony fingers fell from Anneke's wrist.

Anneke held her breath. Now was her chance to escape. Keeping her eyes fixed on Mrs. Tasman, she drew her arm away, but Cobie's mother no longer seemed aware of Anneke's presence. Without a sound, Anneke stood to her feet, grabbed her basket, and limped to the open gate. Not until she had passed through did she dare look back. Still in a trance, Mrs. Tasman watched the rolling water, waiting for her husband's return.

Anneke was free. Her heart beat wildly as she headed down the lane. She could almost hear light footsteps at her heels. Was Mrs. Tasman following her? Trembling, she turned to look, but no one was there. Again she thought she heard them padding softly on the ground, always coming nearer, always close behind her, but each time she glanced back, the road was empty. It had to be her imagination. She tried to ignore them, but the footsteps haunted her until she reached the marketplace. Never again would she go to Cobie's home. Never!

With her wrist bruised and hurting and her ankle swollen and aching, she entered the gates of Kollumdijk. Hot and flushed, she made her way to the town square as the clock struck one. She seemed destined to arrive at closing time. By now, most everything would be sold, and what remained not worth the guilders they were asking.

She wondered if Romke would still be here and if any of his cheese would be left, or if he had even come. Discouraged, she passed the empty booths. She hurried on, catching sight of Jorie's wooden-shoe stall. All of his *klompen* were gone—a rare thing, indeed. He looked happy as he prepared to leave for the day.

"You're late again, Anneke. You won't find anything now," taunted Cobie. She tossed her head and hugged her heaping basket closer.

Anneke looked at Cobie's basket stuffed with eggs and cheese and piled high with produce. Her face flushed with anger, and her fingers tightened on the handle of her own empty basket. "I wouldn't be coming this late if you'd baked your own bread."

Ignoring Anneke's reproach, Cobie tossed her head and pointed to the stand across the way and sneered. "If Jorie's wooden shoes are sold out, you know there's nothing left in the market worth buying." With a snicker, she threw the clog-maker a scornful look as he drew near. Either Jorie didn't notice, or chose not to acknowledge it. Jingling the coins in his pocket, he tipped his hat to them as he passed by. Anneke waved, and then noticed the shabby coat that hung on his shoulders. Poor Jorie, perhaps now he could buy some new clothes.

Anneke headed for the flour stand. To her relief, the vendor had just enough to fill her request. Now she needed to buy cheese, and she would be through with her shopping. Her heart fluttered when she thought of Romke and all that had happened between them two weeks ago, but why should she get her hopes up? He was a true gentleman. He would have helped anyone in need, not just her. How foolish to think there was anything more to it. Maybe she should buy her own village cheese today. She certainly wouldn't want him to think she was taking advantage of him or trying to obligate him to something more. After all, he didn't owe her anything. Yes, that's what she would do—buy her own village cheese and forget about seeing Romke.

She stepped to the counter where her own village cheese lay. All that remained were scanty wedges of the kind her family disliked. She sighed. If only she had arrived earlier. Now she would have to buy Romke's cheese after all. She couldn't go home without any. Although her family loved his cheese, she hesitated. Would Romke think her bold and that she'd come to his booth, hoping for another handout? More than likely he would. No, she wouldn't let that happen. Her family would just have to get along without cheese for a week. She turned and walked away.

Then she remembered his warm brown eyes, his tender smile, how he had gently supported her back with his arm after she had fallen in the marketplace. Oh, she did want to see him—so much. Still, he might not even have come today, but she had to know for sure. With a quick glance toward his booth, she spotted him.

Her heart began racing. She wanted to go to him, but she'd made her resolve, and scores of shoppers were still lined up at his booth, waiting to purchase his cheese. He was too busy, and with all those customers waiting to be served, she was sure there'd be no cheese left for her. She walked on by.

Moments later, sensing someone watching her, she looked back. With their cheese in hand, his customers had left his stand. Romke stood behind his counter, his gaze fixed on her. She paused and his eyes held hers, drawing her to him like a magnet. Her cheeks grew warm and she swallowed to find her voice. "With all those customers lined up, I was sure there'd be no more cheese left." Nervously, she fingered the beads around her neck. Then with one look at his counter, her heart sank. She had guessed right. Only a few thin pieces of cheese remained at his booth as well.

Caught in a dilemma, she swallowed hard, glanced up at him, and tried to say something, but her throat clammed up. His gentle eyes caressed her, making her feel warm and safe. A deep longing for him had consumed her. She didn't dare move or talk, lest this new feeling vanish forever.

Finally, she forced herself to speak. "Do you have enough cheese left for my family?"

He reached below the booth and pulled out a large wedge. "I'm glad you came back. I almost thought you weren't going to."

Had she imagined it, or had she seen hurt on his face? "Well, I wasn't sure if I should or not—I mean—if you'd. . ."

He placed his hand gently over hers.

Her uncertainty melted in the warmth of his touch.

"Here, Anneke, I've been saving this. I set it aside for you before the market opened." He handed her the large wedge of golden cheese.

"Oh, thank you. My whole family loved your cheese."

He cocked an eyebrow and grinned. "Even Kea?"

She nodded. "Even Kea." She reached for her purse.

He shook his head. "No, it's already paid for."

"Oh, I couldn't have you do that. Please let me pay you."

"No, it's my gift to you. I want you to have it."

She hesitated, searched his face, and then relaxed. "I guess you win. *Dank U wel.*" She took the cheese and placed it in her basket.

"How is your ankle? Is it healing well?" His face showed deep concern.

"Yes, it's so much better. Thank you for asking."

"Were you able to make it to market last week?"

"Yes. I didn't see you here, though."

"I'm so sorry, Anneke. Father was sick, and I had to do both his work and mine on our farm." He paused. "I've missed you these last two weeks."

Her cheeks grew warm and her heart raced. A smile broke out on her face. How she cherished those words from him.

"I wish I could offer you a ride home, but I need to pick up my boat. The repairs should be done today."

"That's fine. I can walk home all right."

"I'm glad, but I would rather take you, myself." He paused. "Will you be here next week?"

"I plan to be."

"I'll be waiting for you then."

She caught her breath. Had she heard him right? Had he really said he'd be waiting for her? But next week seemed like a year away. Maybe it wouldn't seem quite so long, just knowing he wanted to see her again.

She patted the cheese in her basket. "Thanks again, Romke. I'll be back next Thursday." She felt like skipping over the cobblestones. She left the marketplace, her heart as light as a blossom just touched by the gentle rays of the sun.

A sudden cry shattered her peace.

"Where did you find *that* cheese?" demanded Cobie, darting from the tree she'd been leaning against.

"In the marketplace behind the regular cheese stand."

"I never saw it, but I won't leave here until I get some." Cobie rushed back through the gates toward the town square.

Anneke walked slowly on. It would be interesting to see if Cobie returned with her golden prize. Pounding footsteps roused Anneke from her musing. She looked back.

Cobie, her headpiece askew, and her face as red as the beets crammed in her basket, bolted down the lane. She headed straight for Anneke, her wooden shoes clacking like thunder. In her haste, she knocked several apples from her basket. She turned from Anneke and chased the bouncing apples down the cobblestone street. At last she reached them, but as she bent to pick them up, more fruit tumbled to the ground.

"This is all your fault!" screamed Cobie, shaking her fist in Anneke's face.

Anneke smothered a laugh. Cobie was like the weather. You were never quite sure when a storm would break loose. Anneke grabbed the apples rolling over the stones and set them in Cobie's basket. Only one piece of cheese lay inside. "Were there no more wedges left of the new cheese?"

Cobie's eyes flashed with anger. "Of course not." She jabbed her finger at the large wedge of cheese in Anneke's basket. "*You* took the last piece from that disgusting man. Why did he come here, anyway?

Don't the women in his own village suit him?" She turned toward the town gates and spat. "I wouldn't trust him or any man from his *dorp*. You know the custom they have in Lijdendorp, don't you?"

Anneke ignored her outburst and watched Cobie rearrange the fruit in her basket. "I wouldn't feel too bad. At least you have one wedge of cheese. You can always get the other kind next week."

"Who cares about next week? I want it *now.*"

"It wouldn't fit in your basket, Cobie."

"I'd make it fit." Even as she spoke, two oranges tumbled out. "Who needs them, anyhow?" she cried, with a jerk of her head. She gave the nearest orange a sharp kick, leaving the second one to roll off the edge of the road to the canal below. The plop of the orange as it struck the water brought a satisfied smile to Cobie's lips. With head held high, she sauntered down the street, watching the other orange roll on ahead.

Anneke cringed. Did it mean nothing to Cobie that their parish provided the means for her and her mother to live comfortably? They had never lacked for food, nor would they in the future. So what Cobie threw away today, she could easily replace next week. Anneke sighed, glad to see her go.

Her thoughts drifted back to the young cheese merchant. How handsome he looked, standing there, talking to her—and such a gentleman. Yet Cobie had found fault with him. What slur had she hurled about Romke, outside the town gates? It was something about the men of his village. All the way home, Anneke tried to remember, but Cobie's words were as lost to her as the orange in the canal was to Cobie.

∽♾∽

While preparing to leave the marketplace, Romke marveled at the turn of events. This was the first time ever, that his father had broken his own command.

With the severe pain that wracked his father's body, it would have been impossible for him to make a trip of that distance. The only alternative was for Romke to go himself.

And though the number of cheeses was doubled, every single one had been sold, with the exception of the wedge he set aside for Anneke and a few bits and pieces for himself—just enough to satisfy his hunger.

But best of all, God had intervened and made it possible for him to see Anneke again. Yes, God had answered his prayers.

Chapter

Chapter

6

Daffodils, tulips, and hyacinths stretched as far as the eye could see, gracing the country fields as Anneke, Moeder, and Kea set off the following week for Kollumdijk. The church and town hall towers soared in the distance.

Today, Moeder planned to shop for material, and Kea hoped for excitement, but Anneke had only one thing on her mind—the handsome, young cheese vendor. Shouts and laughter grew louder as they approached the town gates. The week had dragged for Anneke, but at last she would see Romke. She picked up her pace.

"Why are you in such a hurry today?" asked Kea. "I can hardly keep up with you."

A smile spread across Anneke's face while she stared off in the distance. "Someday you'll understand."

Kea glared at her sister. "Is this what happens to you when you turn seventeen?"

But only a happy sigh escaped Anneke's lips.

Finally they found themselves in the midst of the busy shoppers. Pushcarts and tables heaped with treasures, while the cries of market vendors rang, enticing customers to their stalls.

"Strawberries. Juicy, red strawberries." The merchant gently swung a pail of the plump, rosy fruit before the eyes of potential buyers gathered at his stand.

Anneke's mouth watered at the sight of the strawberries her mother had picked from a crate. As they walked along, a delightful fragrance permeated the air. Blooms of every description blended in colorful profusion: purple and white hyacinths, coral gladiolus, and tulips of rich scarlet, pink, and yellow.

"Flowers here! Roses for your sweetheart, or place them in *your* windows." Stretching his arm toward Anneke, the vendor held out a bouquet of flowers for her to smell. She felt bathed in their perfume, as she inhaled the intoxicating aroma.

The varied chants lured them on from stall to stall. "Tease your tongue with a tasty treat. The flavors we have cannot be beat."

Already, crowds were gathering around the tempting array: sugar cookies, muffins, *makronen*, and the almond-filled *klets koekjes,* all delightfully arranged on doilies.

Moeder paused at the stand. "While we're here, we'll get the lace cookies you girls like and some macaroons for Vader. We might as well buy a few muffins for breakfast, too," said Moeder with a wink.

They moved on to another stand. Ruby-colored candies and salted licorice lay in endless rows with scores of other bonbons. Boys and girls tugged on their mothers' skirts, begging for the tempting treats.

Soon the aroma of chocolate filled the air. The enticing smell caught Anneke's attention, drawing her to the stand. She paused, and then caught her breath. Their warm, brown color reminded her of Romke's dark, tender eyes. She inhaled deeply, and then leaned toward her mother. "We can't pass up the chocolate, can we?"

"Never!" said Kea.

Moeder chuckled, purchased a generous amount, and handed them each a piece.

Anneke placed hers in her mouth almost reverently. What delightful flavor, so rich, and so smooth. She savored the taste, making it last as long as she could. What could be better than chocolate, unless . . . it was Romke.

A snappy polka leaped from the street organ, rousing Anneke from her daydream. Its notes swirled through the air, setting a festive mood. Children in their wooden shoes danced on the cobblestone square, blending their cheerful clomping with the brassy tones of the pipes.

Impatiently, Anneke followed her mother while Kea lagged behind, stopping at each booth.

At a nearby stand, a vendor shouted his pitch in a singsong voice. "Come see the Village Queen. She's selling silk and gabardine."

"There it is, girls; that's what I've been looking for." Moeder directed their footsteps to the yard goods.

Cloth of every description hung from rafters, while pastel silks draped and twirled around posts. Brocades of red and yellow and velvets of purple and blue lay in neatly folded piles on the counter top. The display of colorful fabrics resembled a garden of its own.

"Let's look at lace for the curtains," said Moeder. Reaching the table of lacy hooked-cotton, Moeder examined one pattern after another. Swans glided throughout one bolt, while sailboats drifted across another.

A third one caught Anneke's attention. Tulips bent this way and that along the delicate tatting, as though listening to the wind's secrets.

Time dragged on. Anneke tapped her finger on the counter while Moeder moved between the two designs, studying the tulip material closely, then returning again to the swans. Anneke shuffled her feet. She glanced across the market square, then back to her mother. "Moeder, do you mind if I walk around for a while? Maybe we could meet at the cheese stand."

"Well, I guess that would be all right, dear."

"May I go with her, please?" begged Kea.

Anneke shook her head. "No, I just feel like walking by myself." She knew her sister was bored with the endless rows of material, but she hurried off before Kea's protests could change their mother's mind.

Anneke worked her way through the busy market, hoping Romke would be there. At last, she caught sight of him. Her heart fluttered. Anneke picked up her speed, but before she could reach his stand, Cobie appeared, shouldering her way through the swarm of shoppers straight toward Romke's booth.

Anneke arrived a moment later.

Sashaying about, Cobie stole glances at Romke while fingering the cheeses.

Romke handed the change to his customer, then turned her way.

Cobie leaned toward him. "I'm so glad you've come to our marketplace. It's the best thing that's ever happened around here." She batted her eyelashes "We'd love to have you stay."

Pain shot through Anneke's heart. She watched as Cobie lingered, making a spectacle of herself while she tried to hold his attention. But Romke turned back to the line of waiting customers and concentrated on meeting their requests.

Cobie picked up a wedge of cheese and held out her coins. "Is this the right amount?" With a nod and a word of thanks, Romke focused on the next person in line. Cobie stood with her mouth open, ready to say more, when Jorie, the shoemaker, walked over to her side. The coins in his pocket jingled as he ran his fingers through them.

Anneke watched, amused at Jorie's efforts to impress the girl he loved.

"Cobie?"

She turned and, seeing Jorie, jerked her nose in the air. "Can't you ever leave me alone?"

Jorie took one hand out of his pocket long enough to adjust his cap, then cleared his throat. "Cobie, I uh . . ." Again, he cleared his throat. "Will you come over to my stand with me?"

"Can't you see I'm busy? I have more important things to do than talk to you."

Jorie fidgeted with his coat button. "It'll only be for a minute, Cobie, that's all, only a minute."

Cobie planted her hands on her hips and sneered at him. "I should hope it'd be no more than that." With a deep frown covering her forehead, she left the stand with him.

Jorie's face lit up as brightly as the coin he tossed in his hand.

Anneke watched as they walked to his wooden-shoe stall a few feet away. With a look of entreaty, Jorie leaned toward Cobie. Anneke could almost guess what he was asking her.

Suddenly, Cobie's sharp voice soared above the market din. "I'm telling you, once and for all, Jorie, I'm not interested. I don't care how many shoes you sell, or what your future plans happen to be. I want no part of them. And that's final!"

She marched off, head held high, leaving Jorie staring after her. His hands, sunk in his pockets, no longer jingled the coins. With slumped shoulders and bent legs, Jorie leaned against his stand, watching Cobie until she was out of sight.

Anneke teared up as she witnessed the scene. Would life always be so hopeless for Jorie, she wondered.

Her thoughts turned back to Romke. Anneke wished the people would finish their purchases and leave, so she could talk with him alone. At last the crowd cleared away.

As Romke glanced in her direction, he raised an eyebrow and winked. "Where's your basket? Let me guess. You met up with another raw egg and lost it."

Anneke laughed. "No, not this time. Moeder's carrying it. She and Kea are here today."

"When you're ready to leave, may I take you home? I have room for all of you."

Anneke's heart skipped a beat. "Oh, thank you. I'd be delighted." She was surprised the words had rolled off her lips so easily.

Gradually, more customers wandered over to where she stood. When the crowds dispersed once more, Romke handed her a large wedge of cheese.

"This is for you." His voice fell on her ears like a caress.

"*Dank U wel.* But it's enormous."

"I purposely saved it for you, Anneke."

She caught her breath. How beautiful her name sounded when he spoke it—so soft, so lyrical.

"Anneke!"

She turned at her mother's call.

Her face damp, Moeder stopped in front of the stand and set her basket down. "Has Kea been here with you?" she asked, wiping the perspiration from her brow.

Anneke saw her mother's troubled look. "No. I haven't seen her since I left the yard-goods."

The frown on Moeder's forehead deepened. "Lambertus came over and started talking to her. You know those two never get along, so it surprised me when she asked if she could go off with him. I knew how bored she was, so I said she could—and that's the last I've seen of her."

Chapter

⚭

7

Moeder shook her head and moaned. "I've been searching close to an hour. Kea's nowhere to be found, and I still have some shopping left to do before the market closes."

Anneke glanced to the left, then to her right. "Do you suppose she went home with Lambertus and Tante Zusje?"

"Tante Zusje wouldn't take her without telling me." She shook her head. "No, those two are up to something."

The crowds thinned as the chimes rang out the hour of one. Vendors began packing their wares and closing their stalls.

Anneke scanned the aisles. She checked the young girls passing by, each face encircled by a lacy-white cap. Kea was not among them.

She studied the young boys making their way toward the town gates, their pockets full of candy. One boy grabbed his friend's cap, gave it a toss, and laughed while he watched his friend chase it in the wind. But Lambertus was nowhere around.

"While you finish shopping, Moeder, I'll see if I can find them. They may have gone farther into town." Anneke paused while several customers headed toward Romke's stand.

Romke turned back to Mrs. Haanstra. "I should be done here by the time you're through with your shopping. If you'd like, I'd be more than happy to drive you around town and help you search for the missing persons." He grinned.

Moeder took her basket from the counter. "Thank you for your offer. We certainly could use your help."

"I'll be waiting here with the wagon," said Romke.

As Moeder hurried off to finish her shopping, Anneke turned to Romke with a smirk. "I bet I'll find those two before you even leave the marketplace."

"Or Lambertus will find you first with another one of his raw eggs." Romke winked at her.

Anneke chuckled and hurried on her way in search of the missing two. She gazed down one street after another, but saw only a few stragglers hustling home to their midday meal. Soon the streets emptied, and a whiff of roasting pork and asparagus soup drifted from an open window.

As Anneke turned a corner, laughter rang through the streets like a carillon. A young boy, holding his sides, threw back his head with glee. His wayward, red curls bounced about as though they were giggling too.

Anneke stifled a laugh. That unruly head of hair could belong only to one person. But what could be so funny, and why wasn't Kea with him?

Anneke kept close to the buildings as she hurried toward the scene. She would stay out of her cousin's view, but still get near enough to see the action. She stationed herself a few yards from where Lambertus stood. Peering from the side of an old canning factory, she kept her eyes on her cousin and waited.

Lambertus pushed his glasses up on his freckled nose and gazed upward toward the top of a tall, narrow building across the street. "What's taking you so long? I climbed all the way up and back down in five minutes."

Anneke followed his gaze and gasped at the sight. Across the road, stood an old storage shed, six stories high. Near the top of the building, a stepped gable stretched upward. The gable consisted of eight steps on both the left and right sides. There, on the far-left, on the highest step, her sister wavered in her stocking feet. Only her toes rested on the narrow ledge of the stepped gable.

A stepped gable building.

"Quit laughing," shouted Kea. "You had it twice as easy. I have to deal with long skirts and full petticoats. So there."

"I told you, you couldn't do it," Lambertus yelled back. "You're the funniest thing I've seen in a long time."

"I can too, get down. Just see if I can't."

Balancing on one foot at the left end of the narrow ledge, Kea stretched her right hand toward the knob at the top center of the stepped gable. She caught hold of it, then alternating between her right and left foot, she eased them toward the center and grabbed the knob with her left hand.

Her lace cap shivered in the wind as she clung there, studying the five remaining steps that led down the right side of the gable. After a lengthy pause she relaxed her hold, and slid one foot to the right side of the gable, but her long skirts covered the landing her foot sought.

At last, it appeared as though she had found it. She shifted her weight onto her right foot and cautiously brought her left foot around.

Anneke stared, speechless. Was she imagining this?

Gripping the ledge with one hand, Kea slid her other hand down the bricks, then gingerly lowered one foot. While her foot dangled two feet from the step below, the wind whipped her skirts, billowing them like clouds before a storm.

Lambertus snickered. "Hey, the wind's blowing you up. You look like a hot air balloon about to take off."

"Stop laughing at me, Lambertus Lambeastus. See? I'm not taking off, silly, I'm coming down." But as she spoke, the wind reversed and smacked her skirts against her, wrapping them around her foot.

Anneke caught her breath as her sister tried to kick her foot loose, but her foot held fast, trapped in her skirts. Anneke longed to rush to her aid, but she knew if she did, it could be fatal. She forced herself to remain calm and watch while Kea hung, helpless, from the top of the storage shed.

"What's the matter?" shouted Lambertus. "I thought you said you were coming down. You got cold feet, or did you decide to scrub the bricks while you're up there?"

"It's my foot. It's caught in my petticoat, and I can't pull it loose."

"Aw, you're just chicken. Hurry up and get down."

Kea thrashed her foot again and again but to no avail. "Help, Lambertus, I'm stuck. *Help me!*" Her cry pierced the air.

The more Kea kicked, the harder Lambertus laughed. "Hey, I didn't have that much fun," he said, pretending to pout. "You've been up there a whole lot longer than I was."

"It's scary up here. Help me!" Kea's cry sent shivers through Anneke.

Lambertus pushed his glasses further on his nose. "Remember our bargain? We weren't to give each other any help. You'll just have to figure it out yourself."

"Forget it. Help me. Fast! My fingers—they're slipping!"

Her shriek filled Anneke with terror.

"A bargain's a bargain. I knew you couldn't do it. Girls can't do anything tough. They always get scared and panic. You all cry and scream and pitch a royal fit. You're just a big baby, same as any other girl."

He stepped out to the middle of the road, and then slapped his knee in satisfaction. "I guess you'll never again claim you can do anything I can do. You've just proved you can't."

"Oh yeah? Just watch me." After rubbing the sweat from her hands one at a time onto her skirt, Kea wrapped her fingers around the brick gable. Determined not to let her cousin outdo her, she jerked her foot with all the force she could muster. To her horror, her foot slammed against the ancient structure, loosening the decaying brick. Intense pain surged through her toes, and before she could stop it, she let out a cry, but her throbbing foot broke free from her skirts at last. Pieces of brick rained down from the building, straight toward Lambertus's head. A chunk landed with a thud. Dazed, he staggered backward.

Anneke rushed to catch him, tripped over Kea's shoes, and collided head on with her cousin. Lambertus crumpled to the cobblestones, and Anneke slumped beside him. Stars danced before her eyes, and the buildings whirled in a wild and dizzy chase. A horse and cart joined the confusion, twirling with everything else on the street.

Romke jerked on the reins and jumped from his cart. He gently lifted Anneke to her feet. "Are you hurt?"

"No." She held her forehead. "Once my head stops spinning, I should be all right. I'm just glad you're here." Anneke squeezed her eyes shut as she pressed her head with both hands. "But Lambertus. He's out cold. And Kea. Is she down yet?"

"I'll make sure they're both taken care of," said Romke, while helping her into his cart. "But first, I'll see that your sister gets down safely." He hurried toward Kea, keeping his eye on her as she descended the gable.

Moeder leaned forward to examine Anneke's head. "You're getting quite a bruise here, but I don't think it's anything serious." Moeder sighed. "That Lambertus. Sometimes I wonder what gets into that boy's head, running off like this and taking Kea with him. I sure don't know how we ever would've gotten him home if Romke hadn't offered to help us. But where could Kea be?"

"I told you I could do it," shouted Kea, while lowering herself to the last step of the gable. Standing on the narrow ridge, she swayed one foot in search of the rickety ladder propped against the old, abandoned building. Careful not to distract her, Romke edged closer, watching her every move.

Following the sound of her daughter's voice, Moeder looked up at the storage shed. Her mouth dropped open when she saw Kea descending. The ladder sagged, creaking with each step Kea took. Moeder grasped the seat in front of her. "Well, if this doesn't beat all." Without calling for Romke's help, she climbed down from the cart and marched over to the storage shed, while Kea, oblivious to her mother, continued her descent.

Anneke kept her eyes glued on Kea. At last her sister reached the bottom rung. Anneke let out her breath, and Romke walked away from the shed, leaving Kea in Moeder's hands.

Still facing the building, Kea jumped to the ground with a whoop, her torn petticoat dragging behind her. "So, what did you think of that, Lambertus?" Kea said, rubbing her chafed hands on her skirt. She turned to face him but, instead, Moeder stood before her, hands on her hips, in silent rage. Kea stared back, speechless, her eyes growing as wide as her mother's.

"I'll tell you exactly what *I* think of it when we get home, young lady," said Moeder. "But right now, I want to see those shoes back on your feet." Moeder took Kea by the arm and marched her over to her shoes.

Kea slipped on one wooden shoe, and then let out a cry as she struggled to get her sore, swollen foot inside the other shoe.

Moeder didn't seem to hear Kea's moans or notice her limping. Her hand still clutching Kea's arm, she waited for her to get into the cart, and then climbed in the back seat beside her. From the look on Moeder's face, Anneke knew what was in store for Kea.

Romke lifted Lambertus, and laid the unconscious boy behind the back seat. Once inside the cart, he turned to Moeder behind him. "We'll let your sister know what happened. Which road do I take to get to their home?"

Anneke looked back to see Moeder's expression. It had relaxed somewhat, but Kea kept her eyes averted.

"Thank you so much for your help, Romke. Bear left as you leave town," said Moeder. "Lambertus lives down that road, the third house on the left. You can't miss it. Their home is covered with ivy."

In the distance, the carillon sounded the hour of three. Romke gripped the reins and guided the horse through the town gates, then turned down the country lane.

Anneke thought of the day's events. He had asked to take them home and offered to help them find Kea. Now they were sitting together, and he was driving her home again. Could this really be happening?

Several minutes later, Romke turned to her, his voice low. "By the way, you have quite an adventurous sister, I'd say."

Anneke grinned. "You're right. She gets into more scrapes than any other person I know. Life is never boring when Kea's around." Anneke looked up at Romke. "Do you have any brothers or sisters?"

"Yes, I have a twelve-year-old brother."

"I'll bet he's a handful, too."

A moment passed before Romke spoke. "No, actually he's more quiet. He's a very special brother to me."

Anneke noticed the change in Romke's mood. It left her wondering, but she thought it best not to question him further.

When her cousin's home came into view, Anneke pointed out the cozy farmhouse covered with the luscious, green vine. Her aunt stood peering through the front window, framed in ivy.

Catching sight of the cart, Tante Zusje whipped past the lace curtains and ran outside. After noting each of the passengers, a look of bewilderment crossed her face. "I had hoped you were bringing

Lambertus home." She wrung her hands. "I don't know where that boy ran off to."

"He's here in the back." Romke jumped down from the wagon and walked to the rear.

Tante Zusje followed. She leaned over the side of the cart and peered inside. Lambertus lay motionless, sprawled out before her. She nudged his arm and called to him, but received no response. "He's dead to the world! I can't believe he'd be that tired."

"He's not really asleep," said Anneke. "He got knocked out by a piece of flying brick. He needs to be checked by the doctor."

"A flying brick?" Her face grew pale. "He could have been killed! How did that happen?"

Kea jerked around and stared at her cousin. "Did I do that?" She snickered. "Well, Lambertus, ol' buddy, I guess I got the last laugh after all."

Tante Zusje wheeled around at Kea. "You threw a brick at my son?"

Kea's smile faded. "No, I kicked it."

"You, what?" Tante Zusje's lips quivered.

"I didn't do it on purpose. It happened when the brick crumbled."

"When what brick crumbled? Oh, never mind. We're losing precious time." Tante Zusje sniffed, pulled her handkerchief from her pocket, and wiped her nose. "How will I get him to the doctor?"

"I'll take him. I'm Romke Veenhuizen, a friend of your sister and her family." He helped Tante Zusje into the cart, beside Moeder.

Tante Zusje sank to the seat, still wringing her hands. "Dank U wel. Continue down this road for about a mile. I'll tell you when I see the doctor's home."

It wasn't long before a large, white house with thatched roof came into view. Trees of various kinds spread their branches over the home like a canopy, sending a feeling of love and protection.

"This is it," announced Tante Zusje.

Romke came to a halt, jumped from the cart, and tethered his horse to the hitching post. Before he could assist Tante Zusje, she leaped to the ground and tore across the lawn to the doctor's house. With Lambertus in his arms, Romke followed.

Lambertus's eyes flickered. "Oh, my head . . . it aches." He moaned.

Everyone turned in his direction. A large lump had blossomed on the top of his head, raising his unruly curls a ridiculous inch higher.

Kea shook with laughter. She stood up, poised to jump, but before she could leave the cart, Moeder caught her arm. "You're staying right here, young lady, where I can keep an eye on you. You'll wait in the cart with us."

Kea turned toward Moeder and huffed. "But I *want* to go in. I'll be missing the best part of all." With one glance at her mother, she said no more. She pulled her arm away from her moeder's grasp, plopped back down in her seat, and huffed again.

Tante Zusje grabbed the knocker on the doctor's door and rapped it several times. After receiving no response, she slammed it harder. The front door flew open. Tante Zusje rushed inside, followed by Romke carrying her son.

A half hour passed before they emerged from the doctor's home and returned to the cart. Tears ran down Tante Zusje's face. "My Lambertus has a concussion. The doctor confirmed it. Ohhh, he could have been killed." She pulled out her handkerchief again, and dabbed her eyes.

Moeder placed a hand on her sister's arm. "Please don't worry. I feel confident he'll get better soon."

With everyone back in the cart, Romke started down the path.

"He got what he deserved," Kea muttered.

Anneke looked back and scowled at her sister, but Kea ignored her.

A smile playing on his lips, Romke turned to Anneke. "I can remember, as a boy, doing something similar to what your sister and cousin did, though it was probably worse. My friends and I used to challenge each other to do all kinds of daring things, the more dangerous, the better."

Anneke listened, oblivious to her family in the seat behind them.

Romke lowered his voice. "One time somebody dared me to climb our windmill, and I was ready for the challenge. I hoisted myself up the base until I reached the low end of the nearest sail, then scrambled up the framework. You should have heard the cheers from below. When I made it to the center where the four sails met, I yanked off my cap and waved to my friends. Suddenly the whole gang was shouting, 'Keep going. Let's see you reach the top!'"

The Veenhuizens' Windmill

Anneke sat spellbound. "I wish I could have been there watching you."

He looked over at her and winked. "The wind started to blow, but I was determined to prove I could do it. I kept climbing until I got halfway up the highest sail, but before I could reach the top, a gust of wind set the sail spinning and took me with it. I grasped the slats even tighter. It seemed like I was pressed against the sail for hours."

Anneke could picture this adventurous little boy in her mind, all four limbs clinging like a starfish to the surface of the sail.

"Finally, the wind brought the sail back down again."

Anneke breathed a sigh of relief. "Whew. Did you jump off?"

"No. I thought about it while I had the chance, but I was hanging upside down. Then another gust of wind hit, and before I knew it, I was at the top again. All of a sudden, it was deathly still. No one was cheering anymore. All I could hear was my shirttail flapping. It felt uncanny."

"While I twirled around, I caught glances of my friends. They looked stiff, terrified, like they were frozen in stone. They must have thought I'd never get off, but I was having the time of my life." He grinned.

Anneke leaned toward him, studying his face. "You weren't even the least bit scared?"

"Not at all. I just shut my eyes and clung to the slats of the sail, enjoying every minute of it while the wind spun me about in circles."

Anneke shook her head. "You were brave. But how did you finally get down?"

"When the sail lowered again, the guys yelled, 'Jump, Romke, now!' I don't even remember letting go, but the next thing I knew, I lay flat on the ground with my friends' faces spinning above me. Later, I woke up in bed, not able to figure out how I got there."

"Were your parents upset with you?"

"Were they ever! Father made me bale twice as much hay for a full month, and he wouldn't allow me to play with my friends until the end of that time. I never realized how long a month could be. Yet when the time was up, we were back to our old tricks. But I never did take on the windmill escapade again."

Anneke breathed a sigh of relief. "I'm sure once was enough, even if you did enjoy it."

They both chuckled.

Romke pulled up to Tante Zusje's home and jumped down from the cart. After assisting her, he lifted Lambertus, followed Tante Zusje inside, and returned to the cart.

It wasn't long before they arrived at Anneke's home. She didn't want the trip to come to an end. She could have ridden for hours, even days, listening to him talk.

After Romke helped each of them down from the cart, Anneke's mother turned to him. "Thank you for all your help. We wouldn't have been home yet, if it hadn't been for you. This time you can't refuse us. Please stay for dinner."

"Thank you, Mevrouw Haanstra. I'd love to."

Moeder's eyes twinkled.

When Kea had jumped from the wagon, the axle caught her torn petticoat and ripped it more. From the open doorway, Anneke watched her sister stall for time: petting Romke's horse, feeding him an apple that had fallen to the ground, then meticulously tucking the long strip of jagged petticoat inside her stocking to give the others plenty of time to get ahead of her. Anneke knew Moeder would be even more upset if she saw Kea's ripped petticoat, but since she hadn't mentioned it, perhaps it had gone unnoticed.

Kea helped Moeder prepare the meat and potatoes, while Anneke gathered the ingredients to make *knapperige groentesalade*, her favorite crunchy vegetable salad. She sliced fresh carrots, celery, zucchini and snow peas, still in their pods, into strips. Next she added the cauliflower florets. After frying the vegetables, she transferred them to a serving bowl and sprinkled a mixture of lemon juice and puree over them. She removed the seeds and membrane from a sweet red pepper, cut it into narrow pieces, and added it along with a sliced onion. Anneke sprinkled on the seasoning and brought the bowl to the table.

The Haanstras' Dining room

Before long, the aroma of roast beef wafted through the house as well.

Anneke's father entered the kitchen, closed his eyes, and inhaled. "When I smell food like this, you can bet I'm through working in the fields." After scrubbing his hands, he took his place at the head of the table and turned to Romke, seated on his right. "I see your horse found his way to our home again. Welcome back."

"Thank you, meneer, but this time, I made sure he stayed clear of your flax."

Vader grinned. "I hear you're the one who makes the delicious new cheese we've had lately. In fact, the whole village is talking about it."

A warm smile spread across Romke's face. "I'm pleased you all like it so well. It's always exciting to taste something new."

"But only if the flavor is as good or better than what you're used to," said Vader.

"Moeder, for dessert, let's have the strawberries that we bought at the market today," said Anneke. "I'll bring the cream."

"I can't think of anything that would taste better," said Moeder.

The mention of strawberries and cream brought a smile even to Kea's face.

When dinner came to an end, Moeder began to clear the dishes from the table. "Are you spending the night in Kollumdijk, Romke?"

"No, I'll pick up my boat there and set off up the Zuider Zee toward home."

"That's quite a distance to travel," said Vader.

Romke nodded. "It takes ten to twelve hours in good weather. It's a lovely trip though, very peaceful and quiet."

Anneke caught her breath. How she'd love to make that trip with him. She tried to imagine what it'd be like.

A tinge of sadness flowed through her when she walked out with Romke to his cart. Another long week of waiting before she could see him again. Once more, she wondered why he had come to her town. Surely, his village had a marketplace.

His village. . . What was it Cobie had said about a custom practiced by the men of Lijdendorp? Had it been a warning? She tried to remember, but still, Cobie's words were lost to her.

Seated in the cart, Romke took the reins. "I've enjoyed being with you so much, and thanks for the wonderful meal."

"I'm so glad you could join us, Romke."

All thought of Cobie's warning slipped from her mind. In the brief moment that followed, their eyes spoke to each other in tender communion. She watched him guide his horse down the lane. Several times, he turned to wave. With one last sweep of his hand, he rounded a bend and disappeared from sight.

Her heart told her she could love this man forever. She would follow him to the ends of the earth if he but asked her. And yet, she hardly knew him.

Chapter

⚜

8

Anneke wandered among the stalls at the marketplace, searching for a gift for Kea's birthday. Several objects vied for her attention as she strolled from one booth to another, but none completely satisfied her. She had almost decided on a collector's doll, an import from the East Indies dressed in its native garb, when something sparkling in the sun caught her eye.

Just above the doll, a silver necklace dangled from a cord strung across the booth. The scarlet stones, twinkling in the sunlight, took her breath away. This would be perfect. Kea's favorite color was red.

She reached up and let the jewels lie against her fingers. While she watched a sunbeam play on its facets, a shadow moved across the necklace, dimming its glimmer. Someone must have blocked the light.

Looking behind her, she saw the folds of a faded gray skirt swish by. She turned back to the necklace. Once again, the jewels danced for her. This was the ideal gift for Kea. She could hardly wait to see her sister's face when she opened it.

Anneke made her purchase and hurried to Romke's stand. When she drew near, he greeted her with a lingering smile. She would show him Kea's present when the marketplace closed.

The minutes dragged by as she watched the wedges of cheese dwindle from his stand. But the line continued to grow as more shoppers queued up, some chatting with Romke longer than necessary.

At least Cobie hadn't put in an appearance to mar the day; though it was odd she hadn't seen her. Anneke looked again at the glimmering necklace lying in her basket. Would the carillon never sound the hour of one? While the last customer paid for his purchase, the bells in the church steeple began to chime. At last, Romke was free to close his stand.

She reached into her basket, pulled out the red-jeweled necklace, and held it up. "Look what I found for Kea. Isn't it beautiful?" The scarlet gems shimmered in the sunlight. "I can't wait to give it to her. Her birthday's this Saturday."

He moved closer to see it, then turned and silently gazed on her. "That's beautiful, Anneke, but not near as lovely as you."

Anneke lowered her eyes. She felt her cheeks flush as she placed the necklace back in her basket. They each took a wedge of the cheese that remained on the counter and set it in his cart. When Romke reached for the last one, his hand brushed hers. Anneke's heart raced.

"This cheese is yours," said Romke. He gave it to her, and then laid his hands over hers. "Would you like to share lunch down by the river?"

Anneke was speechless. Soft breezes caressed her cheeks, and a chorus of robins sang in a nearby tree. She felt as if she had stepped into paradise. At last she found her voice. "I'd love to. It's way too nice a day to leave so soon."

The music from the carillon floated on the air as they strolled toward the river. In the distance a dog growled, shattering the silence, but caught up in the enchantment of the moment, they ignored it. Moments later, the growl grew closer. Anneke turned back to look. Something gray ducked behind a tree, but it had moved so quickly, she'd failed to see what it was. *It was probably just some animal.*

Again, she felt the warmth of Romke's hand on hers.

"Let me carry your basket, Anneke."

As he took it, she withdrew her hand.

Wandering in and out among the trees, they finally reached the river, where a chestnut tree spread its canopy, offering them shade. Romke guided her over, and together they sat beneath the tree. He handed her the basket and she set it next to her, glad that she had nothing perishable to worry about. Only the cheese and the necklace lay inside.

Opening his knapsack, Romke pulled out a loaf of bread, broke off a generous piece, and handed it to her.

"That smells wonderful. Do you make your own bread, too?" asked Anneke.

"Yes, my mother does."

She took a bite. "Mmm, it's delicious. It's different from any I've ever had."

"I'm glad you like it." He sliced off a wedge of cheese and held it out to her. Reaching into his knapsack again, he pulled out a container and removed the lid. Bright red strawberries beckoned them.

"Oh, I guess you know how much I love them," said Anneke.

Choosing one, Romke held it for a moment, and then looked at her. "Did you know this matches the color of your cheeks?" He placed the strawberry in her hand.

She chuckled and lowered her eyes.

"Have some more." He held out the container, and she helped herself. Romke leaned back against the tree.

While they ate, they watched the breeze play with the grasses growing on the edge of the river. Endless ripples danced across the water. Around the bend, two swans glided near the bank, and paused. The male tenderly stroked the female's neck with his bill. She raised her head till their bills came together. Lovingly, the cob entwined his neck around his mate's.

Romke lightly placed his hand on Anneke's and gently laced his fingers through hers.

Her heart pounded. "Romke, what do you think about on your long trips home?"

"I think about my life and how I will spend it."

She studied his face. "How do you want to spend it?"

"Most of all, I want to honor God. I want to live my life so I'll have no regrets."

"That's how I feel."

"Then, God is important to you too, Anneke?"

"Important to me? Well, I know God is present everywhere, and yet, He seems so far away."

Romke leaned forward. "Yes, God is everywhere. He's here with us right now. He cares for you and longs to save you."

She looked at him, puzzled. "What would He save me from?"

"Save you from sin and give you a new life in Him."

Anneke grew troubled. Why was he talking about sin? Had she done something he didn't approve of? "What sin have I done?" She hesitated. "Have I displeased you in some way?"

"No, Anneke. You're like an angel to me. But God sees us as we really are. That's why He sent His Son to die on the cross for us, to take the penalty for our sin." He held her hand close in his. "Do you understand what I mean?"

"Not really." She withdrew her hand from his. "I always try to do what's right." Surely she must have done something to offend him. Bewildered, she kept her gaze on the strawberries in her hand as she ate them, one by one. They finished their bread and cheese in silence. Brushing the crumbs from her skirt, she glanced up at Romke, uncertain.

He turned to her, a tender gaze lingering on his face. "Let's walk along the river."

She could tell he had something more on his mind. Neither one spoke as they followed the winding path along the bank.

The pebbles scattered on the river's edge caught Anneke's attention. She moved closer to the water and picked several stones. A larger one caught her eye, one with pink sparkles. Although it was much further out, she had to have it. Pink was her favorite color.

"Look, Romke. See that pink rock out there? Isn't it gorgeous? I'm going to get it." How she loved his smile. It always gave her confidence.

Cautiously, she stepped from stone to stone. Before she reached her destination, she glanced back at Romke. A big grin lingered on his face. She smiled back and moved on toward her prized rock jutting from the water. "Oh, it's even more beautiful close up."

Anneke reached down, grasped the glittering rock, and tried to pull it from the water. It wouldn't budge. She began to wiggle it free, and with a final jerk, up it came, but the rock, covered with algae, slipped from her hands and fell back into the water. Slime covered her hands, but more determined than ever, she scraped the algae from her hands and swished them around in the water. Grabbing the rock once more in a tight grip, she yanked it as hard as she could. Again, her fingers slid from the rock. She lost her balance, screamed, and landed in the river.

Instantly, her wooden shoes filled with water. She could feel the weight of them pulling her down. "It's deep—Romke, help me—I'm sinking!"

Romke had watched her every move and was already by her side. He lifted her from the river and carried her to a grassy plot beneath a nearby tree. After pouring the water from her shoes, he sat beside her. "Are you all right?"

She nodded, but her body trembled. "Thank you, Romke." A tear trickled down her cheek. "What would I have done if you hadn't been here with me? I—I would have drowned." She shivered at the thought.

Romke placed his arm around her back and gave her a tender squeeze. "Wait here. I'll get the rock for you." He removed his shoes and socks, rolled up his pant legs and waded out to Anneke's prized rock. In no time, he was back.

"Here's your rock, Anneke."

"Dank U wel!" She turned the glittering rock this way and that, fascinated by its dancing sparkles.

Romke watched her. "Are you feeling better now?"

"Yes, much better."

"I'm glad to hear that. Come with me, Anneke. I have something special to show you."

After she slipped into her damp shoes, Romke took her hand in his.

Around a bend lay a quiet inlet filled with water lilies, their thick, rubbery pads resting on the water's surface. Here and there upon the almost-circular leaves, the water lilies bloomed, as though a hand had carefully placed each one. The flowers, some with white petals, others with pink, lay opened, displaying their beauty.

Anneke stepped closer to them. "Oh, they're enchanting." They reminded her of the water lilies on her pillowcases. She was glad she hadn't finished embroidering them yet. She would use these same colors. A warm sensation trickled through her. He must love water lilies, too.

Romke bent down and picked the smallest one. Drops of water lay on its waxy white petals. Toward the center, the petals burst into a blushing pink. Standing up, he turned to Anneke. "Just like this flower, if we're attached to Jesus, the life-giving Stem, we are joined to God. He becomes our strength in trouble. Without the Lord, we have no one to sustain us when trials come. We will drift, wither, and die." He handed her the water lily. "I want you to know Him personally, Anneke."

She gazed at the lovely flower. "It's so beautiful." Turning, she watched the river flow in its course. The swans glided in perfect harmony with the river's current. Life was wonderful. What hardships did she know? She had everything she needed and a family who loved her. Surely she was safe. And yet, if Romke hadn't been with her, she could have drowned. She looked again at the water lily in her hand. Did she really need a Savior?

Hand in hand, they wandered through the park and finally made their way back to the chestnut tree. Romke picked up his knapsack, slung it over his shoulder, then handed Anneke her basket. She laid the water lily inside, next to the cheese, and slipped the basket over her arm.

Thoughts of Kea's birthday celebration filled Anneke's mind. She envisioned Kea's face growing radiant as her sister gathered the jewels in her hand to admire them. Anneke longed to see the necklace sparkle in the sunlight again. She glanced inside her basket and stared in disbelief. She lifted the cheese and the water lily to make sure Kea's gift hadn't slid beneath them, but the necklace was gone. A wail escaped her lips.

Romke turned to her in alarm. "What's wrong?"

"The necklace—it's not here!"

"How is that possible?" He leaned over and peered into the basket. "I saw you put it back in after you showed it to me." Romke shook his head. "You don't suppose there's a crack in the basket, do you?"

Anneke shook her head. "No, I would have noticed it if there had been."

Romke reached for her basket. "Let me check it, just to be sure." After examining it, he handed it back to her. "Let's check the grass around the tree."

But the necklace wasn't there. Although they continued to search the lawn as they retraced their steps back to Romke's cart, they saw no sign of the sparkling red jewels.

"I'm so sorry, Anneke. Do you think someone might have taken the necklace while we were further down the river?"

"That's the only time they could have, but I never saw anyone around. What am I going to do now? I can't buy another necklace before Saturday, and besides, I didn't see any other like it. Oh, Romke." Her voice shook. "I wanted so much to get Kea a special gift. She's been acting so different toward me lately. Something's upset her, but I have no idea what. I had hoped my present would mend the rift, and she would see how much I love her."

"I'm sure she'll understand. Just buy her something else next week."

But Anneke knew it wouldn't be the same.

Chapter

⟨❦⟩

9

On Saturday morning, Anneke spent hours in the kitchen making *stroop koekjes* and *appel taart*, two of Kea's favorite desserts. After baking the last sheet of molasses cookies and laying them in a circular pattern on a crystal plate, she set out the ingredients for the *appel taart*.

Though she did her best to push the stolen necklace from her mind while she prepared the cookie crust shell, disappointment plagued her. *When her sister discovers that she has no gift for her, Kea's hurt and disappointment will only widen the rift between us.* She and Kea had always been close in spite of their age difference. How she longed for their relationship to be restored.

Anneke's eyes misted as she pared the apples. One by one, she sliced them in eighths, then spread the crescent-shaped fruit in the pastry shell. While she filled the gaps with smaller pieces of apple, thoughts of love for Kea filled her mind. The thoughts became words, the words became verse, and before Anneke realized it, a poem had evolved. While the appel taart baked in the oven, she copied the verse onto paper.

My Sister

To whom do I run when I want to impart
All the joys and happiness deep in my heart?
Whom do I seek when I'm burdened with care?
My sister who's waiting my sorrows to share.

> *To whom do I go when I've heard some choice news?*
> *To you, my dear Kea, who else would I choose?*
> *It's you that I turn to, whatever the reasons:*
> *My sister, my treasure, my friend through all seasons.*

Anneke folded the paper and slid it under Kea's plate. After setting the table, she brought on the coffee and the warm *chocolade melk*.

Vader and Moeder took their seats, and Kea followed, her face beaming with anticipation.

Anneke removed the appel taart from the oven and placed it near Kea.

"Ummm." Vader inhaled deeply. "Remember to make an appel taart for me, Anneke, when it's my birthday."

"You can count on it, Vader." Anneke finished spooning on the last of the whipped cream in swirls.

After Vader said a special birthday blessing for Kea, they all joined their voices in the celebration song.

> *"Lang zullen wij leven,*
> *Lang zullen wij leven,*
> *Lang zullen wij leven*
> *in de gloria, in de gloria, in de gloria!"*

> *"Long shall we live, Long shall we live, Long shall*
> *we live in glory, in glory, in glory!"*

Kea finished her last bite and sighed. "Thank you, Anneke. That appel taart was delicious!" She looked up at Moeder. "Now may I open my gifts?"

Moeder handed her two presents. Kea tore open the first one and found a beautiful lace headpiece. She ran her finger over the delicate white pattern, then down the length of the soft blue tulle. "Oh, Moeder, it's beautiful. Thank you for making it for me. My old one is way too small and even ripped a little. And tomorrow's Sunday. I can hardly wait to show it off to my friends."

She picked up the second gift and stole a look at Anneke, but when she opened it, a puzzled look crossed her face. She held a dark, wooden pencil box. Carved flowers, painted blue and pink, graced the lid on all four corners; and her name, in flourishing silver script, danced in the center. She knew it was from Vader. Through the years, he had made her many cherished keepsakes out of wood. She looked up at him. "Oh, Vader, I love it!" Her finger traced the swirls flowing from the letters. "I'm so glad you added my name. That makes it specially mine." She opened the lid, and her eyes grew wide. Inside, were two new pencils and a fountain pen. "How did you know I needed these? Now I won't be losing my pencils at school anymore. Thank you so much, Vader." Kea grew silent, hesitant. She fixed her eyes on Anneke as though waiting for something.

Anneke reached across the table and squeezed Kea's hand. "On market day, I bought you a very special gift. But on our way home, I discovered it missing. I'm so sorry, Kea. I'll do my best to find another one next Thursday, but I don't think there were any more like it."

Kea jerked her hand away and scowled at Anneke. "I know better than that. You were so busy talking to Romke, you never even thought of my birthday."

Moeder stood to her feet. "Kea, I'm surprised at you. Certainly, you can believe your sister's word. Think about the hours she spent in the kitchen making your favorite desserts. You owe her an apology."

"She only baked them to cover up her neglect."

Anneke winced at her sister's words. She hesitated for a moment before telling her of the poem she had written for her. "Kea, I do have something else for you. It's under your plate."

Kea made no move to retrieve it. Finally, Moeder rose from the table and gathered the dishes. She picked up Kea's plate last and placed it on top of the others. In front of Kea lay a folded piece of paper. Kea snatched it, shoved back her chair, and marched from the room.

Chapter

⚭

10

The August heat had descended on Zevendorp. The flax was ready to harvest and, in every household, the women were canning their bounty. Anneke made her way to market alone. Moeder had been busy in the kitchen making applesauce and, alongside her, Kea was filling the shiny jars with plum preserves. Baskets of golden pears waited their turn to be sliced and seasoned with cinnamon.

Anneke entered the town gates and hurried to Romke's stand. Deep lines etched his brow. While staring off in the distance, he rubbed his fingers back and forth across his chin. She'd never seen him look so troubled. She stepped up closer, not knowing what to expect. "What's wrong, Romke?" He made no reply, but his fingers never stopped moving. Perplexed, she waited. Perhaps, he hadn't heard her. He hadn't even turned her way.

"Romke...?"

Before she could say more, a customer approached the stand. Romke turned to help him as though Anneke had never spoken. In response to the buyer's request, Romke sliced a wedge of cheese, gave it to the man, and accepted the coins. Blankly, he handed the gentleman his change. With a nod, the man left and was soon lost in the sea of shoppers. No warm welcome or friendly talk accompanied the cheese as Romke filled the requests of the buyers.

She puzzled over his actions. Something must be weighing heavy on his mind, but what? Had she upset him last week because she hadn't understood what he meant by her needing a savior?

She moved closer to his stand, but, before she could speak, a woman rushed to his booth and asked for two large wedges of cheese. Romke never acknowledged Anneke's presence. Instead, he turned to help the woman as though Anneke wasn't there.

Bewildered, she wanted to question him, but more people clustered around his stand, eager to be waited on. She would come back later when his work was done. But maybe he'd rather she didn't. Perhaps, he no longer cared for her. She walked away, trying to suppress the ache in her heart.

"Hey, Anneke!"

She froze at the sound of her name.

Cobie dashed toward her. Hands on her hips, she threw back her head. "What's the matter? Has the cheese peddler lost interest in you?" A smirk played around her lips.

Anneke scowled at her, wishing Cobie hadn't witnessed the scene. "What are you talking about?"

"You didn't notice? It was obvious the way he ignored you. What else could it mean?"

"He looked worried and distracted. But what difference does it make to you?"

"A lot," Cobie whispered under her breath. She turned and sauntered up to Romke's booth.

Anneke watched as Cobie desperately tried to win his attention by her prattle, but he seemed oblivious to her, too.

A sudden wind whirled through the marketplace. The wings of Anneke's cap fluttered in the breeze. Women clutched their lace caps to keep them from flying away. Men pulled their hats down tighter over their heads.

Shoppers ended their bartering with nearby vendors and gathered at Romke's stand, as though determined to have his cheese in hand before the approaching storm forced them to leave.

The mob pressed in on Cobie from both sides, pushing her first to the left, then to the right. She spun around in a rage and glared at the people surrounding her. "Give a body some room, will yuh? What right do you have shoving me around? I got here first!" She rammed her elbows into the sides of those next to her and planted her hands on her hips to keep the crowd at bay.

Romke turned from his patrons and stared speechless at Cobie, while Jorie wound his way through the crowd and appeared at her side.

Anneke edged closer, not wanting to miss any part of the scene.

Jorie selected a wedge of cheese and handed Romke the change. Then, slipping his arm through Cobie's, he ushered her off before she had time to protest. His other hand, sunk deep in his pocket, jingled the coins that lay inside.

Amused, Anneke followed them from a distance.

Cobie jerked her arm away from Jorie. "How dare you drag me off like that!"

Jorie handed her his purchase. "You have your cheese, so there's no more reason for you to be hanging around that stand."

"You have no right to tell me where I should or shouldn't be. Just who do you think you are, anyway?"

Anneke held her breath, wondering what would happen next.

The busy marketplace came to a halt as the villagers stood watching, while ignoring the threatening weather. Even the children stopped their whining and hid behind their mothers' skirts to peer at Cobie.

Jorie spoke with authority, but kindness showed in his voice. "If you can't control your own behavior, you need someone to help you do it."

Cobie's mouth dropped open. She glared at him while strands of hair, blown loose from her cap, waved in the wind. She turned from him with a jerk, only to see the nearby shoppers staring at her. Cobie's face turned crimson as she hurried by, then seeing Anneke, her body stiffened, her hand shook, and the cheese fell to the ground unnoticed. She clenched her jaw and ran from the market, the wind whipping her skirts. Jorie's gaze followed her through the square until she was lost from view.

ᏮᏗᎷᎧᎩ

A light rain began to fall, sending the villagers home, but Anneke barely noticed the drops when she headed back to Romke. His mood hadn't changed. She hesitated a moment, then walked behind the counter. "Romke, is something wrong?"

He set a wedge of cheese in her basket, then, laying his hands on her shoulders, looked deep into her eyes as though searching her heart. "Anneke, I dread having to tell you this, but—just yesterday, I found out this will be the last time I can leave home until next June." He swallowed hard, then paused several moments before continuing, his voice a husky whisper. "Darling, I'm going to miss you terribly."

Her lip trembled. October ended the selling of cheese until the following spring, but this was August. "You mean—you won't be back for almost a year?" Anneke fought the tears that clouded her eyes. "But, why?"

"I kept hoping I could come, at least for a few more weeks, but my father needs me on the farm. Uncle Fons had agreed to help us, but his wife's health took a turn for the worse. Then the continuous rain we've had set us back. If we put off cultivating any longer, we'll be late planting the winter wheat. Then, we'll lose much of our crop."

The thought of not seeing him for so long seemed unbearable. "Romke, I live for Thursdays when I can be with you." She lowered her head but not fast enough to hide her tears.

He gently wiped them from her face, then drew her head to his chest and held her close. "I love you, Anneke. I love you dearly." He tightened his embrace and placed his lips on a soft, blond curl. "Did you know I loved you the first day I saw you, and each time I'm with you, my love for you grows deeper?"

"Oh, Romke, I don't want you to go. I love you so much." She clung to him, afraid he would slip from her life as well as from her arms.

The wind grew stronger and streaks of lightning flashed across the sky. Romke's horse grew skittish: leaping in the air, kicking out, and rearing.

"Anneke, let me help you into the cart before the storm breaks loose. I'll join you just as soon as I calm my horse."

Reluctantly, she climbed into the cart. She watched as Romke quietly walked to his horse, gently rubbed his horse's neck and back, while speaking softly to him. After a short time, his horse relaxed. Romke returned to the cart and sat down beside Anneke, gathered her in his arms once more, and held her close.

All grew quiet. Only the steady "tap, tap, tap" of raindrops pelting the canvas hood above them, could be heard. She didn't want to break the mood, but the eerie cry of a loon shattered the silence, sending a shiver through her body. She glanced up at the sky. Threatening clouds stared down at her. She watched them move across the heavens until a premature darkness covered the sky. The wind whirled and the rain began to beat against the tarp above their heads.

Romke released her from his arms. "Darling, I've got to get you home."

When he left her arms, emptiness gripped her soul. The sinister clouds followed them while they made their way along the road. Each clop of the horse's hooves increased her anxiety as it brought her closer to home and nearer to Romke's departure. Would she ever see him again? Would he still love her a year from now, or would he forget her? In the distance, she could see her house. She turned away and stole a glance at Romke.

Pulling on the reins, he brought the cart to rest beneath a spreading willow. He reached for her hand and sought her eyes. "Anneke, will you wait for me?"

"You mean . . .?"

"Yes, darling." He touched a lock of hair escaping from her cap. "When I return next spring, will you come back with me to my village and be mine forever?"

A trace of thunder sounded in the distance.

Ignoring the thunder, she looked up at him and saw his dark hair, his kind and gentle eyes, and felt the warmth of his hand on hers. She loved him, loved everything about him.

While waiting for her answer, he placed his lips gently over hers. Then he raised his head. His eyes held hers.

Her heart pounded. "I'm yours, Romke," she whispered. "I'm yours forever."

He put her hand in his. "I promise you, *mijn lieveling,* my love, I'll be here for you in early June. And with this kiss, I seal my vow." He cupped her face in his hands, drew her closer, and kissed her lovingly, and then held her close once more.

She didn't want to leave his arms, but the thunder rumbled nearer. He would need to head back home. She felt his cheek next to hers. If only he didn't have to go, but he had promised her he would return next June. In the empty months ahead, she would remember these tender moments. They would bring her comfort and see her through.

Chapter

11

During the lonely fall, when Anneke's mood darkened, the memories of her final hour with Romke brightened her spirits. Day after day while she worked on her wedding gown, her thoughts drifted back to the times they had spent together.

Her longing for him escalated when she remembered that last day they had shared— how he had asked her to go with him to his village, and later when he brought her home, had come inside and asked for her parents' consent. The twinkle in Vader's eye and the contented smile that lingered on Moeder's face spoke surer of their permission than any answer they could have given.

Shopping with Moeder the following week, examining the beautiful fabrics in the marketplace, and choosing the loveliest satin for her wedding gown, had been exhilarating. And, in the most unlikely of stalls, Moeder had found iridescent dewdrops to add the finishing touch to her headpiece.

Anneke picked up the small cloth bag that held them and loosened the drawstring. She smiled as she peered inside and sifted through the stones. How beautiful they would look sprinkled over the delicate tulle flowing down her back and on the attached cap of lacy-silk water lilies. The petals would sparkle like blossoms kissed by the morning dew.

She drew out a handful and held them up to the window. As the light danced across their surfaces, her mind drifted to the things Romke had told her of his family and village.

His village. Again, the haunting words stirred in her mind. What was it Cobie had shouted that day outside the marketplace? She struggled to remember, but nothing surfaced.

She knew she'd be living in his family's home while he continued his responsibilities on the farm, but what would it really be like? Would his village be much different from hers? Would his parents like her? Would she like them? She hoped she would please them. But why should she worry? If they were anything like Romke, their home would be a wonderful place to live.

Moeder's presence usually kept such reflections at bay. Most days, they sewed together, but today other chores occupied Moeder's time. Anneke missed her expertise and companionship. Pensively, she let the tiny dewdrops slip through her fingers and form a pile in her lap. Without Moeder, it wouldn't be nearly as enjoyable stitching them to her headpiece, but—she could ask Kea. She'd love to share the time with her sister. She stood and held her apron over the table, letting the sparkling dewdrops pour out. She would invite Kea to join in the project.

After searching the house without finding her, Anneke stepped outside into the late August air. The breezes ruffled her skirts and played with the fringe on her shawl. She set off in the direction of the tall beech tree, Kea's favorite spot. Perhaps she'd find her there, propped against it, reading *Alice in Wonderland*. How many times had her sister read that? At least a dozen. Anneke chuckled.

A steady thump-thump-thump sounded ahead of her. The pounding grew louder as Anneke approached the tree. Scores of dried bundles of flax lay on the ground. One bundle was open and the woody part of the core had already been removed from the stems. The knife-shaped wooden blade her sister had used to scrape it off with lay next to it. Anneke circled halfway around the huge trunk before she found her. The happy memories of past years when she and Kea worked the flax together flooded her mind. Anneke wondered why her sister hadn't asked her to join her this time. Next year, Kea would be left to do it alone.

With flushed face, firmly set jaw, and a wooden mallet clenched in her fist, Kea pounded away at a pile of flax fibers. Anneke waited, not daring to interrupt her while her sister *beetled* the fibers. Already the strands had softened and glowed in the sun with a silky sheen, but Kea continued to beat them.

Sweat dripped from Kea's brow. She paused and dragged her sleeve across her forehead,

Anneke moved closer. "Kea?"

Kea dropped the mallet and her head shot up. "What are you doing here?"

"I've been looking for you."

"Well, you found me, so you can leave now."

Anneke winced. "Kea, I wanted to ask you…I thought it'd be nice to sew together. Would you like to stop *beetling* for a while and help me stitch the dewdrop stones on my veil? I can help you with this later."

The frown deepened on Kea's brow. "Why should I help *you*?"

"What's the matter? Why are you so upset?"

Kea hung her head. "Just go. I don't feel like talking."

"Look at me, Kea." Anneke waited till she got her sister's attention. "We've always done things together, and we've always had so much fun. I don't understand why you won't sew with me."

"Get Romke to sew with you. You'd rather have him anyway." Kea turned away, picked up the mallet, and resumed her arduous task.

Kea's words chilled Anneke like a winter wind blowing off the Zuider Zee, but she'd try once more. "Won't you please come with me?"

The sharp whacks from Kea's mallet split the air, punctuating the silence.

With heavy steps, Anneke made her way back to the house. The sparkling dewdrops in her mind's eye dimmed and turned to tear drops. She let them fall.

Chapter

12

Swaying her shoulders back & forth, Cobie sauntered up to Anneke, a sneer on her face. "It's a pity you have no one to drive you home from market today."

The words startled Anneke. She hadn't even heard Cobie approach. Anneke kept her back to her as she placed the bright red tomatoes in her basket among the asparagus and parsley. Anneke left the stand, still ignoring Cobie.

Cobie fell in step with her. "Maybe you can find another peddler in the marketplace to take you home—like Jorie." She snickered.

"There's only one man I care to ride with." Anneke hurried off.

Cobie followed her. "Remember, Romke's from Lijdendorp. Surely, you're aware of what those women have to contend with."

Uneasiness gripped Anneke. "What are you talking about?"

"Trial maternity. What else?"

Cobie's words drove a dagger through Anneke's heart. That couldn't be true. Cobie was lying.

"Does Romke really plan to marry you before he takes you to Lijdendorp, or will he wait until you're expecting his child? And what will happen if you can't give him one in the first year? Will he still love you, Anneke? Will he want you then?"

Anneke's heart pounded with rage. How dare Cobie insult her! Even if Romke's village did have such a custom, it didn't mean he agreed with it. "Romke loves me with his whole heart."

Cobie threw back her head and laughed. "It's not you he loves. He has but one motive—to breed farmhands for his own use. And if you can't give them to him, he'll toss you out like any other man from Lijdendorp would do."

Anneke's whole body trembled. "That's a lie. Romke's not like that. He would never send me away."

Cobie's lip curled. "Don't be so sure. What makes you think he's any different from the rest of the men in his village? Haven't you wondered why he came to Kollumdijk? It's obvious. His former woman failed the test."

Anneke gasped. "You don't know that's true."

"It doesn't take much to figure it out. You just don't want to admit it. I'd bet a hundred guilders it was the women who named their village. Ha, *Village of Sorrows*. How appropriate. And you want to go *there*? Sure sounds chancy to me, but if that's the risk you want to take, go ahead." A malicious grin covered Cobie's face while she swung her shoulders. "I hope you won't be *sorry*."

Cobie's taunts stung Anneke with greater force than the brisk autumn winds slashing her cheeks. Anneke clenched her fist. She didn't trust herself to answer. Instead, she left as though she hadn't heard, but fury and hurt consumed her. Cobie's words burned her heart, leaving behind a heavy, black cloud that smothered her joy. "Oh, that despicable girl," she repeated to herself as she hurried on her way. "Only jealousy would prompt her to say what she did."

Troubled thoughts ran through Anneke's mind. Surely, Romke hadn't had another woman. She shuddered. His eyes had always told her she was the only one he'd ever loved. He had even told her that himself. But if she couldn't give him a child in the first year, would he send her away?

Maybe she should write him regarding the maternity custom of his people. No, it would be best to wait until he returned. Then, face-to-face, she would ask him how he and his family felt about it. But it was foolish to borrow trouble. She would certainly have children, so that problem would never show its ugly face to her. Yet Cobie's words haunted her all the long months that followed.

⟨∞∞⟩

March arrived and, with it, Romke's letter saying he would come back for her the first week in June. Anxiously, she counted the days. Excitement and anticipation for his return made her forget her fears and Cobie's taunts. After reading Romke's latest letter, Anneke lived in a dream. She tried to imagine what it would be like to have him for her husband. "Wonderful, absolutely wonderful," she whispered as she spun around before her mirror.

She picked up her purse and joined her family walking down the road to church. During the morning service, her thoughts drifted to their wedding that would take place right here. How lovely the sanctuary would look decorated with ferns and flowers, with candles flickering their little lights throughout the ceremony.

Then the candlelight in her mind's eye faded as Cobie's words came back to her. If Romke's family adhered to their village custom, she might not even have a wedding. She couldn't imagine marrying Romke only after they knew she would have a child. But surely, he would respect her wish and agree to have their wedding here before they traveled to his home, and then to be in Romke's arms forevermore. What bliss. What heavenly happiness. Again, the imaginary candles burned bright.

Anneke roused from her daydream as the congregation sang the closing hymn. After the final "Amen", the people filed out, greeting one another with a smile or a nod.

"Hi, Anneke." Cobie stood before her, all smiles in her Sunday best, a black, wool skirt only slightly better than the worn and faded gray one she wore on weekdays. "Just three months left till June. I bet you're excited. Which week does Romke plan to come for you?"

"Why do you want to know?"

Cobie closed her eyes, and a soft smile spread across her face. "I guess you might say I'm anxious to…" Her smile vanished. "I'm anxious for you, that is."

Why should she give Cobie any information? "You'll know when you see him."

Cobie stiffened, and her eyes burned with hate. "I hope you're ready when he comes."

"I've already made sure of that."

"I don't mean ready for the wedding. I mean ready for the risk!" Cobie spat the last words with venom, turned on her heel and sauntered away.

Anneke stared after her in shock. Had anyone else heard those hateful words? The same black cloud that had had haunted her earlier grew heavy in her heart, blotting out her sunshine once more. It hovered over her, making her feel uneasy and insecure.

⊙ⱮⱮⱲ☉

Several days later, Anneke finished her wedding gown. She tried it on and, after turning this way and that before the mirror, felt pleased with the final results.

"Oh, what a beautiful bride you make!" Her mother stood in the doorway, her eyes shining with admiration.

Like a ballerina, Anneke pivoted, then curtsied, holding out her hand to her mother.

Into Anneke's opened hand, her mother placed her own antique vase of rich Delft Blue porcelain. "Dear, I want you to have this for your wedding gift."

Anneke looked in awe at the treasured heirloom. She loved how the blue-flowered vine swirled gracefully around the pearly-white vase. It had always been her favorite, but she knew it was the one her mother cherished most. "Oh, Moeder, as much as I love it, I couldn't. I know how much it means to you."

"That's all the more reason I want you to have it. Each time you look at this, remember I'm thinking of you and praying for you."

"That's so sweet of you, Moeder. I will treasure it even more now." Mixed emotions surged through her, and the pent-up anxieties of the past months finally gave way. She crumpled in her mother's arms and cried.

Moeder held her close, allowing Anneke's emotions free rein.

As her tears subsided, Anneke looked up at her mother. "Has anyone mentioned anything to you about Romke?"

"How do you mean, dear?"

"Well, like the customs of his people?"

"You mean trial maternity?" asked Moeder.

"Y-yes. Then you know about it too?"

"Only what I've heard different ones say. But you'll be marrying him here before you leave for Lijdendorp, won't you? Didn't he agree to that last August?"

Anneke's finger traced the design on the vase she held. "Well, I assumed we would. We didn't really talk about the wedding. But he told me he loved me and asked me to come with him to his village, and I promised him I would be his forever."

"The only way I'll let you go is if you're married in our church."

"Yes, Moeder, and I'm sure he'll want to be, but..."

Moeder smoothed Anneke's hair. "But what, dear?"

"It's just that, Cobie knows about the maternity custom, too, and she taunts me whenever she sees me. But I trust Romke and even if I were unable to have children, I feel sure he would never send me away, but still it's unsettling."

Anneke's mother gave her a warm hug. "I can't believe Romke would do that to you, but you need to find out how he and his parents feel about this custom. Talk to him when he comes this June. His village may not even practice that anymore.

"But don't let Cobie upset you, dear. She's a troubled girl. All she's ever known is insecurity. When she was only three, her father deserted her and her mother. Mrs. Tasman never got over the shock and hurt." Moeder sighed. "Poor woman. That's the reason she suffers so and has neglected Cobie most of her life. Cobie has never experienced the stability of a normal, loving home. Just try to understand her and forgive her."

Pity stirred in Anneke's heart for Cobie, but the darts that Cobie had thrown at her were too painful to forgive.

Chapter

⌒∞⌒

13

Bitter March winds tore at Anneke and Kea as they made their way through the marketplace. It seemed June would never come to replace the harsh winter months they'd endured. The wind howled more fiercely than ever, as if March had determined to flaunt its cruel weather.

The market teemed with people despite the severe climate, but it lacked the cheery chatter that usually filled the scene. Anneke noticed that Kea acted differently too. Instead of lagging behind, stopping here, loitering there, her sister hovered near her.

They worked their way through the crowd toward the kettle stall. Copper pans of all sizes hung from the rafters while others lay in piles around the merchant.

Catching Anneke's eye, the vendor chanted his sales pitch. "Copper kettles, get 'em here. Tasty meals you'll serve all year!" To accent his jingle, he grabbed the pipe from his mouth and struck a kettle that hung from the rafter above.

Anneke jumped. The unexpected clang reverberated through her body, jarring her nerves. All the while, the man kept his eyes on her, making it difficult for her to concentrate on which kettle to choose. The corner of his mustached mouth turned up in a sneer, accenting a scar that zigzagged like a snake from his right nostril down past his chin. She shivered.

"Sorry if I startled you, *mejuffrouw.* I like to see folks react. It's just my way." He cleared his throat. "Didn't mean to upset you none."

Anneke didn't know how to answer him. She couldn't remember ever seeing him before, yet something about him looked familiar. She knew she didn't trust him. Maybe it was his manner or those long sideburns and dark, greasy hair or the expression in his eyes that made her so uncomfortable—or his snake-like scar. That alone was enough to unnerve her.

Kea tugged on Anneke's arm and shouted. "Come on, let's go! It's getting darker. I don't want to be here when the storm comes."

Her sister's complaint stirred Anneke into action. "We need to get a kettle, and then we'll leave."

"Who needs an ol' kettle, anyway?" said Kea, still tugging on her sister's arm. "I want to go home!"

The merchant continued to stare at Anneke. She felt uneasy as she scanned the display of kettles. She tried to remember what Moeder wanted, but her mind had drawn a blank.

"Come on, Anneke!"

Yes, she would like to leave too, but she couldn't without her purchase. She picked up one, turned it over, and read the words on the back, "Quality Kettles," along with the craftsman's initials, "DT." It looked like the right size.

"I'll take this one." She laid it back down on the counter and fumbled in her purse for the correct change, then handed him the coins.

She reached for the kettle, but he snatched it away and, once again, struck a deafening blow that resounded through the gusty winds.

Anneke jumped back, shaken and perplexed. Should she try to take the kettle from him, or would he only yank it from her again? Then, seeing her chance, she grabbed for it. The stranger's lip curled as he placed the pipe back in his mouth.

With the kettle tucked under her arm and her fingers wrapped tight around the handle, she pulled Kea to her side and turned from the stand. Her body shook, and her mouth quivered. She struggled to distance herself from the vendor, but her legs were as weak as two sardines out of water. After walking several minutes, she still could sense the man's strange power over her.

When they neared the town gates, the wind died down, and an ominous silence took its place. A figure clad in black, its garment trailing the ground, swept through the entrance. A hood half-covered the face, and a bony hand clasped its cape to its chest. With the other hand, it pointed a skeletal finger to all who came near, as though sentencing them to condemnation.

Kea grabbed Anneke's arm. "Oh, look! Who's *that*?" Her voice trembled.

Anneke gasped. She shook her head, unable to respond.

The growing crowd edged closer, but kept a safe distance from the stranger. Curiosity and fear covered each face while a deathlike stillness hung in the air.

The creature moved closer and opened its mouth to speak. Unable to hear the stranger's muffled words, the villagers leaned forward.

The bony finger of the unknown one moved left, then right, pointing to all in its path. Slowly, it edged its way to Anneke, and there the finger stayed.

Anneke held her breath and drew Kea close to her, never taking her eyes off the form standing before them.

"HARK!" The cry echoed through the marketplace.

Kea trembled, and Anneke tightened her arm around her sister.

The mouth of the stranger opened once again, and words poured out in hollow, eerie tones.

> "You citizens of Kollumdijk
> And villages nearby,
> I've come to bring a warning
> To you all before you die."

Kea clung fast to Anneke's arm.
The stranger's voice grew intense.

> "I have seen the elusive mermaid
> On the rolling Zuider Zee.
> In the twilight hour she beckoned,
> Then she swiftly swam my way.

She told me what would happen,
Everything that was in store.
How the floods would come
And drown you all for sure.

You refuse to heed the mermaid,
But her power o'er you will loom;
She's the messenger of evil,
She's the mermaid of our DOOM."

The last few words crescendoed in a raspy screech, then silence returned—a chilling silence that turned Anneke's blood to ice. The lanky finger never wavered as it pointed straight at her.

Sweat broke out on Anneke's face. She wanted to wipe it away, but she didn't dare move.

The draped form edged closer to Anneke, paused, and continued the sentence of destruction.

"Zevendorp will be destroyed,
Though the church tower will remain.
Listen well and hear the warning
That the waterwolf will reign.

Of this prophecy be certain,
Of her words you may be sure:
From the mermaid's bleak foretelling,
Not a one of you'll endure.

You can take or spurn my warning,
But of this you may be sure.
Neither woman, man, nor child,
Not a one of you'll endure."

A deafening silence filled the marketplace paralyzing the villagers: children's faces, white with terror, clung to their mother's skirts; women, hands pressed to their heart, stood hyperventilating; while all around them, men stood motionless like statues.

"**DOOM**!" The final warning poured from the mouth of the eccentric being, followed by an unearthly cry that pierced the air.

Tremors slithered up Anneke's spine. Her feet froze to the cobblestones. Kea's body grew stiff against her.

A shout rose from the crowd. "It's the Devil!"

Another yelled, "It's a witch!"

A rush of voices cried out in unison: "It's Mrs. Tasman! Seize her! Don't let her get away!"

The marketplace went wild. Children screamed, women wailed, while the men pushed their way through the mob, charging across the cobblestones to reach the messenger of doom. The crowd of shoppers followed from a safe distance, determined to see what would become of Mrs. Tasman.

Soon, shouts of victory rose from the men up ahead. "We've got her! That'll be the last of her threats. We'll lock her up for good."

Mrs. Tasman—abducted. Anneke shuddered. Sorrow and relief vied to win the battle in Anneke's heart. She'd never be threatened again by ominous prophecies, but now Cobie would be all alone. How long did they plan to keep her mother locked up— for life?

The mania gradually subsided to a hideous buzz, like a swarm of bees. All around, shoppers had formed groups to discuss the episode. Anneke felt the bees would attack her unless she left the clamor. But now, Kea begged to stay and hear the gossip, rumors, and predictions.

Kea tugged on Anneke's arm. "Let's stay a little longer, please? I want to hear what everyone's saying."

Anneke sighed. She preferred to head home, but she had to admit that now, her curiosity was almost as strong as her sister's.

"What will become of the poor creature?" asked a kind-faced seamstress, her eyes misty as she twisted one end of the measuring tape that dangled from her neck.

"They'll lock her up where she belongs. They should have done it years ago," a vendor retorted.

The seamstress blinked several times to stem the tears threatening to spill. "But her daughter—what will become of her?"

"She'll manage," said the vendor. "The woman's never taken care of her child all these years, and Cobie's of age. Maybe it'll be best for both of them."

The seamstress pulled out her handkerchief and dabbed her eyes. "The woman did us a service if she truly believed what she told us. We should thank her, not punish her."

"Well, I say you can't take the word of a lunatic. I know one thing, I don't intend to lose any sleep over it."

Anneke grew dizzy as the voices persisted in their clashing views. She felt like taffy, pulled first in one direction, and then yanked back in the other. She wished she could see the face of the man who had spoken. He was so insensitive! But his back was to her, and she didn't want to move in front of him and call attention to herself. He had to be the vendor she had met at the kettle stand. She recognized his voice. And if he were, she certainly wouldn't want to catch his eye again. She would stay where she was and listen.

An elderly washerwoman set down her basket of dirty clothes and tapped her cane on the stones to get the attention of the vendor who had just spoken. "You can say all you want, but I, for one, feel there may be some truth to it. It's usually that type of person who has a sixth sense. We might be wise to listen to her."

"You're a fool if you believe that woman's tale." The vendor spat on the ground.

The washerwoman pointed her cane at him. "We'll see who the fools are when you perish in the flood."

A young girl about ten years old moved closer into the circle. "I've read about mermaids cursing towns and villages. It happened just like the mermaid said it would. The dikes broke, the towns flooded, and all the people perished. It's right in my great-great-grandfather's diary. Honest! You can read it yourself!"

The man sneered, but the child's broad-chested mother stepped forward.

"My daughter's right. I have that diary of my great-grandfather, who was a sea merchant. He wrote of several instances when mermaids appeared to him and his shipmates. If they even looked at a mermaid, the waves would churn and the tempests rage. I tell you, I've read that diary many a time. It's enough to make the spinning sails of a windmill stop dead."

"Legends and fairy tales—stuff for kids and lunatics. I suppose you both believe in the waterwolf, too?"

Before the hefty woman could answer, the washerwoman thumped her cane again. "You know as well as I do that the waterwolf has caused disaster to our land throughout history. That's common knowledge, son."

"Floods and tempests, yes. Waterwolf? Sure, if you call the raging waves its claws, and the roaring sea its growl. And I suppose you believe the flooded villages are the result of the waterwolf's greed and hunger for the farms and villages. It's an overactive imagination that fabricates such nonsense. Waterwolf and mermaids, indeed!" He spat again as if spewing the very creatures from his mouth.

The washerwoman stood as tall as her small stature would let her and faced her opponent. "Then, how do you account for the destruction of Wenduine that vanished in a spring tide after a young fisherman saw a mermaid? Or the villagers of Zevenbergen, who perished in a flood, just as a mermaid had prophesied?"

"Enough, enough of this nonsense."

"You will hear me out," insisted the washerwoman. "Remember, Westerschouwen reaped disaster." Her voice rose. "And don't forget the terrible flood of 1717, when a mermaid cursed the town of Namen."

A coarse burst of laughter tore from the vendor's mouth. "Well, I must admit you listened well in school and learned your facts, or should I say fiction." He sneered again and pulled his pipe from his coat pocket. "I'm afraid I've got more sense than to put stock in those old fables."

"Well, just the same, I'm not taking any chances." The washerwoman thumped her cane on the stones at her feet.

A young scholar listening to the conversation from outside the circle moved in and joined the group. "So, what do you propose we do? Pack our bags and flee to Germany?"

A stocky fisherman, huddled inside his thick wool jacket, spoke up. "I don't know about you folks, but I'm staying put. *This* is my country, not Germany. This is where my fathers lived, and it's where I'll live, come what may."

The washerwoman shook her head. "Those are pretty risky words. You may find yourself fleeing with the rest of us."

The fisherman set his jaw. "Well, I'm not leaving. You think I'm pulling up roots just because a lunatic threatens me? What does she know? She can't even function in everyday life."

The scholar broke in. "Even if you did believe in the oaths of mermaids, no one has any proof that that crazy woman ever saw one."

"How true." The vendor rubbed his pipe in his hand with satisfaction. "Here are a couple of men who can think for themselves. Now that they've hauled that crackpot off to the asylum, we won't have to worry about any more threats from mermaids." A coarse burst of laughter poured from the vendor's mouth. He winked at the two men in their circle, turned his pipe upside down and tapped it several times in the palm of his hand, then slipped it between his lips.

"That's him all right," Anneke said under her breath. Instinctively, she grabbed Kea and edged closer, in time to see a cold gleam flash in the man's eyes.

Without warning, the vendor jerked his pipe from his mouth and struck a savage blow against the old washerwoman's cane.

Startled, the woman began to shake.

A wry smile lingered on the man's lips. "Relax, just relax. I wasn't trying to rattle you, granny. I only wanted to wake you out of your dream world." He leaned forward and addressed the trembling woman once more. "Just don't let any mermaids swim into your dreams, mevrouw." His lip curled again, and his scar widened, distorting his face. Puffing on his pipe, he turned and sauntered off to his cart. The small group watched the cart jostle over the cobblestones, the heaps of kettles tumbling and clanging.

"Does anyone know who that man is?" asked the seamstress.

The washerwoman shook her head. "Never saw the man before, but I don't think I've missed much." Her hand still shook as she clutched her cane.

The seamstress nodded. "I don't recall ever seeing him either. He's not from Kollumdijk. Maybe he's from Zevendorp. He seemed to know a lot about Mrs. Tasman. He even knew her daughter's name."

"He also knows no respect," said the older woman. "He can say what he wants, but I'm taking note of the warning, just the same."

Anneke shivered as she clasped Kea's hand and hurried from the marketplace. In the darkening sky every naked branch pointed down at her, every gust of wind echoed the sentence of doom.

Chapter

———— ⚬✤⚬ ————

14

The routine of daily life gradually shoved Mrs. Tasman's message of doom from Anneke's mind. Spring settled in at last, bringing all the promises of life and beauty.

It wouldn't be long before Romke would return to take her to his home, and she must be ready. She placed her valise on her bed, opened it, and stepped over to her wardrobe. After choosing her nicest clothes and her best Sunday outfit, she placed them in the valise. While she worked, her excitement grew, sending dreams wafting through her mind.

Next she'd decide which shoes to take. She walked over to the closet to get them and gasped. One pair was badly scuffed and some of the wood on the other pair was splintering. She didn't remember them looking that bad. She would buy some pretty ones on market day.

Now, she needed to decide on which jewelry to take. After choosing her favorite pieces, she pulled opened a drawstring bag and let the sparkling necklaces, earrings, brooches and rings pour into the bag.

But something was missing. "Oh, the pillowcases." She couldn't leave without those. She opened her cedar chest and drew them out, then closed the lid and sat down. Holding them in her hands, she gazed at them, thrilled with their beauty. How she treasured these. She remembered the first day she began embroidering them, and how she had wondered who would lay his head on the other pillowcase, all the while hoping it'd be Romke. And now that wish would be granted. She ran her finger over the embroidery floss, following the outline of the water lilies. Would Romke love them as much as she did?

∽⦚∾

On the first market day in June, Anneke's heart fluttered as fast as the wings of the windmill along their canal. Today she would see Romke! Those long, lonely months had passed, and now only happiness lay before her. She dressed in her prettiest full skirt and, draping her pastel blue shawl around her shoulders, ran to the kitchen. "Moeder, I'll be ready to leave for market as soon as I eat breakfast."

Moeder set the dishes on the table. "I won't be going to market today. There's too much to do before the wedding. Also I need Kea to stay here and help me. Can you manage everything by yourself?"

"Yes, Moeder."

Anneke felt relieved as she went out the door. Now she could be alone when she saw Romke. And just the two of them could come back home together. She hummed a tune while she walked along, keeping Romke's image in her mind. How wonderful it'll be to see him again. Her face aglow, she quickened her pace, and soon reached the town gates.

Cobie stood inside the entrance. A satisfied smirk hovered about her lips as she stepped to Anneke's side. "Romke's here. I beat you to his stand—as usual." She jerked her chin out, malicious pleasure flashing from her eyes.

Anneke ignored her and kept walking.

Cobie fell in step with her. "How nice it was to talk with him again. I must say, it's been rather boring around here for the past ten months without him."

Anneke refused to answer.

Cobie edged a little closer. "We talked for quite awhile. He even asked my name."

She paused, swaying her shoulders back and forth. "I bet he drives me home today."

Anneke's anger rose. "You make me sick! Don't you know we're getting married this Saturday?" The words caught in her throat sending fear through her. What if Romke decided not to marry her, after all? Her hand flew to her heart. *Oh, Romke, please say you'll marry me. . . before we set sail for Lijdendorp.* Struggling to push the uneasiness from her mind, she faced Cobie. "Why don't you spend your time on someone who loves you, like Jorie."

Cobie spat on the cobblestones. "Jorie? I loathe him! Besides, he's too easy a catch. I prefer a challenge."

"Well, someday you may be begging at his feet."

Cobie came to a halt and gasped.

Anneke took advantage of the situation and sped up, weaving in and out among the people in hopes of losing Cobie in the crowd. Soon, she caught sight of Romke. Her heart beat wildly. Oh, how handsome he looked. How she loved him. She longed to feel his arms around her once again. Forgetting her fear, she hurried to his stand. "Romke."

He looked up. "Anneke!" He took her hand in his. "I've waited so long for this moment. Oh, mijn lieveling." He picked up a red rose from the counter and placed it in her hair. "Seeing you is like having spring in all its beauty stand before me." He studied her face. "You haven't changed a bit, darling, just more lovely."

She felt her body glow in the warmth of his smile. "It's so good to have you back again, Romke. I thought the months would never end."

He gave her hand a gentle squeeze before he released it. More customers had come to buy his cheese.

How thrilling to have him here again. And to think, this time she would go with him when he left for his home. They would go together as husband and wife—or would they?

Tremors fluttered through her body. She wanted to ask him now, but a long line of customers extended from his booth. Then, remembering her own shopping, she waved and hurried off to make her purchases. She found the yard goods, chose several spools of thread, and paid for them. She then made her way to the vegetable stand. After making her selections, she headed to Jorie's booth. This was one place she knew Cobie would stay clear of. Anneke picked up her pace. She'd buy the prettiest pair of shoes to take with her to her new home in Lijdendorp.

Lijdendorp. . . The name reverberated in her mind. All the taunts Cobie had thrown at her threatened Anneke anew. Her heart pounded as she remembered she had but one year to prove she could mother a child. And what if she couldn't? Would Romke really send her away? No, it would never happen. But as she struggled to push the disturbing thoughts from her mind, the sun's soft glow faded. A cloud had passed over it, leaving her uneasy.

A group of women had gathered at Jorie's stand. As she drew closer, a display of cradles out front surprised her. She stepped to the one nearest her and ran her hand over its smooth finish. Another one had ornate scrollwork carved on both the head and footboards. Some cradles had decorative cutout heart shapes, while others were painted with delicate flowers. But one particularly caught her attention. The rims on both sides of the cradle were carved to look like waves. Anneke marveled at its creativity. It almost seemed as though it belonged on the sea instead of by a cozy hearth.

A picture flashed through her mind of an infant in a cradle, tossing over the waves. She shuddered at the thought. Why did that image seem so familiar to her? Then she remembered reading in grade school about the St. Elizabeth's flood of 1421. A baby was found washed ashore in a cradle, the lone survivor of that disaster. The people in the surrounding areas renamed the village Kinderdijk, Child's Dike.

She shivered. *What a nightmare that must have been.* She found herself gently rocking the cradle, wondering what little child would be laid inside. But this was the dawn of the twentieth century. The dikes along the sea arms and the rivers were more secure now than they had been back then. She'd seen severe storms, but never a flood that wiped out towns and villages. The dikes had always proved strong enough to hold back the raging sea.

Then a chilling thought loomed in her memory: Mrs. Tasman, shrouded in hooded garb, warning the villagers of inevitable doom. Recalling the incident made her nervous. She quickly dismissed it from her mind. It was time to forget about cradles, floods, and warnings.

Turning her attention to the shoes, she looked over the huge display. Again, each pair's uniqueness proclaimed Jorie's artistic ability. If only Cobie could see his worth. From the rows of shoes, Anneke chose a bright blue pair with borders of tiny, white flowers circling the opening of each shoe. "How beautiful," she whispered. She tried them on for size.

A perfect fit. She looked over the rows of shoes again, until she found a pair for every-day use. She gathered the shoes in her arms and headed for Jorie's stand.

Jorie had just finished with his customer, when Anneke reached his stand. "Hi, Jorie. I see you've expanded your business. Your cradles are beautiful."

Jorie's smile illuminated his face. With a slight bow, he extended his hand. "That's very kind of you, Anneke. I hear you're planning a wedding soon."

Anneke handed him a *gulden*. "Yes, very soon. It's this Saturday, and you're cordially invited."

"Thank you. I'll be there." With a broad smile, he placed the money in his pocket.

As she turned to go, she could hear the jingle of coins as Jorie ran his fingers through them.

When she reached Romke's stand, he had finished closing up. It reminded her of old times when he helped her into her seat in the wagon. After a short time, Romke brought the cart to rest beneath the shade of a white willow. The tree spread its branches over them in blessing. Even the sunshine had returned, filling the tender moments with warmth.

Romke faced Anneke as he gently took her hand in his. "Do you still love me enough to come back with me?"

A chill ran through her. Had he not received her letters, telling him how much she loved and missed him, and how she longed for his return? Each night she'd crossed out the current day on her calendar, eagerly waiting for this very moment to arrive. "Oh, Romke, my feelings for you haven't changed. They've only grown stronger."

Relief showed on his face. He brought her hand to his lips and kissed it tenderly. "I hoped you would say that."

"Did you doubt that I still loved you?"

"No, I really didn't believe what she said. I've just wanted to hear you tell me so yourself."

Anneke placed her other hand over his. "You didn't believe what who said?"

"Do you know a girl named Cobie?"

Anneke jerked upright. "Yes—what did she tell you?"

"Just that—" He paused before going on. "She said that you had changed your mind about returning with me, and that you never really loved me."

So Cobie had lied to Romke about her. Hate seethed in her heart toward Cobie. She looked up into Romke's face. "Darling, I love you with my whole being. Believe me when I tell you I am yours and only yours."

Romke drew Anneke back into his arms. "Mijn lieveling, those are the words I've been longing to hear."

How wonderful she felt. She was safe in her haven at last. And this haven would be hers forever. She raised her head toward Romke. "The past months have been long and hard. Every chance Cobie had, she ridiculed you to my face. She taunted me with threats that. . ." Anneke couldn't repeat what Cobie had said to her.

Romke cradled her in his arms. "Tell me, Darling."

Her lip trembled. She didn't want their marriage to be a trial one, secure only if she could give him a child. And in a year's time, at that! "Oh, Romke, say it's not true."

"Say what's not true, mijn lieveling?"

"That if the woman cannot..." Her voice caught and a tear rolled down her cheek.

Romke's finger followed the gentle curve of a curl that lay on her forehead. "Are you talking about the trial maternity custom of my people?"

Anneke nodded. "Y-yes."

"When I take you to be mine, Anneke, it will be forever, regardless of any circumstances. My love for you will take precedence over any tradition of our people." He kissed her quivering lips as a lasting promise of his faithfulness.

"And do your parents feel as you do?" She had to know the truth.

A shadow crossed his face as he gently released her and leaned back in the cart. For several minutes, he stared at the wispy branches of the old willow tree that hovered above them. Then, looking down, he ran his finger over the design etched in a silver button on his shirt. It seemed an eternity before he answered. He took her hand in his. "My parents are from the 'old school,' you might say, and quite set in their ways. Yes, they were brought up to follow that custom." He swallowed hard. "But when they see our love for each other, I feel sure they will give us their blessing."

Anneke wished she could be satisfied with his answer, but uneasiness gripped her. Was he trying to convince himself as well as her?

When they started back down the country lane, she forced herself to forget her fears. He was the man she loved. Nothing else mattered. In her mind she repeated the words Romke had said. "When they see our love for each other, I feel sure they will give us their blessing." Maybe he was right. He should know. After all, they were his parents. She pushed the issue from her mind.

Anneke leaned closer, brushing Romke's shoulder with hers. "I've been very busy these past months."

Romke looked down at her with a smile. "Doing what, may I ask?"

"Making my wedding gown." She waited for his response.

Romke released his right hand from the reins and put his arm around her. "And when will I get to see it?"

Anneke blushed. "On our wedding day."

Romke slowed the cart to a stop on a narrow bend in the road. Then his lips found hers. "Have you already planned the wedding?"

"Oh, yes!" Then doubts crept in to smother her joy. "That is all right, isn't it?"

"Of course, darling. I guess I hadn't even thought about a ceremony, since my village doesn't do it that way. My dreams only consisted of whisking you off as my true love and floating over the Zuider Zee with you, in my boeier."

Anneke caught the dreamy look in his eyes. "But what will your folks say? Will they disapprove if we go against your tradition by marrying first?"

He cupped her face in his hands and kissed her tenderly. "It may be the way of our people, but it's not God's way. Holding to a custom like that isn't placing faith in God's perfect will for our lives." His face brightened as he took her hands in his. "So our wedding will be this Saturday?"

Relief filled Anneke's heart. "Yes. Everything's ready."

Romke gathered her in his arms once more. "Oh, mijn lieveling," he whispered. "In two more days you'll be my wife."

Anneke sighed in contentment. Never had she felt so secure--so sure of a happy future.

Chapter

15

Dressed in her bridal attire, Anneke radiated with beauty as she walked with Romke, down the village lane to the church. The birds in the trees above trilled in chorus when the two of them passed by. It seemed all heaven sang as the sun burst forth in splendor, trimming the edges of the cotton-white clouds with gold. The iridescent teardrops on her veil and headpiece shimmered in the morning light and seemed to bring the lacy water lilies to life. Golden rosettes decked with pearls hung like bells from the sides of her *oorijzer* and sparkled on her forehead. She turned toward Romke, admiring him as he walked by her side. He looked down at her and caught her gaze, and simultaneously they broke into smiles.

Anneke's family followed behind. Moeder appeared serene as she watched the happy couple before her, but her eyes, reddened by the tears she had shed earlier, betrayed a mother's sorrow.

Vader's face glowed as he watched his daughter, his pride and joy, and the man about to become her husband. He turned to his wife with a twinkle in his eye. "Remember when we walked down this lane anticipating our new life together?"

Anneke's mother looked up into her husband's face. She took his arm and, drawing strength from his happiness, answered. "Yes, dear. It seems like only yesterday. But we were so much older."

"You were only seventeen when I married you, and Anneke is eighteen."

"But they seem so young. Maybe if she weren't leaving our village, I would feel better about it. It's just that. . ." Moeder paused to clear her throat. "I have this strange feeling we'll never see her again."

"Now, darling, don't borrow sadness, especially on her wedding day."

"You're right. I'm being foolish to think this way." She looked up again into her husband's face and felt reassured.

Kea lagged behind, a deep scowl etched across her brow. Her footsteps matched neither the light ones of her sister, the proud ones of her father, nor the yielding ones of her mother. She trudged along, upset that she'd been forced to come.

Kea gritted her teeth. *What made her sister so happy, anyway? Didn't she realize she was breaking up their family? There'd be no one, now, to wash dishes or scrub the kitchen floor with or share the loathsome job of preparing the flax. Having Anneke there, with her lively chatter, always helped to make the time fly by and ease the drudgery of the dreaded chores. She almost wished she had sewn with her sister when Anneke had begged her to. Now, there would never be another chance to do anything with her sister again.*

Anneke was leaving her forever, the only sister she had. Obviously, Anneke didn't care about her anymore, if she could go off and leave her like this. She'd just up and decided to marry this man, a stranger too. It wouldn't have been quite so bad if he were from their village. But no, he had to be from some remote place called Lijdendorp. . . Village of Sorrows! The name itself should have been warning enough for her sister not to go there.

She and Anneke had always been so close. Somehow their age difference had never mattered. Being sisters, they shared everything they did, even their secrets. But then things changed. Anneke preferred Romke's company to hers. It all started last year when Anneke slipped in the raw egg that Lambertus had thrown. Lambertus the beast—it was all his fault!

She would never forget what had happened the following week, right after Anneke turned seventeen. Kea couldn't keep her frown from growing deeper. *She never wanted to turn seventeen, and that was final. Eleven was a good age to be. Scenes of that market day, so different from the ones before, flashed through her mind. Instead of walking with her, Anneke had hurried ahead. But she wouldn't tell her why she was so* anxious to get there. Then after they had arrived, Anneke went off and left her. She no longer wanted her. Someone else had taken her place.

Several times, Anneke and Moeder had invited her to join them as they worked on Anneke's wedding gown, but she had refused. Why should she help to hasten her sister's departure?

Anneke never should have turned seventeen. That was her mistake, and now she was making another one. If only her sister could realize that things would never be the same again.

"Hurry up, Kea! Why do you always lag behind?" Lambertus pushed on his glasses, setting them back on his small, freckled nose.

She ignored him. *His thick, unruly red curls, matted together like a shrunken wool blanket, actually looked fairly presentable today. How long had Tante Zusje worked on them to get his curls to lie flat?*

"Don't you want to see your sister married?" Lambertus persisted, pushing on his glasses again. "If you don't walk faster, the wedding will be over by the time you get there."

How disgusting Lambertus was. Of all people to be paired up with. As if the wedding wasn't enough of a torture, having him for her partner added insult to injury. She couldn't remember a time when she hadn't detested him. His name was bad enough. When he turned twelve, he had wanted to be called Bertie, but she'd told him straight out, "Anyone as ugly as you are deserves a name like Lambertus, so Lambertus it is!" From that point, their relationship had gone from bad to worse. But she didn't care.

"Come on, Kea, pick up your feet and get moving."

Wrinkling up her nose at him, Kea lunged forward and kicked him in the shin. "There! Did I pick up my feet enough for you that time?"

Lambertus' cheeks vibrated, and his face turned red, then purple with rage.

She gloated as she watched the transformation. *What power she had over him, to make his face turn such a hideous shade.* She felt happy for the first time all day.

Her cousin's eyes began to bulge.

Kea giggled. She couldn't have hoped for anything better.

Then fire lit his eyes. Like a streak of lightening, he bounded toward her.

Kea darted away, but not fast enough.

He lunged at her, grabbed her braid, and yanked till she cried. "Owwww—Stop it! Let go."

Kea's parents turned, saw their nephew's peculiar coloring, and rushed to his side. "Lambertus, are you all right?"

His body shook with fury, but a grin began to play on his purple lips.

Kea's eyes grew wide as his smile reached the size of the Cheshire Cat's— just like the picture in her Alice in Wonderland book.

Lambertus faced the little group standing around him. "Actually, I haven't felt better in a long time."

By the time Anneke's family reached the church, the excitement had died down. Kea and Lambertus stood in their positions at the altar. Lambertus's face had softened. *Kea knew he was ready to forgive and forget, but she wasn't. A tear was jerked loose when he yanked her braid, and he had seen the telltale sign of her weakness.* She determined in her heart to get even. *Just you wait, Lambertus,* she directed the silent threat at him. *Just you wait!* Kea repeated the words to herself over and over again during the ceremony.

⌒∞⌒

Unaware of all that had transpired, Anneke remained in a world of her own, shared by Romke. Her heart filled with ecstasy as they stood side by side at the altar and spoke their vows. After the ceremony, the celebration lasted for hours. Friends, neighbors, and relatives extended their best wishes.

Anneke scanned the many guests seated at the banquet. Then through the crowd she spotted Cobie. *Why had she come? Did she wish to cast a cloud over her wedding day, too?* Anneke turned away but found herself once again searching for Cobie. Now, Cobie was laughing, even flirting, *but with whom?* Anneke looked between the guests and saw Jorie. *So Cobie had settled for him since she couldn't have Romke.* Anneke hoped Cobie would see Jorie's worth and grow to love and appreciate him. With relief, Anneke watched them, glad that she would no longer have to endure her taunts and lies. In only a few hours, Cobie would be out of her life. They would be separated forever.

When the banquet ended, Anneke's family lingered to say a last farewell. After hugging and kissing her parents goodbye, she noticed her sister standing apart, looking as if her best friend had abandoned her. A scowl covered her forehead.

For the first time that day, Anneke realized something was wrong. She walked over to Kea and threw her arms around her. "What's the matter?"

Kea's scowl deepened. "You should know. Things have never been the same since you met *him*." Her eyes flashed as she turned in Romke's direction. "And now you're leaving, and all day you've done nothing but smile, as though you're glad you're going. I don't mean anything to you anymore, and it's all the beast's fault! That Lambertus! He's the one who took you away from me."

Anneke held Kea's shoulders and listened while her sister opened up her heart to her. Now it all made sense. *So she had caused Kea's hurt. Why hadn't she sensed her sister's ache before? She had been blind, seeing only what life had to offer herself but insensitive to the needs of her sister. Could that be why Kea had loosened Romke's horse and cart the first day he brought her home? Had Kea felt threatened even then?*

Her sister was right. The two of them hadn't been that close this year, even the months that Romke was gone. Anneke's throat closed up as she realized the loneliness Kea had suffered. Once again her arms fell around her sister, but this time in a tighter embrace, warmed by the love she felt for her.

"Oh, Kea, I had no idea you felt this way. No one could take your place. You're my dear sister and always will be." Anneke took Kea's hands in hers. "I'll never forget the fun we've had growing up together and all the scrapes you'd get into and how I'd always manage to lighten the punishment that seemed to constantly hang over your head." Anneke leaned over and kissed her sister on the cheek. "Please write me, Kea, and let me know about your new adventures. Write it just like you'd tell it to me if we were sitting side by side. But don't get into too much trouble. Remember, I won't be here to bail you out!" Anneke swallowed several times to get rid of the lump in her throat. "I wish I didn't have to leave you."

The scowl faded from Kea's forehead. She tightened her hold around Anneke's waist. "I promise to write you. It'll make me feel like you're still here with me."

Bittersweet tears fell from both their eyes.

When Anneke walked to the cart, she noticed Lambertus leaning against a tree. He turned away as she glanced at him. How lonely he looked, his head bent over the piece of wood he was whittling. If only Kea would be a friend to him. She watched the shavings fall from his block of wood and hoped the friction between him and Kea would also drift away.

After Romke helped Anneke up to her seat, Vader clasped his new son-in-law's hand in his. "Take good care of my little girl," he said, with a warm smile and a handshake to match.

Romke looked over at Anneke seated in the cart and winked at her, then looked back to Mr. Haanstra. "You have my word of honor on that, Vader."

While Anneke's father set her valise inside their wagon, her mother leaned over and whispered in her ear. "Remember the Delft blue vase."

Her mother's words brought Anneke back to reality. How much her family meant to her, and she was leaving them. Again, Anneke felt tears rising to the surface. She reached out toward her mother and clung to her. "Yes, Moeder, I will never forget. Each time I look at it, I'll remember I'm in your prayers." As they drove away, she waved to her parents and sister until they were mere specks on the horizon.

Chapter

⟨⟩

16

Anneke grew quiet as they continued on to Kollumdijk. She thought back on all that had happened that day, not wanting to forget the beautiful memories. At last her thoughts reached the final moments before they left. *If only she had realized how lonely Kea had been. How thankful she was that the rift had been mended before she left for Lijdendorp. She thought of her father and how good he had been to her. And she would remember the Delft blue vase. It would be a constant reminder of her family's love, especially her mother's prayers and concern for her.*

After accommodations had been made for the night in Kollumdijk, and they had changed out of their wedding attire, Romke turned to her. "Darling, let's go down to the river where we took our first stroll last year."

Anneke looked up into his face and felt the warmth of his tenderness. "I'd love to."

Together they left the inn and followed the white, iron railing that bordered the canal along the narrow, brick sidewalk. Eventually the buildings thinned out where the canal opened into the river. A charming bridge of twisted tree limbs separated them from the park. Romke took her hand in his, and they crossed to the other side. In sweet silence, they walked over the freshly mowed lawn until they found the chestnut tree.

Leaning against the trunk, Romke drew Anneke into his arms. "Do you remember when you asked me last year what I thought about on my trips home?"

Anneke smiled and nodded, waiting to hear what he'd say.

"I wanted to add that I dreamed of taking you back with me to Lijdendorp. But I didn't dare tell you that so soon." He brushed his lips across her forehead. "And now that time has come."

Anneke ran her fingertips through his thick, dark hair. "And do you know when I first wanted to make that trip with you?"

"When, Darling?"

"The first evening you had dinner at our home."

She felt the gentle strength of his arms as he pulled her closer to him. "Mijn lieveling," he whispered. "I think we both knew from the start that we loved each other. That's a sure sign God brought us together."

In the sunset, they shared a picnic lunch beneath the tree. Anneke looked out across the winding river. She thought of the swans they had seen there the year before and hoped they would come again. Before long she saw them gliding over the water. "Look, Romke! The swans have a little family!" She counted the cygnets. "Five babies."

Romke's face beamed.

They watched the brood as they finished their meal. The tiny balls of fluff dove head first to catch a quick snack. Only their soft, yellow tails could be seen above the ripples. Romke and Anneke lingered, amused by the playful cygnets. The moon rose higher in the sky, illuminating the cob and pen as they preened each other's feathers with gentle strokes.

Romke drew Anneke close to his side. Sunshine filled her soul, and a passing thought brought joy to her heart. Someday she and Romke would have a family too.

༄

The morning sky greeted them with a brilliant blue, a perfect day for their honeymoon.

Romke took Anneke's hands in his. "Is my pretty bride ready to cruise with me to her new home?"

"Oh, yes, Romke. And what a lovely day to sail."

He gathered her in his arms and kissed her. "Then that's just what we'll do. But first, I have something to give you." Romke reached into his pocket and handed her a small case of polished wood.

Anneke opened the lid. Inside, lay a sky-blue brooch on which a white water lily with a pink center floated. "How beautiful, Romke! It's just like the one you picked for me last year." She could hardly wait to see his surprise, this evening, when she planned to show him the pillowcases with the water lilies she'd embroidered in the very same colors.

Romke smiled. "I hope it will have a special meaning for you, mijn lieveling."

Anneke gazed at the brooch and fingered its smooth surface. She remembered the symbolism Romke had used when he picked the water lily for her last year. The haunting question tugged at her heart. Was she safely joined to the life-giving Stem? The thought gnawed at her soul. How should she answer him? What could she say? "It—it will always be special to me. Thank you, darling." She turned the brooch over and opened the clasp, to pin it to her clothing.

Romke closed his hand over hers, then took the brooch and pinned it gently to her bodice.

She couldn't return his gaze but wrapped her arms around him and pressed her face to his chest, hoping he hadn't noticed her hesitation.

She shoved the troubling thought aside as they sailed through the arched water gate, its fortified twin towers supporting the covered bridge on both sides. The towers stretched heavenward, each forming a spire, creating a picture of strength and beauty. She would miss Kollumdijk, but someday when she returned, this gate would still be standing tall with open archway to welcome her home.

As they floated over the Zuider Zee, Romke pointed out the various Dutch vessels that came in sight: the hoogaars, the tjalk and the Staverse jol. She watched enthralled as they bobbed and tilted on the spirited sea.

But Anneke preferred Romke's boeier. Painted white with contrasting black ironwork bordering the rim, the small, sturdy yacht with its well-rounded hull reminded her of a wooden shoe drifting over the waves. The wing-like leeboards of varnished wood lay against the hull on the starboard and port sides, ready to be lowered to balance the craft in turbulent water. A beautifully carved mermaid in gold leaf graced the rudderpost behind the stern. Beyond it, a golden pole reached upward, rigged with the Dutch flag, its three wide stripes of red, white, and blue rippling with pride against the azure sky. The two sails caught the wind and billowed, thrusting their yacht over the water past the other vessels.

At noontime, Romke guided their boat off the sea and down a secluded river. Soon they reached a shady bank lined with weeping willows. Their slender branches draped the water. "This looks like an inviting place. How about a picnic beneath this spreading willow?"

Anneke reached out and caught a hanging strand of narrow leaves, letting the length of the stem filter through her fingers. "I was thinking the same thing."

After Romke secured the boat, he and Anneke disembarked. They laid the food that Anneke's mother had packed for them on a mossy patch. While they sat leaning against the tree, Romke took her hand in his and brought it to his lips. "This is just how I imagined our life would be together—peace and happiness. I can hardly believe you are really mine, Anneke. I thank God so much for making us one."

She laid her head on his shoulder. "My dearest Romke. I cherish every moment you're by my side."

He gathered her in his arms and held her close. "You are my jewel, my precious treasure." He kissed her gently on her neck. "I promise to love you and care for you darling. You'll always come first in my life."

Anneke clung to his words as he held her in his arms. "My husband, my love," she breathed. "You are my one desire."

᠔᠊᠊

They took their time traveling home, stopping whenever a landscape or village intrigued them. As the day drew to a close, the heat subsided, and the nighttime coolness brought a pleasant change. The stars glittered down on them like diamonds from the black velvet sky, promising a future of unending joy.

The following afternoon, they reached Oostenhaven. Leaving the Zuider Zee, they entered the lazy Oostelijk River, winding their way past the sleepy villages huddled on the banks. The cozy little homes with step-gabled roofs nestled close together. Beyond the villages, large farmhouses with low-hanging thatched roofs dotted the countryside. As their boat sailed by, windmills waved their arms in greeting.

Romke steered their boat off the river, into the harbor of Zwartland. "It's late, darling. Let's spend the night here and finish the last few hours of sailing tomorrow. That way, you'll be able to see the landscape as we approach our home."

Anneke flashed him a smile. "Extending our honeymoon sounds great to me. I always wanted to take this trip with you, but this adventure has exceeded all my expectations. And I even get to share it with the most handsome pilot in the world."

Romke folded her in his arms. "And this pilot has the most beautiful woman in the world for his passenger. Just think, we have the whole rest of our lives together."

Joy and contentment filled her soul. She looked up at him to share his happiness but saw a shadow darken his face. *What could it mean?* Then, like a vapor, it was gone. Surely, she must have imagined it. His eyes caught hers, and he smiled. Within his gentle arms, she felt secure once more.

Chapter

17

Late the next morning, Romke brought their boat down the Black Canal, then along the narrow canal that bordered his land. He drew Anneke close to him. "It's just a short ways now and we'll be home."

She slipped her arm through his and leaned her head on his shoulder. A new home awaited her—their home. "How good that sounds." She snuggled closer to him. A smile lingered on her lips as she noticed a barge up ahead loaded with cattle. Two young girls guided it with their long poles.

A third sat in the stern. Her vacant, fish-like eyes bulged from her pale face as she watched Anneke and Romke approach. She called to her friends behind her. "Beppie, Wietske. . . look, Romke's back—but not alone." The words, spoken without emotion, reached Anneke across the water.

The two young women in the bow turned and faced Anneke. One, short and plump, showed surprise but smiled good-naturedly. Anneke smiled back. The other stared with narrowed eyes, no hint of welcome on her face. A chill ran through Anneke's body.

"We're here, darling."

She shifted her gaze to Romke as he climbed from the boat to fasten the moorings.

Breezes carried the sound of whispers to her ears. Again, Anneke glanced at the barge. One arm propped on a hefty Holstein, the hostile-looking girl continued to watch her. With no way to escape her hawk-eyed gaze, Anneke grew uncomfortable. Gradually the barge drifted further away.

Anneke turned her gaze to the family dwelling. Set far back from the grassy dike stood a large, brick farmhouse—a pretty home with bright green shutters and a low thatched roof, but it seemed so still, so empty of life. Not one window was open to let in the fresh June air, nor did an open door welcome them home. She gripped Romke's arm. "Are your folks expecting me?"

The Veenhuizens' Home

Intent on fastening the moorings, he didn't seem to hear.

She leaned closer to him. "Romke, do your parents know I'm coming?" While she waited for an answer, the sun sank behind a cloud that hovered above the dwelling, casting a shadow over the house. It reminded her of the shadow that had crossed his face last night—but this one lingered.

Romke finished mooring the vessel, then looked up. "My folks have expected I would take a mate soon. But I'm sure they'll be surprised when they see me walk in with my charming bride." His laugh sounded cheerful, but was it somewhat forced?

She almost pressed him further but decided against it. He seemed so lighthearted. Surely everything would be all right. Romke reached for her valise with one hand. With his other, he helped her from the boat.

When she stepped onto the dike, the grass stirred, each blade trembling like sea waves troubled by the wind's bidding. Were they warning her—waving her away from the house enshrouded in shadow? She hesitated, but feeling Romke's hand clasped in hers, she walked up the path with him to their home.

A white, wrought iron design adorned the window frame above the front door. She paused to study it more closely. It resembled a tree. White, leafy vines of iron swirled at its base, while at the top, the tree branched out on both sides, forming two smaller leafed swirls. A bell-shaped fruit, also of iron, hung from a branch.

"Does this have a special significance?" she asked, fascinated with the ornate object.

"It's the Tree of Life. Each time a child is born to a family, the parents exchange the tree for another with an additional fruit to represent the new baby."

"What a lovely custom. This single fruit must stand for you, Romke."

He nodded, but a flicker of sadness crossed his face. He opened the door and stepped aside, allowing Anneke to walk ahead of him.

She entered a large, charming kitchen. An eight-pointed star adorned the soft-brown tiles on three of the walls. Tiles with circular designs covered the fourth wall, where the fireplace stood. Painted floral sprays swirled across the doors of a tall, red cabinet set on a platform against the far wall. In the center of the room, a round, wooden table of bright red with four matching ladder-backed chairs caught her attention. A feeling of warmth filled her as she gazed about.

Then a silver beam streaked across the room. Startled, she turned toward the light. The sun shining through a window on the side wall reflected off the metal headpiece of a woman seated at a spinning wheel. The effect blinded Anneke. Lowering her eyes, she met the woman's stone-like glare. Anneke froze as the ice-blue eyes stared her down.

Mrs. Veenhuizen turned to her son. "Romke, do you realize you've been gone for almost a week? What were you thinking, leaving all the work for your father to do?"

"I had an important matter to take care of, Mother. I brought back someone very dear to me. I want you to meet Anneke."

His mother's lips tightened.

Anneke tried to smile. "I'm happy to meet you, Mevrouw Veenhuizen."

Mrs. Veenhuizen's eyes bore through her.

A tremor slithered up Anneke's spine.

"Remember, Mother, when I told you about the girl from Zevendorp? I've brought her home. She's now my wife."

Mrs. Veenhuizen's mouth dropped open and a look of disbelief passed over her face, then instantly vanished. As though Anneke were not in the room, she kept her attention on Romke. Again the sunlight struck her silver oorijzer, like the flash of lightning before a storm. "Does it mean nothing to you that your father has had no help in the fields for all this time?"

"I'm sorry, Mother, but I'm free to work now."

"Then see that you waste no time in getting out there."

Romke turned to Anneke. "Come, darling, I'll show you our room." In a state of shock, Anneke didn't realize that he had spoken. He picked up her luggage and led her into a bedroom at the back of the house, set down her valise, and shut the door. "Welcome home, Anneke, my love."

Welcome home? Where was the welcome? Anneke felt her world crumbling. Tears filled her eyes, and her body shook. *Was this to be her new home—her new life—living with a woman who hated her, who hadn't even acknowledged her presence except with an icy stare?*

Romke took her in his arms. "Oh, darling, I'm so sorry Mother responded that way. Just give her time to get used to it. She'll soften, mijn lieveling, I'm sure she will."

Blinking back the tears, Anneke looked up at him. "Why was your mother so hostile toward me? She wasn't even civil to you."

Romke guided her to the bed. "Sit down, Anneke. There are some things I need to tell you." He sat beside her and took her hand.

Anneke wiggled her hand free and faced him. "Why didn't you tell me before? You knew how close-minded your parents are. You must have realized they wouldn't accept me."

Romke sought her hand again and clasped it in his. "Please listen, Anneke. Perhaps then you'll understand." He sighed, then paused and cleared his throat. "For the last two years, my parents have been pressuring me to take a woman. They had a certain girl in mind for me. . ."

Could that have been Wietske, the girl on the barge with the hateful glare, Anneke wondered?

". . . although they wouldn't have minded too much which one of the village girls I took. As you know, it's our custom to take a mate only among our people."

"But you made it sound like everything would be all right."

"I know, mijn lieveling. I was hoping against hope. Please forgive me, Anneke. I love you so much, I couldn't bear to let you go."

"But your father—what will he do when he finds out we're married? Will he send me away?"

"I doubt it. I'm sure he'll be upset, but after his initial explosion, he won't ever mention it again. That's the way Father is."

"But he'll wish I'd never come."

"Don't worry, Anneke, I'm sure it won't be as bad as you think."

"At least he'll be out in the field all day. But your mother—I'll be at the mercy of her tongue and her glare all day long while you're peacefully at work in the fields."

"She'll grow to like you, Anneke, in spite of herself. I'm sure she will. How could she not?"

"How can you think that? Why should she feel anything but hatred for me? We've broken her rules. But I'm the one she'll blame—the one who stole her boy and made him scorn the traditions of his people."

"Anneke, no one could think that of you, least of all, me. Mother and Father can blame me all they want, but I'll never let them put the blame on you. Please—just listen for a moment and try to understand what I was up against. Can't you see, Anneke? I had no feeling for any of the young women here, and I felt I'd be doing them a dishonor to take one without loving her. My parents can't understand this. Sometimes..." a wrenching moan escaped his lips. "Sometimes I wonder if they even love each other. They never speak of it or even show it; they simply co-exist—and argue. I wanted no part of that for my future. So what was I to do?"

Anneke's heart softened as she listened. She could sense the heartache he'd suffered.

"In the meantime, my parents continued to pressure me, but I didn't back down. I wanted to feel genuine love for the woman I chose. I knew I needed God's help, so I prayed that He would guide me to the one of His choosing.

"In answer to my prayer, He gave me the idea of seeking her in a different locality. That was when I decided to sell my cheese in another village. Maybe there, I would find the girl of my dreams." He cleared his throat. "I knew I was going against our tradition, but I could see no alternative. I told my parents that I'd decided to make more cheese and take the extra to sell in a new location. I wasn't sure which village to go to, but as I sailed down the Oostelijk River, I prayed that God would lead me."

Anneke studied his face. God had such a vital part in his life. What an admirable man he was. She could feel her love for him grow deeper, in spite of the hurt.

"When I reached Oostenhaven, I sensed the Lord directing me to go down the coast of the Zuider Zee. Then as I came into Kollumdijk I felt compelled to stop and visit the marketplace there." He paused and encircled Anneke in his arms. "That first day I saw you, I knew why. You'll never know the love that stirred in my heart for you. I've never felt that way toward any other woman."

"All that day and the days following, I prayed if you were the one for me you'd come back to my stand the next week. Then father became sick, and I was needed to work his part of the field as well as mine. So, another week dragged by, but you were in my thoughts day and night. All the while I wondered if you had stopped by my cheese stand. I prayed you would come back the third week and wait for me." He tilted her face toward his and caressed her cheek, then tenderly drew her to him again and held her close. "And you did come to my stand. Darling, when I saw you the second time I knew I could love you forever. It was unthinkable for me to take any of the girls in my village as my woman. You had come into my heart and filled every corner of it."

Anneke laid her head against his shoulder.

"Just being with you, Anneke, I felt complete. When you told me you loved me in return, you can't imagine how thrilled I was. I knew God had brought us together. I longed to make you the happiest woman in the world and satisfy your every need. But the hardest time in my life came when I could no longer see you for all those months. I prayed daily you would wait for me and was ecstatic when June arrived and I could see you again.

"And now. . ." His eyes misted. "And now when I was certain our life was so happy—it's become marred." His voice broke. "If only Mother understood how much I love you. Perhaps then she would adapt. But—maybe I was selfish in bringing you here, subjecting you to this treatment." He released her and covered his face with his hands.

Anneke grasped his shoulders and lifted his face toward her. "No, Romke, I want to be with you. Having you for my husband means more to me than anything."

Again his arms went round her, and he drew her into a warm embrace. "I pray you will always feel that way, mijn lieveling. God brought us together; He can keep us together." He released her. "I'm heading out to the fields now.

Chapter

⟶ ⟜⟝⟞⟟ ⟵

18

The sun did its best to coax Anneke from bed the following morning. She turned her face away from the window. What lay in store for her today? Would Romke's mother make any attempt to be halfway civil to her?

Romke stirred beside her, and she laid her hand on his. His eyes opened and a sleepy smile spread across his face. "Is it morning already?"

"Yes." She lay there, watching him get up. *How adorable he looked when he was half asleep. Whatever I have to bear, I will do it for him."* Gradually she pulled herself out from the covers. Just being with Romke made her feel happy again. *She would try her best to win his mother's acceptance.*

She reached for the pillows to fluff them, and realized she'd forgotten to show him the water lilies she'd embroidered. She held up his pillow. "Did you see what I embroidered on these?"

Romke turned to look and gasped. A big smile spread across his face. "That's amazing. They're just like the one I picked for you last year."

"I purposely chose those same colors."

Romke took her hands in his and kissed them. "How thoughtful of you." He ran his finger over the embroidered water lilies. "They're so beautifully done and very special to me, darling. I love you for doing that." He held her close, softly kissing her hair. Each night, as he laid his head on his pillow, it would remind him to pray that his precious wife would become attached to the life-giving Stem.

When they entered the kitchen, they greeted his parents and stood behind adjacent chairs until his parents were ready to be seated.

Without acknowledging them, Mrs. Veenhuizen kept her head lowered while she finished setting the table. A bowl of steaming oatmeal lay at each place. Ignoring their presence, Mr. Veenhuizen left the room, his large frame barely clearing the doorway. His wife continued to busy herself in the kitchen.

To Anneke's surprise, Mr. Veenhuizen returned, pushing a young boy in a wheelchair. This must be Anton, Romke's younger brother. She had forgotten there was another member in his family. But why hadn't she seen him yesterday?

Romke's face beamed at the arrival of his brother. "Well, how's my pal doing this morning?"

Anton hung his head and said nothing.

Anneke glanced around. Only four chairs surrounded the table. Perhaps Anton ate from his wheelchair. Romke's father wheeled his son over to her side, then lifted the boy out and set him in the chair she stood behind. Baffled, Anneke stepped back. Again, winter filled the room—frigid as the North Sea wind. She had intruded on this household. They didn't want her here. Immediately Romke brought another chair to the table and indicated with a smile that it was for her. The warmth of his hand on her arm reassured her. "Sometimes habits are hard to break," he said, holding the back of her chair as she sat down. He took a bowl and spoon from the shelf, filled the bowl with oatmeal, and set it at her place. His parents seated themselves at opposite ends of the table, their faces as hard and cold as the stone walls of their canal.

The silence pounded in Anneke's ears. Mr. Veenhuizen, with his massive form, aloofness, and sour face lorded over the household with wordless dominance. Mrs. Veenhuizen's steel eyes and taut lips sent chills through Anneke. She glanced at Anton. She thought she remembered Romke telling her last year that he was twelve. He'd be thirteen now. How small he looked for his age. Her heart went out to him as she watched him eat. Noticing he had finished his bread, Anneke forced herself to speak to him. "Would you like another slice, Anton?" She held out the plate to him.

He gave her a quick look, and then lowered his head. Again, she asked him. Although he nodded, Anton made no move to help himself. Anneke laid a slice on his plate. After a moment, he raised his head and stole another glance at her. She smiled at him, and the uncertainty left his face until he met his mother's stony glare.

"You don't deserve that bread, young man. You've done nothing to earn it," mumbled Mrs. Veenhuizen.

No one spoke another word for the rest of the meal.

Anneke couldn't help wondering if mealtime was always this strained at their table. And this was only the first of endless meals to come. She cringed at the thought. How pleasant it had been yesterday when she and Romke had stayed in their room and eaten the rest of the food they'd brought with them. Thankfully, there'd been enough for both their lunch and supper. She'd had no desire to join Mrs. Veenhuizen for either meal after the cold treatment she'd received from her that afternoon.

When the family had finished eating breakfast, Romke and his father rose to their feet. Laying his hands on Anneke's shoulders, Romke bent down and kissed her cheek. "Have a good day, darling. We're heading out to the fields now."

She reached for his hand and brought it to her lips. She didn't want him to leave, but she knew he must. She squeezed his hand, and then released it. How she wished she could go with him. She wouldn't care what kind of work she had to do or how hard it was as long as she could get away from this house.

Romke stepped around to Anton's chair. "Don't get into any trouble while I'm gone." He winked at his brother and tousled his hair.

Anton's face lit up. Anneke sensed the love between them. This time, Romke's attention seemed to bring new life to Anton. Then she caught the sadness in his eyes as he watched Romke leave the house. How hard it must be for him to sit and watch his father and brother leave to work on the farm, while he was confined to the house. He must have endured much hurt and loneliness in his short lifetime.

Anneke gathered the bowls and silverware from the table and carried them to the sink. While setting them down, she heard the whisk of a broom behind her. With vigorous strokes, her mother-in-law zoomed toward her, as if she meant to sweep her out of the house. Anneke stepped aside just in time as the broom came thrashing across the floor where she'd been standing. Why had she even tried to lend a hand? She should have known she was the last person Mrs. Veenhuizen would want helping her. She'd go back to her bedroom and find something to do there.

When she started to walk away, she caught sight of Anton, still seated at the table, watching her. Her heart melted toward him. He had been forgotten. How she yearned to befriend him. If only there was something she could do, but what? He lowered his gaze. The dark shadows under his eyes accented his pale skin.

How long had it been, she wondered, since he had enjoyed the balmy, spring air? How long since he'd seen flowers growing and watched clouds sail overhead? That's what she could do to make his life happier. She would take him outside and let him drink in the beauty of June. But—would his mother object to that, too? Anneke peered over her shoulder. Mrs. Veenhuizen had started washing the dishes and didn't seem to care about Anton. Anneke would risk it. Anton deserved to have some sunshine and happiness. She walked over to him. "Anton, would you like to come outside with me?"

He searched her face, and then glanced at his mother. She stood at the sink, her back to them. His body relaxed. He turned to Anneke and nodded.

She was grateful to see him return her offer of friendship. Anneke helped him into his wheelchair, opened the back door, and wheeled him out to the yard. "Where would you like to go, Anton?"

He suddenly opened up. "To the garden, to the fields, to the barn! Over every stretch of our land!" He looked up at her. His eyes grew misty. "I love it out here. This is the first time I've been out since last fall, and now, it's practically summer!" He sighed, taking in the vastness of the open space. "How I wish I could run across those green meadows." He lowered his head. "But that will never happen. It's only a dream."

"We all have dreams, Anton. Never let go of them. Just add prayer to your dreams." Her words startled her. Why had she said that? Had she ever asked God to fulfill a desire of her heart? Did she really know the God who answers prayer? Romke certainly did. A void filled her soul. Again, she thrust it aside.

Soft breezes blew as they took the winding path to the garden. At the entrance, large lavender clematis with deep purple centers climbed the latticed archway.

Anneke stood entranced. "What gorgeous flowers! Let's stop and get a closer look at them."

Anton leaned toward the blooms fluttering in the breeze. "I never even knew these existed."

As they meandered through the garden, joy filled her heart. What a haven. She would come here often.

A gentle wind drifted their way, bringing with it the fragrance of roses. She paused and looked around. Rose bushes of red, pink and white blossoms filled the center of the garden, surrounding a fountain where a cherub knelt with tilted vessel. Water splashed from his pitcher into a large basin, spraying the roses that encircled the sculpture. The scene beckoned her. She wheeled Anton nearer, and to their delight, the cool mist refreshed their warm faces.

"This is like a paradise," breathed Anneke. "Do you know who landscaped this?"

"Romke did. It's a hobby of his."

"My dear Romke," she whispered. *So this was the work of his hands. A new surge of love welled up in her heart for him. If only he were here with her, showing her the many flowers and bushes he had planted. She wanted to ask him what had been in his thoughts when he designed such enchantment—and then to wander in and out among the flowerbeds with him in his very own garden. After supper, she would invite him to walk in the cool evening with her, and she would bring him here.*

While they headed back to the house at the end of their walk, Anton's eyes shone. "This has been a wonderful morning. Thank you, Anneke."

Her heart ached for him. *How much this dear boy had missed out on.* "We'll do this every day," she promised.

"Let's call it 'our garden hour,'" said Anton, his face beaming.

"Yes, let's." This special time meant as much to her as it did to Anton. When they reached the house, she hesitated. She wasn't ready to go back inside. Then something caught her eye. A short ways off stood a bench. She wheeled Anton next to it and sat down beside him.

Anton leaned his head close to Anneke's. "Romke didn't tell Father and Mother that he planned to bring you back with him, but he told me." A smile lit his face. "He said soon I would have a big sister. He also told me you were wonderful. I wasn't sure how I'd like having an older sister. But I'm so glad he brought you here and you're part of our family now."

His words pulled at her heart and her eyes pooled. "And I'm glad to be your big sister." She gave him a hug. "Were you. . ." Anneke faltered, not sure if she should ask him or not. "Were you away from the house yesterday? I didn't see you."

A cloud spread over Anton's face as he lowered his head to his right hand. His left thumb followed the ridge in the large wheel of his chair. "I was here." He paused for several moments. "After breakfast, Mother wheeled me back to my room and told me I would stay there until Romke returned. She and Father were both upset. Each day Romke didn't come home, Father grew angrier. There's so much work to be done in the fields, and it's my fault. If I could help, with three of us working, the chores would get done on time. But I'm of no use to Father—or Mother, either." He hung his head as his thumb moved along the groove of the wheel.

A sudden movement in the distance caught their attention. A black Scottie, yapping a happy greeting, bounded across the yard, straight for Anton. With a leap, he landed on his lap and licked his hand, then nuzzled his little nose as close to his pal as he could get.

Anneke laughed. "It looks like you have a faithful friend there."

Anton gave his pet a warm hug. "Yes, Scottie and I are great chums."

Anneke leaned over to pet the dog. Scottie looked up at her, cocked his head to one side, and licked her hand, then snuggled back against his master and closed his eyes.

It was good that Anton had a pet. Anneke smiled as she watched them. How strange that his mother hadn't brought him out to join the family last night. She laid her hand gently on his arm. "You said you were here at the house yesterday? We arrived by late afternoon. I never saw you then or in the evening. Did your mother forget to bring you out?"

"No, she didn't forget. She expected Romke would be back late Thursday night, like usual, but when he didn't return, she got really upset. On Saturday, I asked her if she knew why he hadn't come yet. She didn't answer, but by her set jaw, I knew she was furious. When she drew her lips tight, I didn't dare ask anything more. By Monday, she was so livid, I was afraid what she would do. After our noon meal, she told me not to leave my room for the rest of the day. I couldn't understand why she was punishing me. I had nothing to do with it. All that afternoon and evening, I kept listening for my brother's voice, but he never came." Anton's voice broke.

"When I heard Romke come home the following day, I wanted more than anything to come out and see him and meet you, but I didn't dare. I waited until Mother brought me my lunch, and then begged her to let me come out. But she said Father had waited for Romke too long already, and she'd sent him out to the fields immediately. Then she asked me why I wanted to see you." He kept his eyes fixed on Scottie. "She said you wouldn't care to meet me."

Anneke gasped.

Anton's shoulders crumpled. "But still I wanted to see Romke. Last night I felt like I'd lost my brother as well as the sister I'd never met. Sometimes I wonder why Romke cares so much about me." His small form shook as he held Scottie close to him and sobbed.

How unfair life could be. Didn't his mother realize how harshly she treated her son? Her son! Anneke remembered the Tree of Life above the door of their home. Anton was her second child. Then why did only one fruit hang from the tree? She remembered the pained expression that crossed Romke's face when she mentioned that the fruit stood for him. It hurt her that no fruit hung on the tree to represent Anton. It must have hurt Romke, too.

Anneke laid a comforting arm across his shoulder. "You are most deserving of your brother's love, Anton. And you've grown special to me, even in the few hours that I've known you."

Anton remained silent. His arms still clung to his faithful dog, his face pressed in his fur.

Chapter

꧁ꮹꭸꮹ꧂

19

Mrs. Veenhuizen threw open the back door, and let it slam against the house. Anneke tensed, then turned to look behind her. Her mother-in-law's eyes met hers with an icy glare.

"Bring Anton in this house at once! While you're here, you will make yourself useful. There are chores to be done, and the cheese making never ends. If I sat around idle like you're doing, nothing would ever get done around this place."

Anneke looked at her in disbelief.

"I said, get in here!" Mrs. Veenhuizen repeated.

Trembling, Anneke struggled with the wheel chair until at last she succeeded in getting Anton into the kitchen. They followed his mother to the back of the house and entered the room that sheltered the cattle in the winter months.

Mrs. Veenhuizen turned around. "Do you have to take him with you wherever you go? There's work to be done. It's time he went back to his room."

"Oh, Mother, please let me stay and watch," Anton pleaded.

"I'm sure I don't know what good you'll be. You'll be more of a nuisance than anything."

Anton winced. He gripped the arms of the wheelchair and squeezed his eyes shut, but a tear slipped from his eye before he could turn away.

Mrs. Veenhuizen's scowl grew deeper. "Well, just be sure you stay out of my way." With a sigh of disgust, she yanked the lid from a large metal milk can. The cover flew from her hand, spun through the air, and crashed into the row of milk cans against the wall.

Anneke jumped as it hit the first container with a thunderous clank. The lid bounced to the floor, striking each can in succession as it continued its dizzy journey down the length of the room.

Mrs. Veenhuizen lunged at them, shaking her fist in their faces. "Now look what you've made me do! The two of you cause more trouble than a broken dike!"

Anton's face grew pale and his knuckles white as he clung to the arms of his wheelchair.

Anneke squeezed her hands together to keep them from shaking. What would her mother-in-law do next?

Mrs. Veenhuizen heaved the heavy can into her arms and proceeded to pour the milk into a huge wooden vat. Anneke watched closely as her mother-in-law grabbed a rake-like tool from a nearby table. Gripping the handle, she plunged it into the vat and thrashed it about in circles, making the milk first creamy, then lumpy, and once again, smooth. After the whey had drained from the vat, Mrs. Veenhuizen reached for a huge ladle that hung from a nail on the wall.

"Here," she said, thrusting it into Anneke's hand. "Start scooping the cheese into these molds on the table. And don't dawdle. They must all be filled while the curd is still warm."

Anneke's eyes widened when she saw the huge wooden molds. There had to be at least two dozen of them, each one over a foot in diameter. The curd would cool long before she could fill them. Her hand shook as she set to work, dipping the ladle into the vat and pouring the cheese into the first mold. She could feel her mother-in-law watching her from behind.

"Stop!" Mrs. Veenhuizen bellowed. "Watch what you're doing. You're dripping more on the floor than you're getting into the mold. At the rate you're going, we won't have any cheese to sell in the market."

Anneke's hand tensed. "I'm sorry, Mevrouw." She tried to keep the ladle steady as she continued her task. She grew warm, and then damp, as the steam from the vat wafted up into her face. She tried her best to ignore the heat as she struggled to increase her pace, but it seemed like she would never get the first mold filled.

Mrs. Veenhuizen snatched the ladle from her hand. "Such a simple task as this, and all you can do is fumble. Didn't your mother teach you anything?"

Speechless, Anneke watched as her mother-in-law thrust the ladle into the vat, again and again filling the mold in no time. "There! That's the way you do it. Now get busy before all the cheese turns cool." She slammed the ladle into the vat and faced Anneke. "And when you've finished this, you'll need to rub the surface of those pressed cheeses on the next table with salt and melted butter. And..." She pointed a thick, calloused finger at the rows of shelves against the far wall. "...you will also be responsible for turning every one of those cheeses until the right amount of acid has formed. Each week you'll start over with a new batch. Have I made myself clear, or is it necessary to repeat my instructions?"

Anneke was thankful she had occasionally watched Tante Zusje make cheese. There were a few minor differences between the two kinds, but the procedure was basically the same. "Yes, I understand what to do."

"Well, I should hope so. It would be shameful not to know how to make cheese at your age. I certainly hope you perform better with the next two stages of the processing than you did with the first." With hands on her hips, she glared at Anneke, then turned and left the room.

Anneke sighed with relief. She dug out the messy ladle from the vat, wiped off the handle on a towel, and resumed her task. Before long, the second mold was filled. Encouraged, she began filling the third. Soon, she developed a rhythmic motion and realized she was working faster.

Perhaps in the winter months, she and Romke could prepare the cheese together, but winter was a long way off. As she continued to scoop and pour, she noticed how intently Anton watched. Maybe he could help her now. With the two of them working together, they might finish while the curd was still warm. And it surely would while the time away much more pleasantly for both of them. "Have you ever helped with cheese making?" she asked.

"No. Romke makes a lot in the winter when he's not busy in the fields, but Mother does it the rest of the year." He lowered his head and rubbed the arm of his wheel chair with his thumb.

"Would you like to help?"

His head bolted up, and his eyes grew wide. "You really think I could?"

"Of course you can." After he cleaned his hands with a damp cloth, she moved his wheelchair closer to the vat and handed him a ladle.

His face glowed as together they filled the molds. While the two of them worked, the time flew by.

When they had emptied the vat, she wheeled Anton to the table where the earlier batch of cheeses lay. They set to work, rubbing the pressed cheeses with salt and melted butter until they shone. She thought back to the first time Romke had given her his special cheese, after her fall in her marketplace back home. And to think that, now, she had learned how to make it herself. She looked at Anton and smiled. It was pleasant, just the two of them working together. Dear Anton. How grateful she was for him. Perhaps living here would be tolerable, after all.

⟨⟨⟨⟩⟩⟩

When Romke returned from the fields that evening, Anneke ran to meet him. "Did your day go well?" she asked.

Romke threw his arms about her and swung her around. "Yes, mijn lieveling, but this is the best part of all, being with you." He set her down and held her close.

Anneke looked up at him. "I made the most wonderful discovery this morning. Try to guess what it was."

"How to make cheese?"

They both laughed.

"Yes, actually I did. But it's something different. After supper, let's go outside and enjoy the evening for awhile. Then I'll tell you."

"That sounds like a great idea." He took her hand in his, and together they walked inside.

Supper was soon over and the kitchen set in order. Anneke wondered if the atmosphere had been less strained or if she hadn't noticed the tension because she had been so happy with Romke. Although Anneke hadn't offered to help with the dishes again, she had cleared the table.

Once outside, Romke drew Anneke close to his side as they began their walk. The setting sun lingered, casting a crimson glow across the sky. They followed the path she had taken that morning and soon reached the entrance to the garden.

"This was my discovery. Paradise in our own back yard."

"Then you like it?"

"Oh, Romke, I love it! Tell me, when did you make this?"

"I've always wanted to have a garden, a special place where I could come to be alone—to think and dream and pray. So several years ago, I began to plant a little here and a little there. But when I met you, I wanted the garden to be our special haven, our own lovely Eden. I made each addition with you in mind. Every tree I planted, I envisioned us sitting beneath it. I added the fountain and surrounded it with roses, eagerly waiting for the day you would see it."

"I love you for that, Romke. You are so dear." Anneke felt his lips on hers as he took her in his arms.

"There are even beech trees and weeping willows. Did you notice them in the wooded area beyond?" asked Romke.

"No. Let's go there now."

The fragrance of the flowers drew them on as they wandered through the garden. At the end of the path, a large beech tree stood like a sentry on each side. Beyond these, the woods began. Trees of all kinds grew throughout, some familiar, some not. Here and there, statuettes of fairies, rabbits, and birds turned the scene into a fantasyland. One fairy knelt by a rabbit, whispering in its ear. Amused, Anneke wondered what secret passed between them. As they continued their walk, Anneke gazed in every direction, trying not to miss any of the fairy world surrounding them.

The path they took, bordered by lush green ferns, led to a garden seat for two. Romke drew Anneke down beside him and slipped his arm around her. Together in the twilight, they watched the lacy-leafed sky change patterns as the cool night air swept through the branches.

Tranquility settled over Anneke. She laid her head on Romke's shoulder and cuddled closer to him, all thoughts of her trying day forgotten.

Chapter

⊙Ⅲℒ

20

Sunday—at last a day of rest with no chores, a day that Anneke could spend with Romke. No one could separate them today. She smiled, her spirits soaring as high as the church steeple she'd seen in the distance.

Anneke removed the last piece of her Sunday outfit from the wardrobe and laid it on the bed with the others. What would Romke's church service be like? She had heard Sundays were conducted differently here. She slipped her blouse over her head and pulled it down over her neck-cloth, then fastened her black silk skirt around her waist and looked over at Romke.

The sun's morning rays shining through the window touched the silver octagonal buttons on his shirt. It reminded her of the first time they met at the marketplace a year ago and how those buttons, along with his gaze, had magnetized her. How glad she felt to be a part of him. He would be by her side as they walked to church and while they sat in the worship service.

She turned back to the mirror and placed her lace cap over her metal headpiece, securing it with the pearl-headed pins. To complete her outfit, she would wear her coral necklace. When she stepped over to the chest, her silk skirt rustled with every move.

Romke stopped buttoning his shirt and watched. "I almost thought I heard the swish of the Zuider Zee," he teased. He came up behind her and caught her hands. "Let me have the honor." He found the little rings of the clasp and secured the coral beads around her neck, then stepped back to examine her outfit. "How charming my pretty wife is!"

With a smile, she playfully spun around.

Romke reached out, caught her in his arms, and kissed her tenderly. "You're the most beautiful woman I've ever seen." He held her close to his heart.

How happy she felt as Romke opened the front door for her. The bells in the steeple pealed out their silver tones, summoning the village folks to lay aside their work and come together to meet the Lord. She tucked her arm in Romke's as they stepped outside. It reminded her of their wedding day, when dressed in their finery, they had walked side by side to her church.

Romke shut the door behind them, gently removed his arm from hers and took her hand. He paused. "It's customary in our village for the men to walk to church in one group and the women in another."

Anneke stared at him. Had she heard him right?

Romke glanced at the house, then back to her. "I'm sorry. Please try to understand."

She looked out beyond their gate. The villagers passed by—two groups headed in the same direction but on opposite sides of the road. She steeled herself. "Oh, I didn't know. Well, I guess I can't get lost. I'll just follow the crowd." She forced a smile. "Then we'll meet again at the church?"

He gave her hand a gentle squeeze, and then released it. "Our sanctuary has two separate sections, as well."

A wave of desertion swept over her. She struggled to keep back the tears.

Romke swallowed hard. "Aren't the men and women separated for worship in Zevendorp?"

She tried to answer, but her coral beads strangled her reply.

"Oh, Anneke, it never occurred to me to mention it earlier. I thought all churches did it this way. Forgive me, darling." He took her hand in his and brought it to his lips, then released it.

Anneke's feet refused to move. In a trance she watched Romke walk away with his father, who, with lordly air, wheeled Anton before him.

Behind her, the front door opened, then closed with a bang. Roused by the sound, Anneke started down the path that led to the road. Without turning, she knew her mother-in-law had exited, but instead of joining Anneke, she rushed by, intent on reaching her friends. It was just as well.

Near the gate, Anneke lingered beneath the golden chain tree that stood on the Veenhuizen's property. Its blooms hung in clusters of gilded droplets like millions of tears ready to fall to the ground. Her thoughts turned to her family. They were all going to church too, but together. Suddenly she missed her mother and father, but especially Kea. Precious memories flashed through her mind of the many Sundays when they had left for church. Her parents in the lead, she and Kea would huddle together behind them, whispering, giggling.

Now she must walk alone.

A tear fell from her eye. The excitement of her first Sunday dissolved like dewdrops on a petal struck by the blazing sun. It no longer seemed like Sunday. Only the bells in the steeple, tolling out their call to worship, reminded her it was the Lord's Day.

Reluctantly, she left the weeping blossoms and paused at the open gate. The street had filled with young and old, forming a procession that wound its way to the little church. Several young women approached, gawked at her, and nudged each other. She hung back, waiting until the clicking of their shiny, black shoes grew fainter. Mustering up her courage, she stepped through the open gate and followed at a distance.

Now the sound of shuffling rose behind her. She turned to look. A group of older women, huddled together like herring in a barrel, drew near. Their voices ceased and their mouths gaped open. Their scowls deepened, and their faded lips grew paler as they continued to stare. Shaking their heads, they passed on by. Up ahead two little girls wheeled around, peeked at her, then giggled. Moments later they turned again to catch another glimpse, and then broke out in laughter.

Anneke realized she was a spectacle, wearing the clothes of her village. Did it offend these people to have someone dressed differently from them or did they react this way because it was an uncommon sight? Probably for both reasons. But what else could she have worn? She had no clothes like those worn by the women here.

She studied their clothing. She wouldn't mind wearing the gown, but the headpieces—how strange they looked. The women resembled a herd of unicorns, each with a single horn projecting from the front of her cap.

They must insert cardboard in their black satin undercaps. Only that would explain the strange protrusion. But even the beautiful white lace cap that covered their undercap and oorijzer was unusual. Rather than draping gracefully over the back of their neck and shoulders like her own, the tails of their tulle caps were pulled up and extended outward. Would she ever feel comfortable in such a headpiece?

At last she arrived at the church. She paused in the doorway and looked inside. Just as Romke had said, the men sat on one side, the women on the other. She scanned the men, hoping to find him. At last she saw him, sitting toward the center aisle next to Anton.

Quietly she slipped into a back seat in the women's section, and found herself searching for Romke again. Peering over the headpieces, she spotted him. How strange to see her husband sitting rows away from her on the opposite side of the church. If only she were there sitting by his side.

It wasn't long before she heard muffled whispers, then the whispers grew louder, and before long, faces from every direction turned to stare at her. How she wished she could disappear. Maybe she should leave before the service began. But then she'd call more attention to herself than if she remained in her seat. Finally the service began. The heads turned away, and soon the whispers ceased.

She was glad when the final hymn came to an end and she could leave. Three young women stood outside the church talking. Anneke recognized them as the ones she had seen on the barge outside Romke's home the day she arrived in Lijdendorp. She smiled at them but only one returned her greeting.

"Hi, I'm Beppie." Shorter than the other two and somewhat plump, the girl's pretty blond hair and happy smile attracted Anneke at once. "These are my friends, Geertje and Wietske." Her bubbly laughter rang as she turned back toward Anneke.

Anneke introduced herself, centering her attention on Beppie. As she spoke, Geertje, tall, thin, and plain, only stared, her fish-like eyes as dull as the wisps of light brown hair protruding from her cap, but Wietske, the dark haired girl, rolled her eyes and sneered. Anneke shifted uneasily and smoothed the folds of her veil, draping her shoulder. Surely, Wietske had hoped to become Romke's mate.

Beppie looked up at Anneke's cap. "Your headpiece is beautiful. I love the lace crown and fringe in front. What province are you from?"

Anneke relaxed. "Gelderland. My village is Zevendorp, three kilometers from the seaport of Kollumdijk."

Beppie gazed at the lace cap. "I've never seen one like it before. But then, I've never been outside my own village." She reached out and touched the intricate lace, then peered around behind. "And look at this long blue veil in back! It's really outstanding!"

Wietske snickered. "It's outstanding all right. It stands out like a turnip in a tulip patch."

An instant smirk flashed across Geertje's face then vanished.

"Oh, Wietske," cried Beppie, "how could you say such an awful thing?" She clasped Anneke's hand in hers and leaned close to her ear. "She's just jealous. Don't let her bother you."

Anneke felt genuine friendship in Beppie's response. "Thanks, Beppie. I'm so glad we had a chance to meet."

"So am I. Are you coming to market on Thursday?" asked Beppie.

"I think so." Anneke wasn't sure, but more than likely, her mother-in-law would give her the task of carting the cheeses to market and selling them.

"Good, we'll probably see each other then."

"Oh, I hope so."

With a wave of her hand, Beppie followed her friends.

Anneke started for home. Up ahead, Romke walked with a group of men. How she wanted to hurry to his side, but she must not. Elderly matrons shuffled along ahead of her, but she had no desire to pass them. She'd had enough glares and frowns for the day.

She thought of Wietske's remark. So she looked like a turnip in a tulip patch. Wietske was probably right, judging from the stares and giggles she'd received. She would need to buy material to make some clothing in the style worn here.

When Anneke arrived home, she changed into her everyday dress. While she hung her Sunday outfit in the wardrobe, she remembered how Kea had always tried to dress exactly like her big sister, even when she was only three. Anneke could almost hear her sister's pleas: "No,

Moeder, I don't want to wear that blue blouse. I want a blouse with flowers just like Anneke's."

But Anneke could never wear her village clothes again. The final ties that kept her connected to her family—to her heritage, had been severed. Tears filled her eyes and one rolled down her cheek. Too sacred to brush away, she let it fall. She gazed at each item she had hung in the wardrobe—never to be worn by her again. All she had left of her village were memories. Lijdendorp was her home now.

Chapter

21

Mrs. Veenhuizen stood in the doorway to the dairy, her hands on her hips, a deep scowl on her face. "So this is where you're hiding! There are other jobs besides cheese-making to be done in this house. If you're going to amount to anything, it's time you learned to make a decent loaf of bread."

Anneke replaced the lid on the milk can and moved toward the door.

Mrs. Veenhuizen stormed from the room and entered the kitchen. "I never can find you when you're needed. I searched all over this house for you." She lifted her apron off the hook, put it on, and wrapped the strings around her ample waist. She pulled hard on the tips, inhaled audibly, and finally managed to tie a knot. With a deep sigh, she wheeled about to face Anneke. "Well, don't just stand there. Get your own apron."

"It's on me, Mevrouw."

"And is it clean?"

"I put it on fresh this morning."

"Then why are you wasting time watching me? Get out the dishes and ingredients, for goodness sake."

No recipe lay on the table, but Anneke could at least start with the staples. She shoved a bin of flour closer to her work area and found a small container of salt. Then she set out the sugar, butter, and eggs.

With arms akimbo, Mrs. Veenhuizen watched every move Anneke made.

Anneke could feel her mother-in-law's eyes on her, making her more nervous by the minute. She reached for a large bowl she'd seen her mother-in-law use before and placed it in front of her. Next, she took down two small bread pans from the shelf. But without a recipe, she was at a loss as to how to proceed. She glanced up at her mother-in-law. "Mevrouw, do you have a recipe I can follow?"

"What? You need a recipe to make bread, the staple of life? Are you telling me you've never made bread before?" She gasped. "What do they eat in your village, bark?"

Anneke's eyes moistened and her body shook. "There are many kinds of bread, Mevrouw, but I don't know how to make the kind you serve."

Mrs. Veenhuizen pulled open a box, snatched out a piece of paper, and slammed it down on the worktable. "There! I assume you can read."

Anneke stared down at the paper before her, struggling to focus on the faded handwriting, but her eyes were too cloudy to distinguish the words.

"Well, get busy! Or do I need to read it to you?"

Anneke's hand shook as she reached for a wooden spoon. If she could just stall long enough, maybe her eyes would clear. She blinked several times hoping her tears would vanish. In one pan, she poured a small amount of water and placed it on the stove to warm for the yeast. Next, she filled the larger pan with a quart of milk and set it over the heat to scald. While waiting for them to reach the right temperature, she measured the flour, sugar, butter, and salt and put them into the large bowl. Gently, she creamed the mixture. When she cracked the last egg and was about to plop it into the bowl, a blood-curdling scream filled the room. Anneke's hands flew up and the raw egg fell from her fingers to the floor. A mad rush of wind swept past her as Mrs. Veenhuizen flew to the stove to retrieve the scalded milk foaming over the top of the pan. White froth covered the stove.

Trying to avoid stepping in the broken egg, Anneke reached for a towel, lost her balance, and grabbed the table to break her fall. But her hands, covered with egg white, slipped, and her foot landed in the pool of raw egg. Her feet slid out from under her and she fell to the floor.

When her head struck the tiles, a similar scene flashed through her mind. Was she actually in the marketplace, reliving an earlier catastrophe? If so, Romke would surely come. She drifted into unconsciousness.

Voices roused her—Romke's voice. He had come to help her. Where was she and what was she lying on? Her hand felt the cold hardness beneath her. Was this the tiled kitchen floor or the cobblestones in the marketplace? She had almost lost consciousness again when the shouts grew louder.

"What was that scream all about?"

"Your efficient wife let the milk scald on the stove."

"And that merited that deafening cry?"

"I guess you'd have shrieked, too, if you'd seen the milk foaming all over the stove and running to the floor. She can't even make bread without creating a disaster."

"Where is she now?"

"Around here somewhere."

Anneke forced herself to answer him. "Here, Romke."

Familiar footsteps approached her. "Anneke! Mijn lieveling!" He knelt and picked her up.

She was safe—safe in his arms.

"What is the meaning of this, Mother? Why did you leave her on the floor?"

Mrs. Veenhuizen snorted. "She's of no use when she's conscious. She was better off where she was."

"You mean you planned to let her lie there till evening?"

"Well, she can't cause a disaster when she's out cold."

"I can't believe this! That's inhumane! And I wouldn't even have known this had happened if I hadn't come back for my cap."

"Consider yourself lucky, then."

"I'll consider myself blessed if she's not seriously hurt. She needs immediate attention."

Anneke closed her eyes while Romke carried her down the hall to their room and laid her on the bed. She looked up at him. "You were there when I needed you. How can I ever thank you, Darling?" She laid her hand on his arm.

"Mijn lieveling, I was beside myself when I saw you lying there helpless, and Mother making light of the incident as though it were of no consequence." He held her close to him. "Tell me where you hurt."

"My forehead feels warm, and I have a sore lump on the back of my head. I guess that's what's causing my headache. But other than that and feeling tender all over, I think I'm okay."

"Don't attempt to get up, darling. Just rest here. I'll put a cool cloth on your forehead and over the lump. That should relieve a lot of the pain and swelling." He dipped the cloths into the water basin, wrung them, and grabbed his oilskin coat from a hook on the wall. He gently raised her head and slid his coat between her and the pillow. He placed one of the damp cloths on the back of her head, covering the lump, and laid the other across her forehead. "I'll check on you again when I come in at supper time."

She reached for his arm. "Thank you, darling."

He bent down and kissed her, then pulled his cap from off the hook, and closed the door behind him.

Later that evening, Romke came back to their room. "Are you feeling better, Anneke? Has the pain subsided?" His soothing hand on her brow and his soft kisses seemed to banish the lingering soreness as much as the cool compresses he had laid on her bruises.

"I feel much better, thanks to my personal doctor." She smiled and drew him close to her.

"I'm so glad to hear that. Stay in bed, Anneke. I'll bring you your plate of food. After you eat, try walking around the room and see how you do. I'll be back with your dinner in just a few minutes."

In no time, Romke returned with her food, adjusted her pillow, and removed the compresses. "Enjoy your meal, Anneke. I'll be back a little later."

After eating, Anneke felt even better. She laid down her plate on their quilt and slid off the bed, eager to see if she could walk without every bone and muscle in her body aching. Gingerly, she stood to her feet. She took a step and let out a cry. Every bone and muscle in her body did ache. Discouraged, she lay back down. Her bed, she decided, was the best place to be after all.

The following morning, before Romke went to the fields, he brought Anneke's breakfast to her. "How do you feel, darling?"

"I think I'll be fine."

"Fine enough to be left all day? I can come back and check on you at lunch time."

"Thank you, Romke, but I'm sure I'll do okay.

Romke squeezed her hand. "I want to be sure. Let me see you walk around the room before I go."

Anneke pushed back the covers and eased her feet to the floor. Her muscles still ached, but not as severely. As she took her first step, she winced. She hoped he hadn't noticed. Slowly, she made her way around the room and back to the door where Romke stood, watching.

"Be careful, Anneke, and don't overdo." He held her tenderly, and kissed her good-by.

When the door had closed behind him, Anneke climbed back in bed. She was too sore to risk another experience like the one she'd had the day before. One thing she knew for sure. She would never again try to make bread in this house unless she could do it alone—without her mother-in-law watching every move she made and yelling at her. Before long, she drifted back to sleep.

Several hours later, she awoke. Fear seized her. How long had she slept? Her mother-in-law would be even more furious with her lazily sleeping in and shirking her duties. She inched herself to the edge of the bed, then lowered her feet to the rug. Her headache had finally subsided and the pain in her body had lessened. The morning was growing late, and she had dusting and cleaning to do. At least she could do that by herself! After dressing, she left her room and entered the empty kitchen. Still sore, and not very hungry, she wanted only a slice of bread, but none was left. On the table, lay two bread pans filled with dough, along with a note. "*Put these in the oven to bake before you start dusting—if you think you can do it without dropping them.*"

A pain stabbed Anneke's heart. Her mother-in-law would never forget what happened yesterday, and probably would never trust her again to make anything. She opened the oven door and set the first pan inside. While she placed the second one on the rack, a voice bellowed from the next room.

"Come here instantly, young lady!"

Anneke shut the oven door and went to the sitting room.

With a deep frown, Mrs. Veenhuizen pointed toward the floor. "What is the meaning of this?"

Anneke stared at the circular rug. She could see nothing wrong with it.

"Why is that dead grass in here? And look at all that lint over there. Must I stand over you to make sure you do it right?"

"I haven't had a chance to clean this morning."

"You haven't had a chance! What have you been doing all morning? It's nearly ten o'clock!"

"I was very sore when I woke up."

"Well, do you think I felt perky when the cock crowed? The world doesn't come to a halt because you have a sore spot." She tramped over to the far side of the room and pointed a puffy finger toward the huge chest set against the wall. Ornamental scallops in relief surrounded the front of all six drawers. The intricate designs carved in rich wood proclaimed heirloom. "And look here! I doubt you've dusted this chest even once since you've come here. Do you realize how important this antique is to me? Did you think I wouldn't notice the film of dust in the crevices?"

"I'm really sorry, mevrouw. I promise not to forget."

A sigh of disgust escaped Mrs. Veenhuizen's lips. "Well, I should hope not. You realize you're getting your meals and lodging here free."

Anneke fought the tears as she hurried from the room. She had to get away from that wretched woman, dusting or no dusting. Blindly she ran from the house toward the garden, following the path to the bench in the woods. Each day, she felt more and more like *Assepoester*, sitting among the cinders, mistreated by her stepmother and stepsisters. Her mother-in-law more than made up for all three of them. Anneke couldn't claim a fairy godmother, but she did have a Prince Charming. If only Romke were here with her now. How she wanted to cry her heart out in his arms. Time slipped away from her as she tried to gain control of herself.

At last she rose to her feet. How long had she been here? Would her mother-in-law come looking for her and demand an explanation? She hadn't even started dusting yet. She edged her way toward the gate, and stopped. Why should she go back? Most likely, more trouble awaited her at the house. But she had work to do. Again she headed for the gate, but the very thought of facing Mrs. Veenhuizen made her tremble. She turned back to the garden. Seeing a trail she hadn't noticed before, she followed it to a small pond. Her heart quickened when the same variety of water lilies, waxy white with blushing pink centers, lay serenely on their lily pads. Her hand reached for the brooch that Romke had given her. If only she could know such peace—the peace of the water lily.

Dreading what lay in store for her, she left the garden, taking the path that led to the house. As she drew closer, the smell of something burning filled the air. Sudden horror seized her. "The bread! The bread is burning!"

Chapter

⟨⟨⟨⟩⟩⟩

22

Anneke raced across the lawn, bounded up the step and into the kitchen. Black smoke poured from the oven, while Mrs. Veenhuizen, clutching a dish towel with both hands, vigorously fanned it away from the stove. One look at the loaves sitting on the table brought fear to Anneke's heart. They were as black as the soil in their garden. What would her mother-in-law say now?

But Mrs. Veenhuizen never spoke a word. Anneke almost wished she would yell at her and get it over with. The deafening silence unnerved her more than the outbursts. She wanted to apologize and offer her help, but her fear and uncertainty left her speechless. Finally she found her voice. "I'm awfully sorry for what happened." Forgetting the promise she had made to herself, she added, "Please let me make some new bread."

Without even a glance in her direction, Mrs. Veenhuizen yanked the mixing bowl from the kitchen shelf and slammed it down on the table. Grabbing one container after another, she shook each ingredient into her hand, then, with a flick of her wrist, tossed it into the bowl. Exasperated puffs accompanied each addition, the puffs growing louder as the pile rose higher.

Anneke stumbled from the kitchen. She could never please that woman. She was as useless here as the two loaves that were pulled from the oven. She groped her way to her room and threw herself on the bed. Something crinkled beneath her. She rolled over, feeling with her hand. A letter—for her? Her mother-in-law must have gone to the post office while she was in the garden. It was a wonder Mrs. Veenhuizen hadn't considered her letter useless, too, and tossed it in the canal on her way home.

She turned it over and read the return address. Kea Haanstra. "Oh, Kea! You couldn't have picked a better time to write." Again a longing tugged at her heart to see her sister.

The banging of pans in the kitchen jerked Anneke back to the present. Her mother-in-law's anger still burned as hot as her oven. Anneke tried to turn a deaf ear to the clamor as she tore open the letter and began to read. It was almost like being back home, sharing in Kea's adventure.

> *Dear Anneke,*
>
> *I just had to write you of my latest episode with Lambertus, the beast. Vader, Moeder, and I had just returned from a concert with Tante Zusje, Uncle Frits, and the beast. They had invited us over for tea, so, while Moeder and Tante Zusje were busy in the kitchen, and Vader and Uncle Frits were talking politics in the parlor, Lambertus and I slipped out the back door.*
>
> *We no sooner got outside, when Lambertus says: "I bet you can't ride Black Piet around the barnyard without getting thrown off."*
>
> *You know, the mean goat that would just as soon butt you as look at you? I had to circle the area three times without falling off. If I fell, I'd have to start over.*
>
> *I'd seen Lambertus do it many times and it looked so easy. Surely there'd be nothing to it at all. And, of course, I had on my Sunday clothes. Still, I couldn't refuse this challenge. I was determined to prove I could do anything he could do.*
>
> *So Lambertus saunters over to the goat, all the while taunting me in his singsong voice, "I bet you can't do it without falling off. Black Piet's a mean old goat, and doesn't like being messed with."*
>
> *I just ignored him. He's so obnoxious. How did we ever get stuck with him for our cousin? Well, I'd show him I could do anything he could do.*

When he led the goat over to me, I tried to read its thoughts, but who can read the mind of a goat? Before I lost my nerve, I grabbed the hair on his neck and jumped up on his back. I hadn't even gotten settled when the old billy goat took off across the barnyard with me hanging on for dear life.

Wow, what a thrill! It was so much fun, I was planning to go for a second ride. Then, after one and a half times around the field, Black Piet comes to an abrupt stop and sends me soaring through the air. I hardly had time to be scared before I plunged headfirst into the center of the haystack.

I felt like I would suffocate with all that hay up my nose and down my throat. My nose started tickling, and my skin itched. It was so dark I couldn't see anything. I pushed the hay off to the sides until I'd made a large enough hole to see through. And there was Lambertus. It was all I could do to keep from laughing. His eyes as round as guilders, he stood watching Black Piet racing riderless at full speed across the field. All the while he kept calling:

"Hey, Kea, where are you? Where'd you go to?"

I wasn't about to tell him. I lay hidden from view, stretched out on my stomach with my head propped in my hands. Watching Lambertus's torment was even more thrilling than riding Black Piet. I knew he'd be held responsible for whatever happened to me, because it was his goat and his idea for me to ride him. And now, from his perspective, I had disappeared into thin air. His face had turned pasty-white, and his voice had a strange quiver.

"Answer me, Kea! You have to be here somewhere. You're just hiding, that's all."

I wish you could have seen him. He was a sight—his dark freckles against his pale skin and his curls standing on end. I had to force myself not to giggle. Then the tremor in his voice increased.

"Come on, tell me where you are. This isn't funny anymore!"

I still didn't answer him. Lambertus's scare was too good a thing to end so soon. Besides, what better way than this to get back at him. He deserved it. I watched him tear across the yard, shouting my name, and searching the row of bushes. He scanned the last clump with no success. Finally, he threw his arms in the air, trudged back to the haystack, gave it a sharp kick, and collapsed beneath it.

I held my breath. He was only about six inches from me. The hay scratched and poked me. My skin felt crawly. My neck and arms started to itch again, but I didn't dare move. I almost sneezed but stifled it in time. Lambertus moaned and leaned further into the hay. I started gasping for air and wondered how much longer I could hold out.

Just then, the top half of the Dutch door swung open and Tante Zusje appeared. "The slagroomtaart's ready. Come and get it!"

My favorite dessert! My mouth watered. I could almost taste the mandarin orange and whipped cream filling topped with chocolate and almonds. I suddenly realized I was famished.

Lambertus inched forward and stood up. Bending down, he pulled off his shoes and began shaking what little hay there was from them. I knew he was stalling for time. If his mother asked him where I was, he'd be in big trouble.

Tante Zusje rested her elbows on the ledge of the lower Dutch door. "Lambertus, I've never had to call you twice for slagroomtaart. Why are you being so poky?"

Lambertus ignored the question and went right on shaking out his shoes.

Then Tante Zusje noticed the empty barnyard. You should have seen her with her hands planted on her hips, and her eyebrows knitted together. She didn't even look *like our aunt! I knew then he was in trouble. I barely suppressed a laugh.*

"Lambertus, where's Kea?"

"She's out here somewhere."

"Why isn't she with you?"

"I don't know, she just disappeared."

"She can't have disappeared into thin air."

"But that's exactly what she did."

"And you expect me to believe that? I want to know where she is, right now! Where did you see her last?"

Lambertus hung his head. "Riding around the barnyard on Black Piet's back."

"Lambertus de Hoochweg! Was this your idea?"

He stood there, hanging his head in shame, more so, probably, because he hadn't proved he was tougher than a girl.

Tante Zusje stepped outside, shaking her head. "Young man, wait till your father hears about this."

I couldn't hold it any longer and started giggling. I crawled out, waving my arms in victory. "It's me," I shouted. "Alive and well." I could hardly decide whose mouth gaped wider, Tante Zusje's or the beast's

"I've been here the whole time, and Lambertus never even knew it." I looked at his puzzled face and laughed all the harder. Then to my dismay, Tante Zusje made the devastating announcement.

"If you think this is so funny, giving your cousin and me such a scare, young lady, you will go without your dessert tonight. And as for you, Lambertus, instigating this whole affair calls for equal punishment." Without another word, Tante Zusje marched into the house and pulled shut both the top and lower halves of the door, leaving us to lick our wounds.

Lambertus and I looked at each other in disbelief. As I thought about what I was missing, I almost regretted our latest escapade.

> *Let me know what it's like in Romke's village. I hope*
> *I hear from you soon. I miss you.*
> *Moeder and Vader send their love.*
>
> > *Your sis,*
> >
> > *Kea*

Anneke chuckled as she folded the letter and put it back in the envelope. Hardly a day could go by without Kea getting into trouble. Anneke found paper and pen and sat down to answer her sister's letter. Kea had asked what it was like in Romke's village. She wouldn't write about his parents or her Sunday experience. She would only write of pleasant things: of their honeymoon trip to Lijdendorp, of Anton and the lovely garden Romke had landscaped, of her new friend, Beppie, and of how to make cheese. She closed her letter asking Kea to give Moeder and Vader her love and promising to write them soon. After signing her name, she addressed the envelope to Kea.

Anneke laughed as she visualized her sister flying through the air. She would have to share this episode with Romke. Her own troubles forgotten for the moment, she ran to meet him coming from the fields.

Chapter

❦

23

Thursday morning dawned bright and balmy, but anxiety filled Anneke's spirit. Today was market day and she would need to buy material to make a dress like those the women of Lijdendorp wore. But how would she know what to buy and who would help her? Though she didn't feel like eating, she came to the table with Romke and took her seat.

Mrs. Veenhuizen set down a platter of *poffertjes*; left over from tea the day before, plopped into her chair, and cleared her throat. Looking across the table at Anneke, she paused before speaking. "We will take turns going to market each week. You will go today and sell our cheese, and while you're there, you will see to it that you buy material to make a proper outfit. I'm sick of looking at those strange clothes you wear. The very sight of them infuriates me!" The flame in her eyes burned as she stared at Anneke's cap and dress.

Anneke's lips quivered, and her clothes grew unbearably warm.

Romke's fork dropped to his plate with a clatter. "Mother, please!"

Mrs. Veenhuizen turned on her son, her eyes flashing. "What does this have to do with you?"

"It has everything to do with me. Anneke's my wife!"

Mrs. Veenhuizen's scowl deepened as she turned back to Anneke. "And another thing. You had better make sure you get what you need today because you won't have a chance to do it next Thursday. I'll be going to market that day, seeing as how Romke no longer finds it necessary to sell our cheese in Kollumdijk." She rapped her fork on the wooden table. "And—I want to make one thing clear. After today, you will not leave this house again, disgracing the family in those despicable clothes!"

She lifted her fork and stabbed it into the heaping pile of *poffertjes*. White puffs of powdered sugar whiffed from her plate like a dragon's breath.

Anneke coughed as she fanned the powdery cloud from her face. Her anxiety turned to fear and hurt. So she had disgraced them last Sunday. She tried her best to eat, but the *poffertjes* stuck in her throat

Mr. Veenhuizen never spoke a word, but he didn't need to. His massive build, his sour face and stern eyes, the mighty bearing of his presence filled her heart with terror.

She could feel Anton's eyes on her. She turned and watched him as he gazed from her cap down to her skirt. Then as if pleased with what he saw, he gave her a loving smile. She smiled back. Dear Anton. He had grown to mean so much to her. She forced herself to eat, knowing that the day would be long. Finished at last, she went back to the bedroom for her purse.

Romke followed her in. "I'm so sorry, Anneke. I will never understand why Mother's heart is so full of hatred." The deep hurt in his eyes pained her heart. He drew her into his arms. "Darling, you'll look just as beautiful in your new clothes, but I think I will always love these best." He fingered the filigree tips of her golden oorijzer. "Because this is what you wore when I first met you." He lowered her head to his chest and held her close. "Mijn lieveling," he whispered.

Drawing comfort from his arms, she smiled up at him. He was truly her haven. Then her smile faded. "But what if I don't find everything I need? Your mother never offered her help. All she gave me were threats." Her lip trembled.

"I'm sure the cloth vendor can show you. Don't worry, darling, you'll do just fine."

Loneliness and anxiety crept through her. If only Romke were going with her, but his father needed him on the farm, and he probably wouldn't know much more about the clothing than she did.

Romke stepped over to the chest, opened the top drawer, and pulled out a handful of guilders. He placed them in her hand. "This should be enough to buy material for two outfits." He looked at her and smiled. "I can't wait to see what you'll bring home."

She laid her head against his shoulder. All the excitement of going to market had gone. Now she dreaded it. But she would have to go. It was her turn to sell the family cheese and her only chance to buy fabric. And she had to have her outfit made by Sunday—two and a half days away! She lingered in Romke's arms, drawing strength from his embrace.

On her way to market, Anneke held the reins while she walked alongside the dogcart. She thought of how minutes earlier her mother-in-law had handed her more and more cheeses to place in the cart, until Anneke's arms ached from the heavy load, but she hadn't dared complain. She was grateful, at least, not to be carrying them. But still she would have to lift the twenty-pound cheeses again as she transferred each one from the cart to the counter at the market. Yet, their faithful dog didn't seem to mind the weight but pulled the cart as though it were filled with bunches of tulips instead of the stacks of cheeses it held.

At last she came to the square and found the family's booth. Once she removed the burdensome load from the dogcart, her spirits lifted. What a relief to be away from her mother-in-law's constant outbursts and out from under her disapproving eye, if only for a brief respite.

Then she remembered what lay in store for her. The thought of trying to pick out what she needed, with no one to help her, weighed her down more than the load of cheeses she had handled. But she had no choice. She decided to wait until noon to shop for the fabric when there would be fewer customers milling around.

Perhaps after she had some clothes like the other women, the villagers would accept her. It hurt to be treated like an outsider. How much she wanted to belong, but she probably never would. It would take more than the right kind of clothes, of that she was sure. She sighed while she laid the cheeses out on the stand.

Gradually the marketplace came alive. She looked across the way at a group of older women hunched together. Anneke watched as one, leading the conversation, wagged her long, spindly finger to the others, her lips moving incessantly. Then, like the blades of a windmill rotating in unison, all four heads turned toward Anneke. Were those women staring at her? Catching Anneke's eye, the four turned back to their own little circle, heads bent together, lips moving swiftly. They looked familiar. Surely she'd seen them at church last Sunday. The spindly woman with beady eyes and pointed nose stood eight or more inches above the others. She resembled Geertje. Another one, as short as she was plump, giggled constantly. Could that be Beppie's mother? The third one, a harried-looking soul, continually called to her son to stay close by. Anneke had no idea who she could be, nor the fourth woman, who stood so prim and proper.

While Anneke rearranged some cheeses to keep her hands busy, Wietske, Geertje and Beppie approached her stand. Geertje Bosboom's face, as usual, showed no expression, seeing all but saying little. Although she resembled her mother in appearance, how different they were in personality. Figuring out Mrs. Bosboom's opinions involved no guesswork, yet, reading Geertje's thoughts proved next to impossible.

Beppie bounded up, her face aglow.

Anneke smiled. "Hi!"

Beppie moved closer. She smiled back as laughter rang from her mouth. "You make a pretty picture selling farmer's cheese in Lijdendorp in your charming clothes of Zevendorp."

Anneke forced a laugh. "I'm sure it's never happened before."

"You're right about that, but I like it," Beppie assured her. "It adds a unique flavor to our marketplace."

Anneke smiled as she struggled to keep back the tears. Again, she was the turnip in a tulip patch. Well this would be the last time, she'd make sure of that. She glanced over at Wietske.

Wietske met her look with narrowed eyes. "Do you enjoy your life here in Lijdendorp?"

Last Sunday's scene came to Anneke's mind. How isolated she had felt, separated from Romke, walking to church alone. Her father-in-law's stern aloofness once more loomed before her, making her cower before him in her mind's eye. And the sound of her mother-in-law's fork striking the table at breakfast this morning resounded in her ear! A shiver passed through her. She had disgraced the family by wearing the clothes of her village.

Still, she had Romke. Her love for him was stronger than the fear or loneliness that gripped her. And Anton, sharing the hours of work with her, made the days more tolerable. With hesitancy she answered. "Yes, thank you."

"Is it much different from where you're from?" came Wietske's next question.

Anneke couldn't think of anything here that resembled her life back home, except perhaps some daily chores. "Well, yes, there are differences."

Wietske's eyes grew narrower. "How long are the Veenhuizens allowing you to stay?"

What a strange thing to ask. Anneke struggled to think of an answer. She understood all too well Wietske's real meaning and wished the quizzing would end. Before she could think what to say, the same young boy she had seen earlier with the group of women came tearing up to them, while his exhausted-looking mother trailed behind.

Arriving at the cheese stand, the boy stopped and, pointing his finger at Anneke, yelled to his mother. "Is this the woman Mevrouw Bosboom was talking about, Moeder? Is she the one who took Romke away from Wietske?"

Anneke felt the blood rush to her face while her heart pounded. So Wietske *had* hoped to marry Romke. No wonder Wietske hated her. Would she have to deal with this girl's bitterness and resentment indefinitely?

Wietske turned on her brother and, grabbing him by the collar, jerked him away from the stand.

"Moeder, Wietske hurt me. Punish her, Moeder! Punish her!" he screamed.

The frazzled woman appeared not to hear her son. She trudged over to Anneke's stand, reached in her purse and, pulling out the proper change, handed it to Anneke. "I've always loved your family's cheese." With a weary smile, she placed the cheese in her basket. She turned to Wietske. "Don't be too long, dear. I'll be leaving right away." She reached for her son. "Come along now. We have one last purchase before we head home."

Wietske sneered at her mother, then turned back to Anneke.

At that moment, several customers came up. Taking advantage of the situation, Anneke stayed involved with each one for as long as she could. She'd make sure that Wietske had no chance to repeat her last question.

Finally the three girls left. Anneke breathed a sigh of relief as she watched Wietske walk away. The longing for a child gripped Anneke's heart. Once she became a mother, Romke would no longer be a potential husband for Wietske, and Anneke would be secure.

Chapter

⟨∞⟩

24

The village chimes rang out the hour of noon. Anneke closed her stand and walked alongside her empty dogcart to the yard goods. She stared at the sea of bolts, their countless flowery designs spread out before her. She had no idea how much material she needed for the different articles of clothing or what was necessary to complete the outfits. Or even the names of the various pieces. Who would bother to help her when she didn't even know what to ask for?

She lingered, undecided. She would have to talk to the cloth vendor. She looked down the length of the table. The tall, bony woman had just finished waiting on a customer and was straightening the piles of material. As she looked up from her work, Anneke gasped. That was Geertje Bosboom's mother—the beady-eyed woman who had bent halfway over to reach the ears of her friends this morning in the marketplace. No, she couldn't ask that woman for assistance. That would be almost as bad as having to ask her mother-in-law.

"Would you like some help, Anneke?"

She turned to see who had spoken. "Oh, Beppie, I'm so glad you're still here. I need to buy material but I don't know where to begin."

Beppie fingered the fabric in front of them. "This is good quality here," she said, as she felt the black satin cloth covered with stipples.

"These designs are beautiful," exclaimed Anneke. "I feel like I'm in a dream, walking through a meadow of make-believe flowers."

Beppie beamed as brightly as though she had designed the patterns herself. "I'm glad you like them. We make these stipple flowers by dipping the heads of pins and nails into a special paint, then pressing them onto the black satin. When we use nails and pins of several sizes and dip them into different colors, we can fashion numerous patterns. You can also make stamps by placing pins and nails in cork and arranging them in creative designs. We learned stippling in sewing class."

"How unique!" Anneke fingered the fabric, admiring the intricate art.

"You'll want some of this material for both the cap and the kraplap. That's what we call this. She pointed to the bib-like vest that covered her underbodice. Do you have a favorite design?"

Anneke scanned the patterns once more. "This blue and white snowflake fabric is beautiful. And this one's pretty over here with the red and blue flowers. I'll get those two."

Beppie unrolled some from each bolt and held them up to Anneke's face. "You'll be pleased with them. They look lovely on you! The snowflake one especially accents your blue eyes." Beppie finished helping Anneke pick out the rest of the material for the outfits. "Would you like to buy material to make a headpiece, too?"

"Yes. I'm so glad you thought of that." With a headpiece that didn't match, she would have been stared down, again, on her way to church.

Beppie led her over to the piles of lace and the bolts of tulle. "On Sundays, you'll want to wear the dressy, lace kornetmuts cap over your oorijzer. On the next table is the fluted bobbin lace for the rim of the cap." Beppie gathered some of each material, as she explained what comprised the outfit.

Mrs. Bosboom watched from a distance, her nose twitching as her eyes followed their every move. Anneke knew she was itching for someone to gossip to. What she was thinking was anybody's guess.

When Anneke had paid for her purchases, she gathered them in her arms. "Thank you for your help, Beppie. I can't wait to begin sewing on them."

"If you have any questions on how to put it together, I'll be glad to help you. I could even come over, and we could make it together. Would you want me to?"

Anneke felt like she had found a true friend. "Oh, Beppie, you can't imagine what that means to me. Would you like to come over tomorrow morning?"

"I'd love to." Beppie grew more serious. "I'm sorry for the awful scene today with Wietske and her brother. Sometimes I wonder how their mother puts up with them. All I can say is, I'm glad Romke took you for his wife and not Wietske. She doesn't deserve a man like him." Beppie switched her basket to her other hand. "I probably shouldn't tell you this, but it wasn't easy for Romke to do what he did. He went against all the traditions of our village to bring you back with him. I heard he even married you. That would never happen here, not until the woman could prove. . . ." She stopped mid-sentence, and placed her hand on Anneke's arm. "Romke must love you dearly."

Anneke's eyes smarted. How Romke must have suffered for her. "And my love for him is just as strong."

"That's the way it should be."

Anneke had never seen her so solemn.

Beppie's face brightened. "I'll come over tomorrow about nine."

With a wave, they headed home in opposite directions. Anneke glanced at the beautiful material in the dogcart. She could hardly believe she was actually looking forward to making her Lijdendorp outfit.

⚬ﾐﾐﾐﾐ⚬

Friday proved to be one of Anneke's happiest days since coming to Romke's village. With Beppie at the house, Mrs. Veenhuizen kept to herself. The hours flew by as the two girls laughed and talked while sewing together on the blue and white snowflake outfit. The process had gone so much faster with Beppie sharing her expertise. After Anneke completed the hem, she tried on her dress to show Beppie and Anton.

"It's beautiful!" Anton exclaimed. "Now you really look like my sister."

"Oh, Anneke." Beppie sighed. "That was the best color you could have chosen. You look gorgeous. Romke will be absolutely mesmerized."

"Dank U wel, both of you." Anneke hugged Anton and Beppie in turn. Pleased by their compliments, she decided to leave it on. Romke would be coming in soon, and she could hardly wait to see his reaction. How surprised he'd be that she had already finished one dress. Tomorrow she would work on her second one. Now that Beppie had shown her so many tips and shortcuts, Anneke felt confident enough to make the second dress by herself.

She watched Beppie gather up her needles, pins, and scissors and place them in her basket. "I can't thank you enough for coming," said Anneke, folding the last piece of leftover material. "Please stay for supper tonight. We would enjoy having you so much." As soon as she spoke the words, horror gripped her. What had she done? She had no right to invite a guest to her in-laws' table! And she was sure her mother-in-law would never agree to it. She felt as though she'd stepped into quicksand, with no one to pull her out.

Beppie looked up. "Thank you. Maybe I can another time. I promised my mother I'd be home by six."

The quicksand released its hold on her. Beppie had pulled her free!

Beppie grinned as she leaned closer to Anneke. "We're having company tonight and I really must be there. It's my brother's best friend from the university who's coming and…" She blushed and lowered her eyes.

"Have you met him yet?" Anneke asked.

"No, but I have his picture, and we've written several times." She unclasped her purse, pulled out a small photo, and handed it to Anneke.

A boyish face, with laughing eyes, blond hair, and ruddy complexion, smiled back at her. He could have easily passed for Beppie's older brother. The signature in the bottom corner read "Jaap."

"He looks so nice. I hope you have a wonderful time this evening," Anneke handed it back.

Beppie's face glowed as she headed for the door.

"Don't forget to tell me all about it when I see you Sunday," said Anneke as she held open the door. "I can't wait to hear."

Beppie fluttered down the steps, then turned back. "You'll hear about it, all right. I won't be able to keep it quiet!" She chuckled.

Anneke grinned, then glanced up at the old cuckoo clock above the mantle. Its hands stood almost at six. She would wait outside for Romke.

The warmth of the June-day sun lingered in the air. Anneke paused before a rose bush, sniffing the delicate pink blossoms. How fragrant they smelled. They would make a beautiful centerpiece for the dinner table tonight. After picking several, she noticed a perfect white rose a few yards beyond. She stepped deeper into the garden, found the bush, and picked the lovely flower. More blossoms caught her attention. She bent over to gather them, unaware of footsteps going past her. As she turned, she saw Romke heading toward the house. She started toward him. "Romke."

He turned back. A look of surprise crossed his face. He blinked twice and stared, then hurried to her side. "Anneke! I can't believe it's you."

She giggled.

"Where did you get it? I mean, how could you have made the dress so fast?"

"Beppie came and helped me. She also helped me pick out what I needed. She's a wonderful friend, Romke. I don't know what I would have done without her."

"We'll do something special for her. Oh, darling, you look lovely. Our women's clothing never looked so good to me before. And your eyes, so blue! They glisten like the dancing waves of Holland's waters." They fell into each other's arms. "I love you so much, mijn lieveling," he whispered.

⟨∞⟩

Sunday morning Anneke dressed quickly, eager to leave the house early. She hoped to see Beppie before the church service to find out how her evening with Jaap had gone. She could hardly wait to hear about it. Perhaps Jaap had spent the weekend with Beppie's family and Anneke would have a chance to meet him after church.

Today, as she walked through the narrow streets, she blended in with the other women. She hadn't met with a single sidelong glance of disapproval. Maybe now this little community would accept her. But would Romke's parents?

When she arrived at the church, Wietske, Geertje and Beppie stood on one side of the step and two young men on the other. She recognized Beppie's brother, Albert, and, remembering the jovial face in the photograph, knew the second one was Jaap.

The two were engaged in conversation, but Jaap kept glancing toward Beppie. Each time their eyes met, his would sparkle, and a mischievous grin would steal across his face. Beppie would turn a flattering shade of pink, lower her eyelids, and sigh.

Anneke chuckled; glad she'd arrived in time to see this romantic exchange. As soon as Wietske and Geertje left, she'd get the whole story from Beppie.

Just then, Beppie looked up. When she saw Anneke, she left her friends and ran to her side. "We had the most wonderful time. My brother took Jaap and me for a boat ride on the river." Her face reddened, and she leaned closer. "I like him so much!" she whispered. "I wish he didn't have to leave. But he promised he would come to see me again when school closed for the summer. That's only a couple weeks away." She swung around to catch another glimpse of Jaap. He had been watching her, and again a big smile spread across his face.

With flushed cheeks, Beppie turned to Anneke. "And guess what? Jaap is from the same area that you're from."

Anneke nodded. "I felt sure he was, from his clothing. The university he attends is in Kollumdijk, the seaport where our market is held."

"Yes. I told him you were from Zevendorp. He has a cousin who lives there, too."

When the church bells pealed their final call, Anneke and Beppie hurried inside and sat down. Anneke watched Jaap while he and Albert took a seat within view of Beppie. The smiles and glances they exchanged throughout the service made her wonder what lay ahead for them. Dear Beppie, she deserved the best. But if their friendship blossomed into love, would they encounter the same opposition from her parents that she and Romke had from his?

Chapter

⬥

25

When July brought the close of the university for the summer, Jaap returned with Albert to spend a week at Beppie's. Anneke could see their relationship deepening. She longed to hear the details firsthand, but all that week there had been no opportunity to talk to Beppie.

The following Thursday, Mrs. Veenhuizen left for market, the dogcart filled to the brim with cheeses. Anneke had just finished sweeping the kitchen when a knock sounded on the door. Opening it, she found Beppie twisting the leather handle of her purse, her smile gone.

Anneke drew Beppie inside. "What's wrong?"

Beppie's lip quivered. "I need to talk to you."

Anneke shut the door behind them and motioned for Beppie to sit down. "We have the house to ourselves. Tell me what happened."

Beppie wiped a tear from her eye. "My father told Jaap he'd have to leave Lijdendorp tonight. Five days early!" She gave her purse strap another twist. "Father let Jaap come only because he thought Jaap was coming to visit Albert, my brother. As soon as he realized Jaap was interested in me, Father made it clear he didn't want a repeat of what happened at the Veenhuizens' home." She paused to blow her nose. "Why does it have to be that way?"

The words stung Anneke with their truth. The villagers still did not accept her. Would they ever?

Beppie wadded up her handkerchief. "Jaap loves me and wants to marry me, but how? Unless I go with him to Gelderland without my father's blessing." Another tear slipped from her eye. "But I want Father to accept Jaap. I don't want a split family."

So Beppie had tasted the bittersweet cup of love, too. Anneke understood her grief all too well. She sat eyeing the pattern on the tiled wall. What words of comfort could she give? She was experiencing the same situation with her in-laws, and she hadn't found a solution.

Beppie sighed. "If only there was something I could do. It's so tense at our house, Jaap doesn't even want to stay for the evening meal." She stopped short. "Anneke, do you suppose you and Romke could come to dinner tonight? I know Jaap would feel more at ease."

Anneke looked at Beppie in disbelief. "Would your parents want me at their table?"

"You're my friend, Anneke, my dearest friend. I'm sure I could convince Mother to let you come. Father usually lets Mother have her way, and my parents have nothing against Romke."

Anneke lowered her head. "Except that he married me—an outsider."

"Well, I don't think of you as an outsider. You're like a sister to me."

Anneke remembered her first meal in the Veenhuizens' home, how her in-laws had ignored her. Not even a chair had been placed at the table for her. Would there be a chair for her at Beppie's?

Beppie clutched her purse strap. "Please, Anneke, you would be doing me a huge favor. Say you will."

Anneke saw the pleading in her eyes. "Beppie, I do want to help you. But how will I know for sure it'll be all right to come?"

"If you don't see me back here in an hour, you'll know that my mother has agreed to it."

Anneke steeled herself. Even if she were ignored, it'd be nothing new. And if it would help Beppie and Jaap, it'd be worth it. "For you, Beppie, I'll do it. We'll be there this evening at six."

Beppie's face relaxed. "Thank you, Anneke. This means so much to me." Beppie rose. "I'll tell Jaap right away. I know it'll make him feel better just knowing you and Romke will be there."

Anneke gave her friend a hug. "Would you like me to bring a special dessert that's popular in Gelderland?"

"Oh, I'd love that. And I know Jaap would welcome a familiar dish from his province."

"Good. I know the perfect recipe. No one can resist it. I'll make it this morning and bring it over when we come."

Beppie grabbed Anneke's hands and squeezed them. "Thank you so much! I can hardly wait to tell Jaap."

Anneke watched her friend hurry down the road. She was glad she could do something for Beppie, but would her presence at the Botterman's table diminish or intensify their prejudice toward her and Jaap?

◯⦚⦚⦚◯

Anneke met Romke in the yard as he came in from the fields. "Tonight's our chance to do something special for Beppie," said Anneke.

"And what is that?" he asked.

Anneke filled Romke in on the stressful situation at the Bottermans' home. "Beppie's been such a good friend. How could I refuse to help her when she begged me to come? I offered to make Gelderland's favorite strawberry dessert to take with us. Beppie was so pleased, but I'm not sure how her parents will react. They may think it's my way of saying their food isn't good enough, or that I'm flaunting what Gelderland has to offer." Anneke looked up at Romke. "How can one group of people be so blind as not to see the good in another group?"

Romke shook his head. "Our village has been isolated for so long that it's become bigoted and self-righteous. Everyone here believes that nothing good could possibly lie beyond it." His voice softened as he drew her close to him. "But what a treasure I found when I ventured from the confines of our settlement."

She laid her head against his shoulder. "I'm so glad you did, Romke. I love you, darling. And you made the first step. Perhaps others will follow in your path."

When they set off for the Bottermans' home with the prize dessert, Anneke wondered what lay in store for the evening. The summer sky calmed her spirits as she watched the birds soar among the fleecy clouds. The balmy breeze swirled around the strawberry dessert, wafting the pleasing aroma through the air.

When they arrived at the Bottermans', Beppie met them at the door. "Oh, that looks so good," she exclaimed, reaching for the dessert. "What do you call it?"

Jaap walked up, a smile transforming his face. "Why, that's strawberry tart, the irresistible delicacy from Gelderland!" He ran his tongue over his lips. "We're in for a real treat tonight. It looks just like how my mother makes it."

Beppie motioned for them to follow her. "Have a seat, won't you?"

Beppie's father acknowledged their presence with nothing more than a nod then took his place at the table. Her mother smiled and giggled as she fluttered around the room, making sure the needs of her guests were met. A constant chatter poured from her mouth, but Anneke wondered if it was more from nervousness than friendliness. Even so, she couldn't help liking Mrs. Botterman and felt sure that most of the animosity had originated from her husband.

When all were seated, a hush fell over the group and Mr. Botterman led in prayer. His cold voice suddenly raged with heat as he concluded his prayer. "...God bless our home, God bless Lijdendorp! Protect her and keep her pure, uncontaminated by outsiders such as these—these Gelderlanders among us. Amen!"

An icy chill spread through the room. After a long pause, heads slowly rose. Anneke looked around the table. No one spoke a word. Not even Mrs. Botterman. Anneke glanced over at Jaap. His face had grown pale. All trace of the elation brought on by the sight of the strawberry tart had vanished. He tugged at his collar.

Mrs. Botterman picked up the dish of smoked eel and handed it to Beppie. Beppie served herself, and passed it to Jaap. His hand shook as he reached for it, and his fingers slipped. The platter hit the table with a thud, and the eel somersaulted into the air. They landed on the table and slithered over the cloth.

"Now, look what you've done!" shouted Mr. Botterman, jumping to his feet, his chair scraping across the tile floor.

Jaap stared at the mess before him, his white face growing as red as the straight-backed chair he sat in. One eel seemed almost alive as it stared up at them. Beppie giggled, laughter trickled from Mrs. Botterman, and Albert burst out laughing. Chuckles followed from

Anneke and Romke. Mr. Botterman tightened his lips to smother a laugh, but the eel, wagging his head at them, was too much. He broke down and joined the others in laughter, holding his side and wiping his tears with the rest of them—all except Jaap, who still sat paralyzed in his seat.

Then, like teamwork, everyone jumped to his rescue. Still chuckling, they began to scoop the eel back onto the platter. Anneke could feel them being drawn together like—like a family! Soon Jaap was laughing with the rest of them.

Mrs. Botterman spread clean napkins over the messy tablecloth. Then, one by one, they took turns telling embarrassing incidents that had happened to them in the past.

When both the main course and the last funny story came to an end, Beppie rose from the table. "We have something special tonight," she announced. She left her place, reached for the dessert, and laid it in front of Anneke.

Mr. and Mrs. Botterman's eyes widened when they saw the golden brown tart topped with a swirled mound of whipped cream, garnished lavishly with strawberries and sprinkled with almonds.

Mrs. Botterman drew in her breath. "Oh, strawberries are my favorite!" Her laughter rang as she turned to her husband. "And his, too."

Jaap beamed at the luscious dessert. "I can't wait to sink my teeth into it!"

Beppie picked up the knife and handed it to Anneke. "The cook who baked it gets the honor of cutting it."

Anneke stood and cut a piece, laid it on a plate, and handed it to Mr. Botterman. Next she served his wife. After the remaining slices were passed around the table, she sat down. Albert winked at Jaap and Beppie, Romke winked at Anneke, then all five turned to watch Beppie's parents take their first bite.

A low, satisfied sigh escaped their lips. "Where did you find such a delicious dessert?" asked Mrs. Botterman, turning to Anneke.

"I'm not sure, but it's been the family's favorite dessert for generations."

Albert broke in. "You can cook for me any day," he said, smacking his lips.

Romke gave Anneke an affectionate pat on the back. "Sorry, she's my cook."

Beppie took a bite of hers. "Anneke, this is wonderful! And to think, this dessert comes from Gelderland..." She smiled at Jaap then stole a quick glance at her father and added, "...the province of many a good thing."

Beppie's father looked up at her. "Well, I have to admit it's the best dessert I've had in a long time."

Beppie glanced at Jaap again, then at Romke and Anneke. Their eyes sparkled as they grinned at each other, thrilled at the turn of events.

Mr. Botterman took another bite. As he chewed, he studied Anneke, then Jaap. Gradually a smile played on his lips. "Well, young man, I guess you two Gelderlanders have proved good things can come from other places. This evening has been quite an eye-opener. In fact, I can't remember when I've had so much fun."

Mrs. Botterman laughed. "You see, dear? Haven't I told you, again and again, what delightful people these two are? Why, Beppie couldn't have a better friend than Anneke. And as far as Jaap goes, well, he could turn this whole village upside down with his hilarious entertainment."

Mr. Botterman dug his fork into the strawberry tart and nodded. "Well, I guess I have to agree with that."

When it was time to leave, Beppie and Jaap walked out the door with Romke and Anneke.

Beppie turned to them. "I've never seen Father enjoy visitors like he has tonight. I really feel like he's accepted Jaap now." She placed her hand on Anneke's arm. "I could never thank you enough for what you did."

Anneke gave Beppie a hug. "There isn't anything I wouldn't do for you, but Jaap deserves most of the credit."

Beppie's eyes twinkled. "Dear Jaap. He broke the barrier by breaking the silence." When their laughter subsided, Beppie leaned over and whispered in Anneke's ear. "I'm just glad he didn't break the platter, too."

Anneke chuckled and took the empty pie plate Beppie held out to her.

Jaap extended his hand toward Romke, who received it with a warm clasp. "There just may be a wedding after all. And if that's the case, this is a special invitation to you and Anneke to be our honored guests."

A broad smile covered Romke's face. "We wouldn't miss it for the world."

Chapter

26

Some of Anneke's favorite times were the hours she spent at the spinning wheel. She had learned to spin as a child, so she felt at home seated before the large wheel, listening to the hum as it whirled around, turning the soft, dyed wool into bright threads of blue, red, or white. Other times she spun the long fibers of flax into threads to be used for lace or linen.

All year long, while she spun or sewed, Anton would sit beside her, captivated by the stories she told him of her life back home in Gelderland. She enjoyed sharing with him the happy times she and her sister had had together, and Anton relished hearing about Kea's antics. But during the hours Anneke spent alone, she dreamed of the time when she and Romke would have their first child. But now, fear accompanied her anxiety. She was only to have had 12 months to prove to her in-laws that she would have a child. But sixteen months had passed, and still no sign of proof that she could supply the Veenhuizen's farm with workers. She was surprised that she hadn't already been forced to leave.

Finished sewing for the day, she smoothed out the remaining piece of linen in her lap— the perfect size for a baby's gown. She placed it in her sewing chest along with the other remnants she had saved. Her eyes wandered over to the lace that lay on the table nearby. How lovely that would look on the tiny white gown. And it was just the right length. She gathered the lace, laid it on top of the linen material, and closed the chest.

Pots clanging in the kitchen brought her back to the present. She should be helping her mother-in-law prepare the evening meal. Rising from her chair, she felt a hand on her arm. Romke stood before her, his eyes shining.

"Are you saving left over material to make something special—for a little person I should know about?"

"Oh, I did have remnants of linen and lace left over today. I'm keeping pieces in my sewing chest for the future but not for anyone in particular, yet."

The gleam faded from Romke's eyes, and his hand slid away from her arm. Hurt pulled at Anneke's heart as she watched him leave the room. She made her way to the kitchen, blinking back a tear that threatened to fall.

Anneke longed for the day when she could share the good news with Romke that they would soon be parents, but week after week passed by with no change.

⁂

The bitter October wind stung Anneke's cheeks while she moved from stall to stall. Thankful to be through with her shopping at last, she clutched the handle of her basket and headed for the town gates. The final market day of the year was over. With a sigh of relief, she picked up her pace. Bracing herself against the wind, she held her shawl tightly around her, glad that she had brought her warmest one this morning. The gusts continued to whip at her, driving their frosty needles against her face and hands. To keep her hands from getting chapped, she tucked them, along with her basket, inside her shawl. At a distance she could see Wietske and Geertje standing by the pump at the town gates. There was no way she could avoid them. With head bent against the wind, she struggled on until she drew near where they stood.

Wietske eyed Anneke up and down. Her lip curled. "Is it really true?"

"Is what true?" asked Anneke.

"Is it possible you're going to have his child?" Wietske stared at the bulk beneath Anneke's shawl.

Anneke followed Wietske's gaze. "You mean this?" she asked, pulling the basket out from under her shawl.

Wietske gasped. "Then I still have a chance."

The last words were spoken under her breath, but Anneke had heard them.

Wietske narrowed her eyes at Anneke. "Why are you so special? No other woman in our village was given extra months beyond the first year. Romke should have tossed you out four moths ago."

Despite the frigid wind, Anneke's face grew warm, and her clothing uncomfortable. A tear formed in her eye.

Wietske nudged Geertje and snickered. They left Anneke, heads bent together, whispering while they ambled on their way.

Again, Anneke felt her heart wrench. Her eyes stung with tears. Half walking, half running, she finally reached the house. Lowering her head as she entered, she set the basket on the table and fled to her room. She shut the door and threw herself across the bed. All she wanted was to cry her heart out. "Oh, God, I want a baby so much! Please give Romke and me a child to love," she pleaded, "a child of our own!" But did He hear her prayer, she wondered? Did God really love her? Did He even care that she was childless? Bitter tears fell from her eyes. She couldn't stop them, nor did she want to. When no more tears were left to cry, she lay exhausted and soon succumbed to sleep.

Angry voices wakened Anneke.

"What do you mean, Romke, that you'll bring her to the table?" her mother-in-law roared. "Does she have to be coddled and carried like a toddler?"

The deep voice of her father-in-law confirmed that trouble awaited her. "And didn't the dominee read from scripture last Sunday that 'He who works not, eats not?' She wasn't in the kitchen tonight, helping your mother prepare the meal. If she's not willing to do her share, she'll have to go."

"She always does her share!" said Romke. "And I know she went to market this morning. Something must have happened there. Did you try to find out if she was all right?"

Neither one answered him.

Anneke sat up when the doorknob turned.

Romke entered, closed the door behind him, and stepped to her side. "Tell me what's wrong, darling."

She threw herself into his arms. "I could never let your parents know, Romke." Her voice caught and her body shook. "They would only make it harder for me."

He smoothed her hair and held her close. "What happened, darling?"

"As I was leaving the marketplace, Wietske..." Anneke lowered her eyes and shook her head. "I can't, Romke. I can't repeat what she said."

"I think I know. Don't worry, mijn lieveling. You're the only one I've ever wanted. You mean more to me than anything." He ran his fingers through her hair and kissed her neck.

Anneke clung to him. His words stilled her heart. But from then on, each time Anneke saw Wietske, whether at church or elsewhere, she caught Wietske eyeing her in the same manner as she had at the town gates. She could sense Wietske biding her time until Romke grew tired of waiting, and it would be Wietske's turn at last to have Romke.

⚬୧୧୧୧⚬

Winter passed, and spring came to Lijdendorp. New hope filled Anneke's heart as she wheeled Anton through the garden. Seeing new life come to the barren ground and watching the seedlings sprout and bloom, she felt sure that new life would come to their home, too, but spring flew by, and summer took its place. Their second year of marriage had come to a close, and still no sign of a child to bless their home. She knew this was causing the rift between her and the village folks to become even greater, but especially so with her in-laws. Daily she could feel the tension growing in the household. Each morning and every night, she prayed God would fill her empty arms, but it seemed her prayers went no further than the thick walls of her in-laws' home.

⚬୧୧୧୧⚬

One Sunday, as the brisk autumn wind whistled through the windows, all were seated at breakfast. Mrs. Veenhuizen made her way around the table, pouring tea into everyone's cup, except Anneke's. When she finished, she set the teapot back on the stove and sat down.

165

Mr. Veenhuizen's usually short prayer droned solemnly on, no end in sight. "Lord, bless this food that we are about to partake of. Help us to finish harvesting our crops before the wintry winds and frost destroy all that we've labored for. We beseech Thy mercy. Thou, alone, dost control the weather. Look kindly on us and endue us with strength to carry out this satisfying but strenuous task."

At the opposite end of the table, Mrs. Veenhuizen shuffled in her chair as though anxious for her husband to finish.

"We need Thy help; in ourselves, we are weak. Thou art the almighty God of both Heaven and earth, and we are Thy people, Thy humble servants, who seek to do thy will."

Still the prayer continued.

"Pour out Thy blessings upon us, we pray; bestow Thy bounty upon our household. Drive out the adversary that would do us harm."

Soon, whispering joined the shuffling. Anneke raised her eyes just enough to glance at her mother-in-law. Mrs. Veenhuizen was mouthing something under her breath, as though rehearsing some treasured piece of news.

"If we have sinned, Father, forgive us, so that we can come boldly before Thy presence with our requests and Thou wilt look favorably upon us and hear our cries. Amen."

A long sigh escaped his wife's lips. She sat up straight and cleared her throat. "Well, did you hear what happened last night?" She adjusted her skirts long enough to be sure she had everyone's attention. "Last night at ten-thirty, Mevrouw Derksen's lovely daughter, Lena, gave birth to a beautiful son!" Mrs. Veenhuizen glared at Anneke, then turned to Romke. "And in only ten months after her man took her to be his woman."

She turned to Anneke, hatred burning in her eyes. "What do you have to say for yourself? Are you less of a woman than Lena? Maybe you need to seek advice from her? Or is barrenness a curse visited upon the females of Zevendorp?"

Romke's fist came down heavy on the table. "Mother, how could you?"

Mrs. Veenhuizen shifted her gaze to her son. "It's time you two took this seriously. You aren't here to play games. You have a duty to perform, and the sooner, the better."

Anneke's face burned with humiliation. She lowered her eyes and tried to focus on eating, but her hunger had vanished. She would force herself to eat anyway. She knew if she didn't, she'd be hungry long before the noonday meal. But she'd eat fast. She didn't want to stay at this table any longer than necessary.

She reached for the silver cup that held her boiled egg and spooned out a large amount. Fragments of egg yolk dropped on the tablecloth. She picked up the pieces that had fallen and put them on her plate. What was left on the spoon, she put in her mouth. Before she finished chewing, she crammed more egg into her mouth. All the while, she could feel her mother-in-law's eyes on her.

Anneke tried to swallow, but her mouth had become dry, and the egg yolk stuck in her throat. A few sips of tea would wash it down. She reached for her cup, but it was empty.

Mrs. Veenhuizen laid down her fork. "Oh, did I miss your cup? Let me pour you some tea." Grabbing the teapot from the stove, she filled Anneke's cup.

"Thank you, Mevrouw." Anneke took a drink, and screamed. The boiling-hot tea formed blisters on her lips, tongue, and upper palate. She grabbed her bread and pressed it to her burning mouth, hoping to absorb the heat. There was no way she could she finish her breakfast now.

Romke had run from the table and now returned with a pitcher of cold water from their stream. He poured some into a cup and held it to Anneke's lips. "Drink as much of this as you can, Anneke. The cold water will lessen the pain, and prevent the blisters from getting worse."

The chilly water refreshed her mouth. She squeezed his hand and mouthed her thanks. Leaving the rest of her food, she left the table with the cup to her lips.

Romke walked beside her, down the hall to their room. "Do you feel up to going to church, Anneke?"

"I'm not sure, but I'm going to try." She didn't feel like staying home, and what would she do here, anyway? Being in church would help take her mind off the pain.

Romke slipped on his coat and grabbed his hat. "There's a lots more water in the pitcher. Drink as much as you can before you leave. Your mouth should feel better by tomorrow."

"It feels some better all ready. Thank you so much, Romke."

"I'm glad to hear that." He held her close. Moments later, he opened their door. "I'm heading off to church now. Will you be all right?"

"I'll be fine." After Romke left, Anneke poured another cup of water and gingerly drank it down. Her stomach grew queasy. She needed fresh air—fast! She grabbed her purse and left for church, inhaling the crisp autumn air.

The dark clouds of autumn hung heavy over her spirit as she walked alone to the morning service. She thought back to her first day in the marketplace, a year ago, when she saw the four women huddled together gossiping. That fourth lady in the group standing there so prim and proper was Lena's mother, Mrs. Derksen, of course. Anneke remembered her well—nose high in the air, eyelids half closed, and head bobbing while Mrs. Bosboom's lips flapped open and closed.

So Mrs. Derksen's daughter was blessed with a son. Of course Lena would have a child within a year's time. That family did everything right and proper. That made Lena's the fifth child born in Lijdendorp since June. Emptiness filled Anneke's soul as the leaves crackled beneath her feet. Why couldn't she have had a baby, too?

The clicking of women's shoes roused her from her thoughts. Turning, she saw two young mothers walking together, carrying their babies wrapped snugly beneath their warm shawls. Little round faces peered from the woolen fringe. The women's smiles reflected their joy as they passed by, chatting together.

The pain in Anneke's heart deepened. How her arms ached to hold a wee one—her and Romke's own child. While she walked along, brisk winds blew the leaves from off the beech and willows. Anneke watched the dying leaves fall to the ground and felt her long-desired hope of mothering a child die within her.

The wind whistled past, its shrill laugh mocking her. She could almost hear the wailing winds whisper as the gusts surged and died, surged and died. Were they trying to tell her something? She pulled her shawl tightly about her and listened closely to the mocking winds.

"All around her leaves are falling,
Torn by winds with dismal sound.
Hope that once lived bright within her
Now lies crushed upon the ground."

Anneke shivered as the words stung her ears. Had she really heard those words or had it been her imagination? She could almost visualize Cobie standing before her, throwing taunts like arrows. And now, Cobie's threats had become reality! More than two years had passed, and she remained childless. One by one Cobie's darts pierced her heart anew, leaving wounds she knew would never heal. *"Romke will no longer love you." "He's no different from all the other men of his village." "He'll send you back in shame and take a new mate."*

Would Wietske now share Romke's days, his nights, his love? "Noooo! Oh, Romke, tell me again, it's not true. Tell me again you will keep me for your own, forever!"

With aching heart she entered the church and sat down, fighting the tears that filled her eyes.

The pastor faced the congregation, and a hush fell over his people. "Let us turn our attention to the forty-sixth Chapter of the book of Psalms, verses 1-3. *'God is our refuge and strength, a very present help in trouble.'*"

Anneke caught her breath. Wasn't that the verse Romke quoted when he gave her the water lily two summers ago? She forced her attention back to the pastor.

"'Therefore we will not fear, though the earth be removed, and though the mountains be carried into the midst of the sea; though the waters thereof roar and be troubled...'"

The pastor seemed to be directing his message to her. What a rich promise. But was it meant for her? Could she claim it as her own?

After the service, the women gathered in groups outside the church, sharing the latest gossip with one another. Romke's mother paused to join her circle of friends. Then, Anneke heard a sharp, inquisitive voice directed toward her mother-in-law.

"Mevrouw Veenhuizen, does it look promising *yet* for you and your household?"

Anneke caught the emphasis on the word "yet" and glanced over to see who had spoken. Mrs. Bosboom, of course. With bony hands on her hips and nose twitching, she waited for an answer.

Mrs. Veenhuizen looked behind her and caught Anneke's eye, then faced the woman before her. "I doubt that day is going to come, at least under the present conditions."

Anneke froze.

"Well!" Mrs. Bosboom exclaimed, her beady eyes growing more intense, taking on the fish-eyed stare of her daughter, Geertje. "You can change those conditions, you know. I dare say, I would never have waited this long."

"That's exactly what we intend to do," Mrs. Veenhuizen snapped, "but I can assure you, it won't be your daughter Romke will take."

Mrs. Bosboom's face grew as red as the shawl that covered her shoulders. The other women in the circle winked at each other as she slunk away, speechless for the first time in her life.

Wietske's mother, frazzled as ever, stood in the group. Her son tugged on her sleeve. "Moeder, does this mean that Wietske will get Romke? Does it, Moeder? Does it?"

Again the women winked at each other in their circle.

Wietske's mother grabbed her son by the arm. "Oh, hush, child. Won't you ever learn to hold your tongue?"

Chills ripped through Anneke's body. She forced her legs to move, leaving a wide berth between her and her mother-in-law's group of friends. How could her mother-in-law and Mrs. Bosboom talk about her, knowing she could hear every word they were saying? They had crushed her heart just as callously as they had crushed the leaves beneath their feet. They didn't care how deeply her heart ached. They only condemned her—condemned her for what she had no control over.

Romke stepped over to her side and slipped his hand in hers. "God understands." He gave her hand a tender squeeze. "And I love you, *mijn lieveling.*"

So Romke had heard it, too. How precious he was to her. She turned to him and saw the concern in his eyes. "I know, darling. I will never forget that. But sometimes it seems like it's more than I can bear."

Romke walked with her the rest of the way home. She didn't care if the villagers stood watching them, incredulous stares on their faces. Romke must not have cared either. In silence they climbed the front step to the house. Anneke looked up at the Tree of Life above the door, its branches spread like open arms, waiting to receive another fruit. A tear fell from her eye.

Chapter

27

Anneke stepped inside the empty house with Romke. His mother was probably still talking with her friends, and more than likely, about her. She sighed as she lay down on the bed in their room. "Romke, I don't feel very well. I won't be eating dinner." How she wished she never had to eat at that table again.

He sat down beside her. "Please join us. You'll feel better after you've eaten. Why don't you rest until my folks get home?"

With a slight nod, she closed her eyes. Quietly, Romke left the room.

When dinner was ready, Anneke felt no better, but for Romke's sake, she forced herself to get up. She sat down as Mrs. Veenhuizen, with fixed jaw, finished setting the table. The air hung icy and tense.

Mrs. Veenhuizen took her seat. With a scowl, she turned to Anneke and cleared her throat. "There need to be some changes made in this household."

Anton's eyes grew wide as he followed his mother's gaze toward Anneke.

Mr. Veenhuizen took a bite of smoked eel before he spoke. "Well, you know the old saying, 'No farmer buys a cow until he is sure of the calf.' If the women weren't productive, our village would soon die out. Isn't that right, Romke?"

Anneke gasped.

Romke gave her a tender smile. "I have the dearest, most beautiful wife in the world."

Mrs. Veenhuizen slammed down her fork. "And what good is beauty without propagation?"

Anneke's throat closed up and her eyes stung. It was impossible to eat any more. She shoved back her chair, but a tear escaped before she could leave. She could feel Mrs. Veenhuizen's cold stare follow her out of the room.

Romke stood up. "Excuse us both."

Mr. Veenhuizen continued to eat as though nothing had happened, his fork clinking hard against his Delft Blue plate while he sliced through the smoked eel.

Alone in their room, Romke drew Anneke into his arms. "I know this has been so hard on you." He fell silent.

"No, it was my fault. I shouldn't have let them upset me."

"It's not your fault, Anneke. You've been kind, patient, and loving, while they've been ruthless. I keep thinking this will resolve itself, but it hasn't. Let me give it some thought. Maybe by tomorrow I'll know what to do."

Anneke's eyes swam with tears. "Like what? What could we possibly do? Nothing is going to change their way of thinking. And certainly nothing could happen overnight that would alter the situation."

His arm moved across her shoulder. "Let's ask the Lord to help us, Anneke. I know He'll hear our prayer."

Anneke squirmed from his arms. "You can, if you want to. I've begged God to give us a child. Why hasn't He answered my prayer? I'm not sure if He's even interested."

Romke winced.

As soon as she had spoken those words, she wished she hadn't. The hurt in Romke's eyes pained her and made her feel estranged from him. But how could she have prayed with him? She didn't have that close relationship with God that he had. It made her feel awkward. He prayed to God as though he were talking to his father, a loving father, that is, but she didn't know God that way. To her, He was only a powerful being in the heavens, not an intimate friend who cared for her.

Romke lowered his head to his hands. She wanted to go back to his arms, but she couldn't. She'd be intruding. She felt like an outsider as she stood there, watching him pray.

That night, Anneke lay awake for hours. Not wanting Romke to know how distressed she felt, she lay as still as possible. Romke was troubled as well. Her heart ached for him as he tossed and turned throughout the night. He especially needed the rest. His duties required both strength and endurance.

At last she drifted off to sleep. It seemed like only minutes had passed when a heavy knocking sounded at the door.

Romke woke with a start. "What is it?"

"Do you intend to sleep the whole morning?" shouted his mother through the closed door. "I would think you'd know your father needs your help harvesting the wheat."

"I must have overslept. I'll be out right away."

"I should hope so. You're already over an hour late!"

Shaken from her sleep, Anneke raised herself on her elbow. "Have you thought of anything yet?" Her voice trembled.

"No," said Romke, "but don't worry. Everything will work out all right." He splashed water on his face and climbed into his clothes. Purple shadows beneath his eyes confirmed his sleepless night. And she didn't feel any better. Romke kissed her, then hurried out the door, closing it behind him.

"Well, it's high time you got here, young man." His father's voice boomed with anger. "This means a late dinner tonight, Romke. We'll be forced to work till dark this evening, to make up for the time we've lost."

"And furthermore, Romke," said his mother, "there's something we need to settle before you leave." She paused.

Anneke slid out of bed and tiptoed to the door to listen. Her heart pounded while she waited for her mother-in-law to continue.

"We have tried to be patient with you two, but Anneke is not doing her part. In ten years your father will no longer be able to carry out the heavy duties on the farm. It's up to you to show loyalty to your parents. You have no other recourse but to send her back to her family and take a woman from our village."

"Never! She's my wife. We were married in her church before I brought. . ."

"You've gone against the tradition of our people and taken things into your own hands," interrupted his father. "You had the audacity to marry a woman from outside our village, without our knowledge or permission and without prior assurance of her fertility. Nor was your marriage sanctioned in our church. Therefore your marriage is illegal, and we will see that it's annulled. You will tell her tonight that she must be out by tomorrow."

Anneke trembled. Then they really did mean to separate her from Romke—forever! She pressed her ear to the crack in the door to hear Romke's answer.

"You can't do this! Anneke's my wife. No one can take her from me! I love her with my whole being."

"This is not a matter of love, this is a matter of life," said his father. "We need a new generation to carry on the farm work. God has frowned upon your union and is punishing you. We think we are being reasonable, Romke. You never sought our approval concerning this marriage. Think about that while you're working in the fields today, and be prepared to send her away tomorrow morning."

"I'll never send her away."

"You have no alternative!" roared his father.

Anneke heard no more. The back door slammed shut, already separating her from Romke.

She threw herself on the bed, thoughts running madly through her mind. She had failed him! His parents hated her. They had claimed her marriage to Romke was illegal. They were demanding she leave by tomorrow morning!

"They'll never have the chance to tell me that to my face," she cried. Her mother-in-law would be going to market shortly. As soon as Romke's mother left, she would leave.

She forced herself from the bed and frantically began to throw things into her valise. Then she stopped. Where could she go? Home was the only place she wanted to be, but Cobie was there. How Cobie would gloat at her rejection. No, she could never face Cobie now, but where else could she go? She sank to the bed in despair.

While she lay there, her eyes wandered to the Delft blue vase. Rising from her bed, she walked over and picked it up. The blue-flowered vine wound aimlessly over the curves of the vase. Was she destined to wander too—with no purpose—with no journey's end? The image of her mother came to mind. Moeder loved her and would understand her problem. She held the vase to her heart. She must go home.

Anneke scanned the room, the room she'd shared with Romke for more than two years. Her gaze took in every corner and every article that filled it and finally rested on the washbasin. She remembered the times they'd dipped their hands together in the water and playfully splashed each other on warm summer evenings. How she'd cherished those times of fun and laughter.

A chasm of loneliness engulfed her. She flopped back down on the bed and laid her head on Romke's pillow, dampening it with her tears. "Romke, Romke!" His masculine scent she loved so much filled her with longing for him.

She sobbed. *How could she think of leaving him? The one she loved with her whole being—but how could she stay?* She jolted upward. *If she didn't leave now, her in-laws would throw her out tomorrow—in shame!*

Never would she give them the satisfaction of watching her leave in disgrace. Never!

She removed her pillowcase, then Romke's. She slipped hers on Romke's pillow, then tenderly wrapped Romke's pillowcase around the vase. *She would keep a part of him forever.*

She forced herself off the bed. *She had better write her parting note to Romke before she fell to pieces.* When she crossed the room, she saw her reflection in the mirror. She paused. *How often when she stood there, he would come up behind her, and before she could secure her coral beads around her neck, he would find the rings and clasp them for her. Then he would draw her into his warm embrace.*

Oh, to never feel his arms around her again—never to share another day with him!

"*How can I do this? Oh, Romke!*"

Tears streamed down her face as she stepped to the desk in search of paper. With pen in hand, she poured out her heart.

> *My Dear Romke,*
> *I love you so much! It's tearing my heart out to leave you, but I wasn't given a choice, only a command. In all fairness to you, I must go. I've failed you, the one for*

whom I'd do anything in my power. But the one thing I desire to do, I can't. I've caused division and contention between you and your parents. It's only right that I should go. I release you from your promise to me. You are free to take another who will bring not only children, but also peace to you and your family.

I know God will bless you, Romke. I pray someday I will know Him like you know Him.

My love for you will never change. In my heart, I am yours forever.

All my love,
Anneke

A tear slipped from her eye and fell to the note. When she placed her letter on the washstand, she left behind her heart and soul. Pain and loneliness now filled her empty shell.

Anneke put the last of her belongings in the valise, added a pile of letters she retrieved from her chest of drawers, then carefully laid the Delft blue vase, wrapped in Romke's pillow case, between her clothing. Last of all, she placed her jewelry box among her clothes. When she'd finished packing, she gazed around the room, making sure she hadn't forgotten anything. How bare it looked. It didn't even resemble their bedroom. She longed to place everything back where it belonged, but this was no longer her room—Romke was no longer hers, either!

The very thought of it drained her body and soul. Exhaustion overpowered her. Her legs no longer held her up, and she sank to the chair in a heap.

A thunderous bang roused Anneke. Mrs. Veenhuizen had left the house, letting the front door slam behind her. Now was the time for Anneke to leave, but she couldn't go without saying goodbye to Anton.

Clutching the handle of her valise, she opened the bedroom door and headed for Anton's room. Did he know that she'd been turned away from their home? She knocked and the door opened. Anton's eyes were moist and swollen. Yes, he knew. Her heart went out to him. She dropped her valise and threw her arms around him.

Anton's body shook while he clung to her. "I don't want you to leave, Anneke. You're my sister-in-law, and you always will be to me." A deep sob followed.

"I wish I didn't have to go, Anton, but I've been ordered to leave."

Anton blinked back the tears that threatened to spill. "It'll never be the same again. You made every day an adventure worth living." His voice broke, and he drew his sleeve across his eyes.

Anneke laid her hand on his arm. "And I enjoyed every minute of the days we shared."

"Won't you ever come back again, Anneke?"

"Only if I'm accepted back. But I'll never forget you, Anton, and I'll never forget my dear Romke. It tears me apart to leave you both, but I wasn't given a choice, only a command. I'd better go now." Anneke could feel the tears gathering in her eyes. She reached for Anton once more, and they gave each other a parting hug. Anneke closed his door behind her. She would have to hurry. She wanted to be gone before Mrs. Veenhuizen returned home.

Hoping no one would see her leave, she ran to the canal that bordered their property. She remembered when she and Romke had sailed up this very canal, thrilled with the joy of sharing their new life together. It had seemed like the beginning of lasting happiness. But then Wietske, floating up ahead in her barge, had appeared in that scene to mar her joy. She remembered the cloud that hung over the Veenhuizen's home, and how the blades of grass, like a warning, had seemed to wave her away. Now, her in-laws, who had never accepted her, had demanded she leave their home.

And Romke, her own, dear husband, would be forced to take Wietske for his mate. She recoiled at the thought. It was more than she could bear. She remembered how he'd promised he would keep her for his wife regardless of any circumstance. But how could he hold to that promise when his parents had changed their destiny?

She paused, and looking out across their land, remembered the fields of flax in August, rippling like waves as the breezes passed through them. Now the fields were covered with wheat, their spiked heads shivering in the chilly autumn winds. She could visualize Romke harvesting the stalks, struggling to keep his mind on his work. She sensed his heart yearning for her.

Longing for him surged through her. She wanted to leave the dike and tear across the fields to find him. For a moment she swayed, like the sea of blue blossoms tossing to and fro in springtime on the flax. Dropping her bag, she faced the fields, ready to answer his silent call. She started to run toward the fields, keeping the image of Romke before her.

Instantly, she came to an abrupt stop. In her mind's eye, her father-in-law loomed before her, blocking Romke from view. With pitchfork held high, her father-in-law faced her with a threatening glare, preventing her from coming nearer. She held her breath as he advanced in her direction. She tried to back away, but his form swelled, stretching closer and closer until she almost felt the pitchfork's metal prongs against her face.

She stumbled backward, then turned on her heel and ran. Up ahead lay her valise. She snatched it from the grass and fled toward the canal.

Chapter

⟨∞⟩

28

Anneke's heart pounded with fear as she staggered along the edge of the dike. The trees overhead stirred in the wind, creating eerie reflections in the water below. On she trudged, until at last the water broadened, merging with the sluggish Black Canal.

Up ahead, a weeping willow offered rest and safety. She hobbled to it, slumped to the ground, and wrapped her arms around her knees. Her body shook and, regardless of the chill in the air, beads of sweat covered her face and hands. She lowered her head to her arms.

Had Mr. Veenhuizen really challenged her? How could something that real have been imagined? Perhaps it had happened. She might never know for sure. But one thing she did know: she had escaped his threatening power. She leaned her head against the tree trunk, closed her eyes, and tried to relax. Gradually her fears subsided.

With heavy heart, she forced herself to her feet and resumed her trek along the Black Canal. How much longer it took by foot than when they had sailed by boat. If only the June sun were warming her back with its rays. Instead, October's brisk winds added discomfort to her misery. Her luggage grew heavier by the moment, and her legs more tired with each step.

Half running, half tripping, she arrived at the dock in Zwartland. She could smell the damp air of the Zuider Zee, probably no more than four kilometers away. With a sigh of relief, she set her valise down on the pier and rubbed her aching arm. A sea breeze blew past her, leaving behind the stench of fish. Sea gulls soared overhead. Their screeches pierced the silence, hanging in the air like evil omens. *Were they meant for her?*

The midday sun lingering overhead still refused to warm the air. She wrapped her arms around herself, trying to stay warm, but she couldn't stop shivering. The gnawing in her stomach reminded her she had left without bringing any lunch. *She hadn't even eaten breakfast. If only she had thought to bring some food with her. But she couldn't go back. Romke's mother would be home from market by now.* She tried to push her hunger from her mind.

She would have to hitch a ride on a riverboat heading down the Oostelijk River to Oostenhaven. Did she have the courage to ask them to take her on board? Would they refuse her? She stared at the myriads of boats, unsure of which to approach. *Romke would know what to do if he were with her—but she was on her own.* Anneke fought to keep back the tears. She longed for him, but she could never return to his home. His parents had made that final. Loneliness swept over her like a giant wave, sucking the life from her soul.

The scene before her both intimidated and threatened her. On the far side of the harbor, iron cranes scraped the sky as they stretched and yawned. Their giant arms hovered over the cargo ships, then reached down to attack what lay beneath them. Barges of all kinds lined the quay. Everywhere, crewmen scurried to complete their jobs, loading and unloading, hauling and pitching. The assembly line of workers moved the crates from one vessel to another.

Along a nearby pier, sailboats and fishing boats formed an uneven row, resembling unmatched beads on a string. Their constant rubbing against the posts grated on her nerves, and the unrelenting water, lapping the vessels like hungry dogs, made her uneasy.

When she walked along the dock, the creaking boards sounded like the rattling bones of ancient seamen. She trembled and tried to lighten her footsteps, but still the wooden planks scraped and knocked against each other. It made her think of Mrs. Tasman and the time she had taken bread to her. And when at last she had gotten free of the woman, how those ghostly footsteps had followed her all the way to the marketplace. She shuddered. At least it was daytime. She would hate to be out here alone at night.

A barge, stacked high with beets, drifted in to dock. She watched the cranes descend upon them, driving their claws deep into the pile. The iron-gray claws, covered with blood-like stains where they had pierced the beets, rose with their load and turned to pour it out onto a waiting freighter. Hungry for more, the giant claws found their way back to the loaded barge where the beets lay helpless, at the mercy of the mighty claws.

She felt like one of them, a lifeless lump, vulnerable, her heart bleeding. But unlike her, the beets had a place to lie. That was all she wanted now. The lack of sleep the night before, the trauma of the day, and the lack of food had taken its toll on her. *Perhaps this barge would accept her.* She hesitated to approach them. She would wait till the beets were unloaded. When the shouts of the crew proclaimed their task finished, she sought out the captain.

"Excuse me, meneer, are you heading south?"

The captain studied her before answering. "Are you running away from home?"

Anneke could feel her face flush. "I'm going home." Nervously, she waited for the man's answer.

"Oh, you're running away from your husband. Hasn't he treated you right?"

She regretted having asked him. If he intended to quiz her the whole time she was on his boat, she would leave now. "Never mind, meneer, I'm sorry I bothered you." She turned to leave.

He gave her a sidelong glance. "I guess we could take you on—as long as you don't get in our way." He turned to a group of men hosing down the barge and shouted to get their attention. "Hey, have we got a spare berth on board for a passenger?"

The crew stopped what they were doing and looked up.

The smiles that lit their faces made Anneke uneasy as she stood there, the object of their ogling. One in particular, muscularly built, with sandy hair and eyebrows, studied her with interest.

"Sure, Dad. If not, she can share mine." The young man leaned toward the others and whispered to them. Loud chuckles rang out. The group of men watched as the captain's son walked toward her.

Again, the call of a sea gull rent the air, confirming her fear of imminent danger. A feeling of weakness coursed through her. *This was a mistake. She would leave and find another boat.* She leaned down and grabbed her valise, but before she could get away, the young man had reached her side.

"My name's Ard. Let me carry your valise for you, mevrouw." He reached over and placed his hand over hers.

Quickly she released her hand, letting Ard take her bag.

"Come. I'll show you where to board."

In spite of the doubts that filled her mind, she followed him, too exhausted to do otherwise. The sooner she found a place to lie down, the better.

"Am I right to assume you're running away? Don't worry, you'll be safe here with us."

Furious, she eyed him with disgust. "I never implied anything of the kind." *If only she hadn't been so hasty in choosing the first riverboat that came along.*

Ard gave her an amused smile. "Oh, I don't expect you to tell me about it or even admit it, but it's rather obvious when a woman is traveling by herself. You're not the first one it's happened to, though."

She ought to insist on taking her luggage back and find another boat, but they had reached the ramp. Here at last was a bed. Perhaps it would be best to stay after all. Besides, another barge might not accept her. Suddenly her legs buckled. As she grabbed for the railing, Ard caught her arm and steadied her.

Anneke paused to get her bearings. "Thank you for your help. I should be fine now."

"Are you sure?" His face drew nearer.

"Quite sure."

He released her arm. When they came on board, he led her down the stairs through a dimly lit hall. "We always have room for runaways." He grinned at her knowingly and slid his arm around her waist.

She jerked away. "I've already told you, I can walk quite well by myself."

He slipped his arm from her waist. At the end of the hall, he paused outside the open doorway to the cabin. "Here we are. Both the upper and lower berths inside that cupboard on the far wall are empty."

Uneasiness gripped her. She followed as he walked to the cupboard bed and set down her bag. Anneke tried one of the cupboard doors, and found it opened easily. She picked up her bag and set it on the top bunk. Ard stepped up behind her. She felt his arms around her waist, his warm breath on her neck. Anneke spun around. "Thank you for showing me to my bunk. If you'll excuse me now, I need some rest."

"But don't you plan to pay me?" He moved toward her again.

"If you don't leave now, I'll get your father to make you leave."

"I didn't mean any harm. Only asking for my just reward. If you change your mind, just let me know. I won't be far away." He gave a slight bow and left, closing the cabin door behind him.

Anneke scrambled up the short ladder to the top bunk, secured the latch, and sank to the bed. Reality hit her. "Oh, Romke, what have I done?" Tears filled her eyes. Why had she run off without him? What would he do when he came in from the fields and found her gone? Why had she acted so rashly? She should have waited until Romke came back at suppertime to decide what to do. And they still would have been together. Maybe if she hurried she could get off the boat before it left the dock.

She forced herself to get up and climb down from the bed. How weak her legs felt, and the gnawing in her stomach had grown worse. She wasn't sure if she could make the three-hour trek back to Romke's house, fatigued as she was, but she must try. Standing beside the bed, she froze. Someone had called her name. She must be mistaken. No one on board would know her. Or would they? Yes, her name was on her traveling bag. Ard must have seen it. She listened again.

"Anneke!" The throaty voice grew louder.

Her heart pounding, she sprang back up onto the bunk, pulled both doors shut and locked them. She waited.

"Anneke!"

She felt safe answering, now that a locked door separated them. "Who is it?"

"Your friend. Open the door."

Anneke hesitated. "What do you want?"

"I have your lunch for you."

It had to be Ard. She felt trapped—at his mercy. Yet, as much as she feared opening the door, she couldn't stay locked in the cupboard bed forever. Hunger overpowered her. If she ate, she would have the strength to go back to Romke. She held the latch. Should she open the door? No, it might be a ruse. How foolish she'd been to come here alone.

She tried to sound nonchalant. "When I'm ready to eat, I'll come upstairs and get it. Thanks, anyway." Anneke waited to hear what he'd say next.

"There may not be any left by that time. But I guess that's your choice."

She heard footsteps fade and knew she'd lost her chance to eat. *Would she ever get off this boat? Would she be held captive here indefinitely, until Ard had gotten from her what he wanted?* She waited several minutes. All was quiet. Maybe now she could leave. Still she hesitated to open the cupboard door. She sat on the bed, listening. Muffled sounds verified her suspicions. Someone still lingered at the cabin door. Panic seized her. *How long could she go on like this, trapped on a boat with no food and no one aware of her plight—except Ard?*

Desperate, she gazed out the porthole. The men had finished hosing down the barge and would probably be leaving the dock shortly. *If she were going to get off, it would have to be soon. But her legs felt limp, and she ached all over. She would lie down for only a minute.* She sank to the bed, exhausted.

Chapter

⟨⟨⟨∞⟩⟩⟩

29

When Romke and his father left for the fields, the door slammed behind them, accenting Mr. Veenhuizen's final command. In silence, Romke trudged across the open land, oppressed by the order that crushed his heart. All day he struggled with his thoughts while harvesting the never-ending rows of wheat. He tried to convince himself that the situation would resolve itself, but he knew it couldn't. It was too late for that, and his parents had meant what they said. He longed to pray, but the cold, domineering presence of his father froze the words on Romke's lips.

How much of the conversation had Anneke heard through the closed door? Probably all of it. How he had wanted to go back to her—to hold her in his arms and reassure her that he would never send her away, but glancing up at his father, he had thought it best not to. He had already wasted precious time by oversleeping—time that was needed to harvest the abundance of wheat God had granted them. Then the episode with his parents had caused them to get an even later start. His father would tolerate no further delay.

The hours dragged. Several times he almost left his work to return to Anneke and comfort her. He also thought of going to the garden to seek God's help. He had often prayed there during the months apart before their marriage, when loneliness for Anneke engulfed him. Many times he had pled with God to keep her for him. The garden became a special place to him, a place where he could feel God's presence. *If only he could go there now. But it was out of the question.*

He wondered how the day had gone for Anneke. *Had she suffered more trauma from his mother? What was she doing now? Preparing the evening meal with her? Or waiting for him in the garden until it was time for him to come in from the fields?*

The setting sun mocked him. Six o'clock! Any other day, he would be done. But today, the additional hours thrust upon him burdened him more than he could bear. At last his father gathered his tools. Finally, they were finished. He put up his own implements and ran to the house, hoping he would find Anneke outside waiting for him as he so often did. But only the empty yard greeted him. As he came near the house, he scanned each window to see if she were watching for him. The windows, too, were empty. *Would she have gone to the garden? He would check inside first before looking for her there.*

He opened the back door and entered the kitchen. His mother, intent on preparing the meal, never looked up. A sickening feeling clenched at his stomach. Where was Anneke? He flew down the hall to their room and threw open the door. The empty bedroom stared back at him.

"Anneke!" The room echoed her name. His eyes fell on the note beside the basin. He reached for it, his hands trembling. "No, this can't be! She wouldn't have done this!" He fell to the bed with the note in his hand. "Oh! Lord, I'll never forgive myself. I knew I should have come back to her earlier. Forgive me for not seeing her this morning before leaving the house!" He felt his whole life collapsing around him. Struggling to gain control of himself, he looked down at the note again. "Oh, my Anneke, mijn lieveling. How much you've suffered. If only you had waited and trusted me to find a way—God's way."

How strange the room felt. Everything that spoke of her—gone, as though she'd never shared this room with him!

"I've got to find her. I'll keep searching until I do. But where should I start?"

In anguish he read her note once more, then folding it, placed it in his shirt pocket close to his heart. *Surely she would have gone back to her family.* He would head down the familiar route to her village. With tear-stained eyes he staggered from his room. Supper was on the table and his family already seated, but he could never eat now. The hunger he had felt earlier in the fields had vanished.

He trudged past his family to the door. "I'm leaving. Anneke's gone, and I won't return without her."

A pathetic sob broke the silence. Romke's hand froze on the knob. Looking back, he saw Anton, his head buried in his arm on the table. Romke came over and placed a comforting hand on his shoulder. "I'll do my best to bring your sister back to you, Anton."

Anton's body shook. "She was so kind. She really cared about me."

"I know, Anton. Our life will never be the same without her. Pray that I find her. Pray that the Lord will answer our prayers."

Their mother stormed to her feet. "Pray? Pray, did you say? You have no right to pray. You've deliberately gone against your parents' rules and our village law, and you continue to do so. Don't even expect God to hear. He'll turn a deaf ear to you!"

At the sound of his mother's raging voice, Anton lifted his head in alarm.

"When I became your father's mate, I prayed too. Has God ever heard my prayers? Have my desires ever been fulfilled? And I never defied any rule or law. I prayed for sons, many sons to carry on your father's work. But one son is all I have."

Anton writhed under her words. Again his head sank to his arm.

"And now his wife couldn't even give him one!" With a snort, she plopped back down in her chair.

The cruel words flung at Anton crushed Romke's heart far more than those his mother threw at him. Her words clanged in his ears. *One son is all I have.* He knew what this had done to Anton as well.

A scene from the past flashed through Romke's mind. He had just turned eight when Anton was born. He hovered over his little brother constantly, excited about this new addition to the family. Their parents had ordered a new Tree of Life to replace the present one above their front door. But when it arrived, they found the second hanging fruit defective.

Concern pulled at Romke. "You'll exchange it, won't you, mother?" She assured him she would, but time passed by and it was never replaced.

A painful memory followed. Several months after they had celebrated Anton's first birthday, Romke had been playing with his toy sailboat in their canal. How he wished his little brother could join him.

But Anton was too young to play outside. Then Romke would go inside to play with him.

When he ran toward the house, the Tree of Life above the door caught his eye. Still, only one fruit hung from its branches. Romke threw open the door and hurried inside.

"Mother, we need a new Tree of Life, remember? One with a second perfect fruit for Anton."

Even now, Romke cringed, remembering his mother's strange expression and the answer she'd given him. "Why a perfect fruit to represent an imperfect child?"

Imperfect child? What could she mean? Anton was his brother, the best little brother in the world! Romke looked down at him on the floor. Anton's chubby face broke into a smile at the sight of his big *broeder*. At once he started toward Romke, using his arms to propel himself, his useless legs dragging behind him.

Dropping his sailboat on a table, Romke ran to Anton and picked him up. He looked up at his mother. "Please, please exchange the old Tree of Life for a new one."

The soft hum of the spinning wheel ceased. His mother's eyes grew cold, her lips thin and set. "We will keep the Tree of Life that's hanging there now. I have but one son, Romke. Anton is not worthy to be called a son."

For the first time, Romke became aware of Anton's handicap. But that never changed his love for his baby brother. Instead, it drew him closer to him, and through the years, it was Romke whom Anton learned to depend on, and Romke was always there to support his brother.

And now his mother had repeated those same cruel words.

"You have two sons, Mother. You've never taken the time to see the value of your second son. Anneke has. She took the time to teach him how to make cheese, as well as showing him other useful things. If it weren't for Anton, Anneke's days would have been unbearable here."

Mrs. Veenhuizen's lip curled. "But what can he do in the fields? Can he help you and your father plow and harvest?"

"Daily he shares in the work around here. Why don't you thank God for the things he can do?"

"Thank Him? Thank Him for limiting my child? I know this was a punishment from God, and I've never forgiven Him. Now He has punished me again through Anneke's infertility."

Romke walked to the door, and paused. "Sometimes things happen in our lives that we don't understand. Perhaps it's for our good so we'll lean close to God instead of depending on our own sufficiency. In any case, if this is God's will, who are we to challenge it? We must accept it and make something beautiful from it that will bring glory to Him."

His mother clenched her jaw.

A deep sigh poured from Romke's heart. It was useless to say any more. "I'm going now."

A rapid pounding shook the door. Romke stepped back, startled by the sudden noise. Grasping the knob, he opened the door. Beppie stood in the entrance, her eyes red, her face tear-stained, and her lips forming words that had no sound.

"Beppie, come in." Romke closed the door behind her, and brought a chair for her. "What's wrong?"

She sank into the chair. Her body trembled as she tried to gain control of herself. "I came as quick as I could! I knew you'd want to know."

Tension hung over the room like a black cloud. All eyes were fixed on Beppie.

Pulling his chair away from the table, Romke sat down facing her. "What happened?"

Beppie dabbed the tears from her eyes. "A flood! At four this morning! It struck scores of villages in Gelderland along the Zuider Zee." Her voice shook. "They say that when the dikes broke, the waters rushed in, covering seventy-five villages, and. . . and drowning thousands in just a few hours!" She caught her breath. "I can't bear to think I'll never see Jaap again." She lowered her face to her hands. "And Anneke—her family. . ." Beppie's voice trailed off to a whisper.

Romke jumped to his feet, his fists clenched. "Where did you hear this?"

Beppie looked up. "In the marketplace. The whole village square was in a turmoil and. . ." She paused and looked around the table. "Where's Anneke?"

No one spoke.

She looked again at each family member. The room screamed with silence. Fear filled her eyes as she turned to Romke. She moved to the edge of her chair. "Romke, where is she?"

"Gone!"

The word echoed in the stillness of the room.

Beppie faced him in disbelief. "Gone? What do you mean?"

He sat down heavily in his chair. "She's gone." His words were lost as his head sank to his hands. It was dangerous enough that Anneke had left by herself but, now, with a massive flood, too, what chance did he have of finding her? Even if she had made it to the Zuider Zee, the deluge could have swallowed her before she ever reached her village. The thought jolted him back to reality. His heart pounded. Yes, gone— driven away by his own parents! The truth cut his heart like a knife.

He glanced first at his father, then his mother, hoping to see a sign of remorse, or at least a softening. But neither one had budged. Their hearts were as cold and unbreakable as their frozen canals in winter.

He sprang from his chair and faced them. "How could you have done this to Anneke, forcing her to leave our home?"

His mother ignored the question. With her eyes on her food, she picked up her fork and began to eat.

Romke's voice rose. "She's everything to me, and you've sent her to her death!" His lip quivered as he struggled to continue. "Don't either of you care?" He turned to his father.

Mr. Veenhuizen continued to butter his bread as though Romke had never spoken.

"No, of course you don't care! I should have known. But in destroying Anneke's life, you've destroyed mine, and Anton's—our entire home! She was the one ray of sunshine in this dark and miserable place; and you, both of you, in your bigotry and hatred have utterly demolished it."

Beppie's eyes grew wide.

Romke grabbed several slices of bread from the table and a wedge of cheese, and took the bowl of strawberries that lay at his place. It wasn't much but it would sustain him on this painful, wretched trip. The ticking of the old Frisian clock filled the room. Each tick reminded him that seconds were becoming minutes. Soon, the minutes would be hours. He couldn't let the fleeting time steal his chances. He had to reach her before it was too late.

He rushed to the door, and paused. Again he faced his parents. "Some things are worth fighting for, and Anneke's one of them. I'll keep looking until I find her, even if I have to search all eleven provinces. And one thing's certain, I'll not come back without her." He laid his hand on Anton's shoulder, and then disappeared into the night.

Her body shaking, Beppie quickly left the house.

Chapter

──────── ⌀⛾⌀ ────────

30

Anneke turned over in bed. "Romke?" She heard no reply, only his name, echoing through the darkness. She called again, louder this time. "Romke?" His name seemed to hang in the air, and then all grew deathly still. She reached out her hand, but the bed lay empty beside her. She stiffened. "Romke? Romke, where are you?" Goosebumps broke out on her skin. The nightmare of the previous day rushed to her mind. She felt the rhythmic current beneath her. Panic seized her. Could she still get off the boat? She leaned across the berth and looked out the porthole. The night was black. They were no longer docked. It was too late!

"Oh, Romke, forgive me!" Her soul ached for him. "I love you, I love you so much. Why did I leave you? If only you were with me now." Then the figures of Romke's mother and father loomed in her mind. Their commands for her to leave their home resounded in her ears. How could she go back? They would never allow her to enter their house.

No, she could never return. Anneke clutched the shawl that draped her shoulders. Why had this happened to her? A sickening feeling engulfed her. She was alone, completely alone.

Anneke's fingers wrapped around the water lily brooch fastened to her bodice. Tears filled her eyes. Besides his pillowcase and handkerchief, this was all she had left of him. She ran her hand over the smooth surface of the brooch. Why couldn't her life be serene like this flower?

She remembered Romke's words as he handed her the water lily by the quiet inlet. 'Like this flower, if we're not attached to the life-giving Stem, we have no one to sustain us when trials come. We will drift, wither, and die. But if we are joined to God, we can withstand the hardships of life. God becomes our strength, a very present help in trouble.'

But how did one become attached to the life-giving Stem? "Oh, God, I don't understand, I don't understand!" Her mind in turmoil, she collapsed back down on the berth.

Hours later, shouts woke Anneke from her sleep. Through the porthole, pale pink clouds rose over the horizon. The emptiness in her stomach grew stronger. Would it be safe now to leave her cupboard berth?

The shouts coming from the deck above grew louder. They must be about to dock. Minutes later, the barge lurched to a stop. Gazing out the porthole, she read the sign: *Oostenhaven*. She was halfway home.

Still, Anneke found herself torn between two desires: one to go back to Romke and the other to continue on to Zevendorp. But she needed to get off this boat as quickly as possible.

She listened but heard no sound. Surely, Ard would be too busy to be thinking of her now. Quietly she unlatched the cupboard doors, and pushing them slightly, peered through the crack. The room was empty. Opening them wider, she slipped down from the berth, grabbed her valise, and shut the double doors behind her. After freshening up, Anneke prepared to leave. With bag in hand, she hurried noiselessly across the room and into the corridor, the smell of coffee and fresh-baked pastry driving her on.

At the top of the stairs, she peered through the galley. A woman with ruddy complexion stood before the open oven, heat waves blowing the strands of hair fallen loose from her bun. This must be the captain's wife, Anneke thought. Surely she would give her something to eat.

"Excuse me, mevrouw. May I have some breakfast before I leave?"

Removing a sheet of steaming rolls from the oven, the woman looked up in surprise. Her surprise turned to pleasure, her face lighting up as she broke into a smile. "Why, I didn't even know there was a lady passenger on board." She grabbed the end of her apron and dabbed the moisture from her face. "Please do have a seat. It's so seldom I get to talk to another woman." Bustling about, she had the food on the table in seconds. Then, reaching for a chair, she joined Anneke. "It'll be awhile before the men are ready to eat. We might as well enjoy a quiet meal by ourselves." The cook set a cup of coffee on the table for Anneke.

Anneke took a sip. "Aahhh, delicious. I can't thank you enough." She hesitated. "But I have no money to pay you."

"That's the least of my worries." The older woman sighed. "You're doing me a favor sharing a meal with me. It gets mighty lonely week after week, month after month, sailing the same route with no one to share it with."

Anneke studied her closer. "You're not the captain's wife?"

"Oh, no, my dear. My husband was lost at sea ten years ago. He often spoke of the legend of the waterwolf, but he feared nothing. No frothy jaw could keep him from the sea. No upraised claw descending toward his ship could make him cower. But, alas, the enemy of the Netherlands challenged him to a final match and won."

"I'm awfully sorry."

"No, don't you waste time feeling sorry for me. I want you to know he was a good man. We were only together for four years when he met with his tragic death." She reached for a napkin and dabbed her eyes. "That's his picture on the wall above the table. I always feel comforted when I see his face so near."

Anneke looked up at the portrait. A shiver raced through her body. That face. Why did he look so familiar to her? She studied his features. Was it the arrogance in his eyes that gave her an uncanny feeling? The scar! She felt the blood drain from her face. She knew that man—she was sure of it. But how could she? She couldn't have seen him in Lijdendorp. And he certainly didn't come from her village. Or did he? No, he didn't live among her people. She must be mistaken.

The cook turned again to her husband's picture. "You know, it's a strange thing. I can't explain it, but every time I look at his portrait, I have a suspicion that he's still alive."

At the woman's words, Anneke glanced up at the portrait again. Shivers ran through her body, as the man's scar seemed to widen.

"And yet," the woman continued, "I know he was shipwrecked and all his crewmen were drowned." She turned back to her coffee, taking a long sip. Then, laying her cup down, she pushed it aside as if trying to shove the past from her memory. "But forgive me for troubling you with my problems. Tell me about yourself. That is, if you don't mind." The woman sounded hungry for companionship.

"I'm headed home to Zevendorp, three kilometers outside of Kollumdijk."

The woman caught her breath. "Oh, my dear! Haven't you heard? That whole area was flooded two nights ago!"

Anneke looked at her in disbelief. "Flooded?"

"Indeed it was. The deluge hit all along the eastern coast of the Zuider Zee. They say that scores of villages were washed under, and thousands of people drowned in a matter of hours!" Pulling a strand of hair away from her face, she tucked it inside her bun, then grabbed another napkin from the table and blew her nose. "Yes, my dear, the waterwolf has risen again."

Anneke's lips trembled. "Nooo, it can't be! It just can't be!" She forgot the food that lay on her plate. "Where did you hear this?"

"When we pulled into Oostenhaven, that was the first thing we heard. Yes, this one sounds as devastating as the Saint Elizabeth's Flood of 1421—only I doubt there are any survivors in this one. You remember the legend, don't you, how one, lone baby outwitted the waterwolf?"

"Yes, I know the story well. I learned about it in grade school. But we're in the early 1900s, now. Surely, the dikes would have withstood the raging sea."

"No, my dear. Few dikes could withstand a storm like this one. All I know is what I've heard; and I can tell you, you don't want to go there. I wouldn't think there'd be any way you could reach Zevendorp now, anyway. No barges will be going that way for weeks, maybe months. But we're headed south down the IJssel River, so it won't affect us. You're welcome to stay on board our boat. Why, you could even share my work, and that would still give us both plenty to do."

Anneke no longer heard the woman speaking. Her home, her family—gone in a matter of hours, during her last sleepless night in Lijdendorp! It made no difference what the cook told her. She had to go home. She had to see for herself. Maybe, just maybe her family's village had been spared. Rising to her feet, she mumbled, only half aware of the woman in the room. "I've got to go home. I've got to go home." She rushed to the door.

"Oh, wait, mevrouw. Please consider what I've told you. At least take what you didn't finish eating. And here's some fruit. There's plenty here." The cook thrust the bundle of food into Anneke's hand, and followed her out of the galley. "Take care, mevrouw. Oh, do be careful." She squeezed her napkin into a tight ball, then dabbed at her eyes. "May God protect you, my dear."

As if in a nightmare, Anneke ran down the ramp and onto the dock. Frantically she looked around. *How in the world would she ever find a boat going to Kollumdijk where the drastic flood took place, and then for the boat to go further inland to Zevendorp, her own village? Like the cook had said, nothing would be headed that way.*

Chapter

───────── ❧ ─────────

31

A sudden wind stirred the air. Anneke looked up, enthralled by the panorama unfolding before her. Massive gray clouds rolled in from the west. The gentle breezes turned chilly. The river responded, lifting its waves higher and higher, almost reaching the dock where she stood. Within minutes, low-hanging clouds covered the sky and darkness closed in around her.

The first pellets of rain soon grew to a downpour. The wind whipped her skirts and lashed at her face. She grabbed her bag of food and held it close to her. Lowering her head from the driving rain, she felt a hand on her arm.

"You can't stay out in a torrent like this. Hurry, let's get back inside the boat."

She knew that voice. She shuddered and reached for her valise, and then saw that the man who had spoken had already picked it up. Without protest, she let him guide her back to the barge. Once inside, she shook the water from her cap and dried her face with her sleeve. She looked up and her body tensed. Ard stood watching her, an amused smile on his face.

"Do you always stay out in the rain, mevrouw?" He spoke more gently than he had the day before.

"No. It came on so suddenly, I didn't have time to react."

Ard removed his cap and studied it, then looked up at her. "I'm sorry, mevrouw, for the way I acted yesterday. He looked down, and then sought her eyes again. "Please accept my apology."

She shook the last drops of rain from her cap and placed it back on her head. "I accept it."

"Tell me, mevrouw, what are your plans for today? Maybe I can help you."

Anneke sighed. "It looks like the weather has done a lot to try to change them. But I'm still determined to go home."

"And where is your home?"

"Three kilometers from Kollumdijk."

Ard's eyes grew wide. "Kollumdijk? There's no way you can go there now. Surely, you've heard about the flood?"

Anneke nodded.

"Perhaps after the storm lets up and the water subsides, but it would be insanity to try to go there now. You need to stay on board. We're headed south, down the IJssel River. In a week or so we'll be back at this dock. Then maybe you might think of trying to go home. I don't believe you'll find much there, though." He paused as if not knowing how to break the news to her.

"I realize the area is badly flooded, but that's not going to keep me from going there. I have to know for sure if my family's still. . ." Anneke's voice broke and tears escaped her eyes.

"The only way you could possibly go would be by rescue boat if one should happen to come along. But it would probably be hours, even days before you would see one. Any survivors would have already been rescued by now. Why don't you stay on board until we come back this way? Think about it while you're drying off."

He carried her valise to a sofa in the living quarters, and motioned for her to have a seat. "I need to head back to the crew. They won't be too happy if I leave all the work for them." With a grin and a wave of his hand, Ard disappeared from the living area as quickly as he had appeared on the dock.

Her thoughts went back to Romke. What had he done when he came in from the fields last night and found her gone? Had she caused him to have another sleepless night? And what was he doing now? It was probably around eight o'clock. He would be harvesting in the fields with his father. But not only would he be working, she knew he'd be suffering.

"Oh, Romke, why did I leave you? Will I ever see you again?" The thought tore at her soul.

She sat staring out the window, watching the clouds float by. The sky didn't look as dark as it had an hour ago. The rain had let up too. Yes, the storm was dying down. She stuffed the bag of food into her valise and headed back down the ramp as the crew made preparations to leave the landing. She had disembarked just in time. Alone on the wharf, she watched the barge edge toward the IJssel River, then sail away. All around her, raindrops beat on the weathered planks, making her uneasy. Each plop resounded in her ears with a hollow echo, warning her to turn *back, back, back*—but it was too late.

The rain splattered her face, and slid down her neck, chilling her while the winds blew. She kept her eyes on the boat ahead—the barge that had offered her shelter, sustenance, and perhaps a new life. Both Ard and the cook had advised her to stay on board, not to go where life had been snatched from the land. She watched the barge sail further and further away, down the IJssel on its southward journey. Had she made another mistake? She felt a sudden urge to cry out, "Wait!" But the barge was growing smaller. They would never hear her now. And she knew she had to go home.

How long would she have to wait for a boat that was headed down the Zuider Zee? She gazed up and down the river. Nothing but miles of empty water stared back at her. Then in the distance, a fishing boat appeared. Hope filled her. The markings, KD 87 in black paint stood out against the pale-blue boat. A boat from Kollumdijk—could it really be possible? Then maybe the fisherman would be returning soon. Anxiously, she waited for him to dock.

She tried to constrain herself while the short, stout fisherman secured the moorings. "Excuse me, meneer. Are you heading back to Kollumdijk any time soon?"

The man uttered an oath, and straightening up, pushed back his fishing cap to see who had addressed him. The scowl across his forehead deepened.

She was sure he wouldn't be the best company, and his boat was not in the greatest condition either, but she couldn't be choosy at a time like this. She would have to accept what was available.

He looked at her in disbelief. "Heading back, did you say? I've just come from there. I'm lucky to have made it out alive! I can't say I wasn't warned, though. *Ja, ja.* Two years ago, I heard the warning in the marketplace. If only I had listened. But nee, I would not heed, I would not listen to the lunatic or to the washerwoman with the cane. And now I'm paying the miller. *Ja,* now I'm paying the miller."

The fisherman stood staring at his damaged boat, then thrust out his hand toward his vessel. "My sails are ripped to shreds, my masts are bent and twisted. Fifty-pound herring couldn't entice me to go back. *Ja, ja,* I should have listened to them both." He wiped his brow and shook his head. "If you have any plans of going there, I'd forget them in a hurry!"

An ominous feeling enveloped her. She had forgotten that foreboding March day in the market when Mrs. Tasman had pronounced the mermaid's doom on Kollumdijk and its surrounding villages. So the prophecy had come true.

"I'm very sorry about your fishing boat."

"Well, I guess I can be grateful that I survived. Not many escaped the fangs of the waterwolf this time."

Anneke walked back to her valise. Kollumdijk—gone! Should she still try to go home, or was she being foolish? Well, where else could she go? And there always remained the slim chance that her family had been spared, since her little village of Zevendorp lay a few kilometers inland from Kollumdijk.

The hours dragged by, and still she waited. She glanced back at the fisherman, making minor repairs on his vessel. Maybe she should have stayed on the riverboat. But to be halfway home and then turn her back on her family? No, she couldn't. She had to know for sure if they were still alive. They might even need her.

Exhausted, she plopped down on the wharf. The rumbling in her stomach drove her to pull out the sack lunch the cook had packed for her. Grabbing the half-eaten breakfast roll, she dug her teeth into it, hardly noticing how dry it was.

She had just finished eating an apple when something on the water caught her eye. A rowboat. In bright red letters, VOLUNTEER RESCUE SQUAD marched across its length. Her heart leaped. She stood to her feet and jerked off her blue and white cap. As the boat drew nearer, she waved it until she caught the boatman's attention.

The young man veered toward the dock. "Do you need help?"

"Yes, meneer. I need a ride down the Zuider Zee."

He leaned forward and arched his brows. "I'm here to take survivors out of that area, not bring people in."

"I have to go there! Please take me on board."

"Space, in a time like this, can be crucial." He hesitated. "How far did you want to go?"

"Near Kollumdijk."

His boat reached the landing. "All the way to Kollumdijk?"

She clenched her fists. "Oh, please. You've got to take me!" Clutching her bag of food in one hand, she snatched up her valise with her other hand and hurried to the edge of the peer where his boat bobbed with the current.

"Kollumdijk probably doesn't even exist anymore."

She gasped. "Oh, don't say that! We won't know until we see for ourselves."

"Well, come on, then, but I'm not promising we'll even make it."

Before he could change his mind, she climbed aboard. "You don't know what this means to me." She choked on her words.

The young man looked at her quizzically. "Why are you so set on going to Kollumdijk? Surely, you've heard about the horrendous flood there, haven't you?"

"My family!" She broke down in sobs.

The rescue worker reached into his pocket and pulled out a handkerchief. "Here, mevrouw. I'm awfully sorry."

Anneke wiped her eyes and cleared her throat. "My family lives near there. I have to know if they're still—alive. I won't take anyone else's word." Fresh sobs racked her body.

The young man nodded. "I guess I'd feel the same."

They sailed on in silence. Anneke struggled to gain control of herself, but the words of the boatman continued to haunt her. *"Kollumdijk doesn't exist anymore. Kollumdijk doesn't exist anymore. Kollumdijk doesn't exist anymore."* Like the grinding gears of a windmill, the words grated on her mind and would give her no rest.

She looked out across the water. Beams and planks, torn from homes, surged on the waves. Moments later, a beautiful door with a brass knocker floated past them. Chairs and tables circled and danced in confusion. Deserted boats rose and fell on the rushing sea, their torn sails beating against their twisted masts.

Hour after hour brought her closer to her destination, but also to greater destruction.

By late afternoon they had reached the ravaged areas. She stared at the scene before her. Where were the pretty little villages she remembered so well from her honeymoon trip? No, they couldn't all be gone!

She clutched the side of the rescue boat and searched in vain for people, cattle, any living thing. Her anxiety turned to horror as she found village after village flooded and forsaken. Was there not one dorp left unharmed along the shore? The restless waves answered her question. What had once been land was now sea.

She watched the raging waters and violent winds rip open fallen vegetable crates and rob them of their treasure. In frenzied freedom, beets and potatoes tossed on the surging waves.

Toy trains and rocking horses circled aimlessly on the crests. Carriages, stripped of blankets and pillows, bounced and collided. A doll spun past, arms outstretched, its golden curls fluttering. Anneke could almost read fear on its face. She shuddered at the horror that had descended on these people.

Then a body floated by, its clothes trailing behind it. Anneke gagged, stood and leaned over the gunwale and retched. In a state of shock, her legs gave out, and she collapsed on the seat, almost as limp as the body she'd just seen.

Everywhere she looked, windmills moaned in desperation as though grieving for their lost land. Their upper arms flailed in helplessness, their lower limbs lay buried in tempestuous graves.

And what of her own village? She trembled. No! It couldn't possibly be like this. She thought of her family: Vader, Moeder, Kea. Each in turn rose before her mind's eye. "No—No—No!" her heart screamed.

Chapter

32

Romke cast off the moorings of his boat and climbed inside. He laid his knapsack, stuffed with water, bread and cheese, and the bowl of strawberries, on the seat beside him. His small yacht was equipped with blankets and sweaters for the cold autumn nights, but still, he didn't feel ready to leave. He bowed his head in his hands.

"Oh, Lord, I feel so lost and alone. I need Your help, God. Please guide me once again to Anneke. Help me find her before it's too late."

Romke steered his boat along the canal. He welcomed the darkness—there would be fewer people out on the water. In his grief he wanted only to be left alone. He thought of Beppie and her heartache. Could Jaap and Albert have escaped such a sudden disaster? Everyone in Kollumdijk and Zevendorp would have been asleep the hour the flood struck. He trembled at the thought and feared even more for Beppie.

When he entered the Black Canal, his mind turned back to Anneke. Where was she now? Probably on some riverboat. She might have had a good nine hours' lead on him, but then again, the boat she was on may have made several lengthy stops along its route. Scenarios of risks and dangers plagued his mind. And she'd be at the mercy of the boatmen, too. Would she be safe? Again Romke prayed for her. When he reached the Oostelijk River, he stayed alert for vessels along the way. He approached each one and asked the crew if they'd seen a young woman of Anneke's description. Always he received the same answer. No one had seen her.

The journey dragged on as he followed the course of the river, ever winding, like a lost child wandering through the heather on the moor.

He knew it would take several more hours to reach Oostenhaven, just halfway to her village. He sighed. If only the moon was out to lighten his way. If only this river ran straight, like the canals, he could make the distance in half the time, or even less. He remembered his previous trips down the Oostelijk to sell his cheese, but especially to see Anneke. He had enjoyed the slow, lazy trek then. But now it tortured him to circle the endless bends, only to find more waiting beyond.

His boat inched along, creeping, crawling, like a windmill on a windless day, and he not knowing where Anneke was or the dangers that faced her. Grief filled his soul. He raised his eyes toward heaven. "Lord, please help me to trust fully in You and fill me with Your peace. Help me to remember that wherever Anneke is, she's in Your care. Oh, God, I beg of You to bring us back together again."

The smell of the sea permeated the air. He had reached the halfway point to Oostenhaven. Here, the river wound its way to the edge of the shore to embrace the Zuider Zee, only to desert it a mile down the coast and become a river once more. It preferred to wander aimlessly over the land, rather than follow the sea's bidding. Here, Romke, too, would turn off, following the Oostelijk River to Oostenhaven.

The darkness grew thicker, making it impossible to stay on course, and now the snail-like boat had crawled to a stop. He had hoisted the sails, so why wasn't the boat moving?

Was he on a sandbar—in the dead of night? He must be encountering the effects of the storm already. Romke climbed from his boat and strained his eyes to see through the gloom. Along with the sandbar, debris lay everywhere. Rocks, limbs, silt and seaweed impeded his progress, but there was no way he could free himself tonight.

He was stranded, forced to wait out the long, dismal hours until daybreak. Only then would he be able to free his boat from all that held it captive. And he would have to wait for the tide to come in to replenish the mouth of the river, as well. All this would put him even further behind. A deep sigh escaped his lips. He could feel his heart sink—sink to the depths of the Zuider Zee.

Helplessness overpowered him. He turned from the disaster and walked to his berth. He might as well try to get some sleep. He lay down and closed his eyes, but vivid images tormented him. Stranded in the sea, Anneke flailed against the waves, crying for help. He squeezed his eyes tight, opened them, then tried again to sleep; but now in his mind's eye, he saw her running frantically across the moor, someone close at her heels. He wanted to rush to her aid. Then he remembered it was only his mind playing tricks on him. Or was it?

He bolted from the berth and paced the deck. "What if she *is* in some kind of danger? And here I am, stuck on this sandbar, unable to rescue her?" Exhausted, he collapsed on the berth, tossing and praying for hours, until sleep overtook him.

Romke woke with a start. What time was it? Had he overslept? He peered out the window. "Mid-morning, already?" Dawn had slipped past him. With heavy heart, he set to work, hauling off the logs, branches, and rocks surrounding his boat.

When he had finished clearing a path, he looked out across the sea. The tide was coming in, leaping and splashing as though anxious to reach him. He stood in awe. He couldn't remember a scene more beautiful or a sight more welcome than those mighty waves heading his way, coming to his aid. It wouldn't be long now before that rolling tide would reach the river. Romke stood watching, captivated by the powerful sea. What force, what strength. But how much stronger was his God. The sea's power was confined, doing only as much as God would allow it.

The thought comforted him as he climbed aboard his boat. Tiny wavelets, like fingers, had reached his craft on the edge of the river. Then came waves, and soon breakers, lapping and overlapping with a constant rush and roar. Gradually he could feel his boeier rise and wobble, then bounce as the water lifted him from the shoal. With a sigh of relief, he once again followed the Oostelijk River as it moved inland toward Oostenhaven. Only a few hours remained before he would arrive. No other vessels were in sight as he made the lonely journey south on the quiet water. It was almost too still, like the waterwolf pausing before pouncing again.

At last the church tower of Oostenhaven rose in the distance. Activity on the river increased. While the bell chimed the hour of one p. m., Romke sailed into port. New hope surged through him. Hopefully, someone here had seen Anneke. His hunger reminded him he'd had nothing to eat for hours, but there would be time for that later.

Finding a vacant berth, he guided his yacht between two fishing boats, then jumped onto the dock and fastened the moorings. A few yards ahead, massive cranes with gaping mouths descended to the mountains of coal heaped high on a barge. Clamping their mouths shut over their prey, the cranes moved toward the waiting cargo ship and opened their mighty jaws to unload the ebony rocks.

Romke rushed over to the men supervising the operation. Perhaps someone from this very ship had talked with Anneke or seen her if she had come this way. His heart pounding, he faced the crew. "Have any of you seen a young woman here alone on the dock?" He searched each face for a trace of hope.

"If we had, she wouldn't have been alone for long." The man who spoke nudged his mate and laughed.

Romke set his jaw. "It's urgent that I find her."

The men eyed Romke in amusement. Another spoke up. "You looking for a pickup?"

Romke clenched and unclenched his fists. "You don't understand. She's my wife."

A third one joined in. "You mean, was your wife?" He winked at his mates. Guffaws poured from the mouths of some of the crew, while others whistled and jeered.

He was getting nowhere with this bunch. Disheartened and exhausted, Romke turned to leave.

Another crewman spoke up. "We pulled in about a half hour ago. The dock was clear at that time."

Thanking him, Romke headed back to his boat in defeat. He had been so sure that he would find some trace of Anneke. There was no point in staying here any longer. If she had come this way, she probably had left hours before anyone here had arrived. He dragged himself over to his craft, bobbing on the waves. Untying the mooring lines, he felt a hand on his arm. In surprise, he looked up into the concerned face of a fisherman.

"Did I hear you asking about a young woman?"

The line slid from Romke's hand. "Yes. You saw one here today?"

"*Ja*. When I pulled in sometime around nine, this morning, I saw her standing here alone on the dock. She asked me if I was going back toward Kollumdijk any time soon."

Romke swallowed hard. "What did she look like?"

"A beautiful woman. Her eyes were the loveliest shade of blue and her figure, unsurpassable. But she wasn't dressed like the women of Kollumdijk."

"That must have been her. What happened then?"

"I'm afraid I wasn't very helpful. I was too upset over the damage to my fishing boat from that storm in Gelderland. Worst one I've ever seen, and I've lived in that area all my life. You've heard about it, haven't you?"

"Yes. I understand it was a pretty bad one."

The fisherman straightened the cap on his head. "That's putting it mildly, meneer. I have my doubts that I'll ever head back that way again." He lowered his head, shaking it from side to side. "*Ja*, I should have listened. I should have listened to the mermaid's warning."

Romke cocked his head at the fisherman. "A mermaid's warning?"

The fisherman looked startled. He shook his head. "Oh, just forget what I said. It was nothing."

Romke looked at the pitiful sight that the fisherman called his boat. And Anneke was headed for the very place from which this man had fled. Fear rose in his heart. He faced the fisherman. "Then what happened?"

"Well, I tried to discourage her from going, but she had her mind made up. About half-past noon another boat came by, a rescue boat, is my guess. She hailed him and convinced the boatman to take her on." The fisherman rubbed his chin. "That's the last I saw of her."

Romke's voice quivered as he tried to speak. "Then I need to find her fast. If she's heading on toward Kollumdijk, it may be too late." He reached down and picked up the moorings, then faced the fisherman once more. "You've been a big help to me, meneer. I appreciate your coming over and telling me."

The fisherman clapped his brawny hand on Romke's shoulder. "I only wish I could help you more."

Chapter

33

Hours passed as the rescue boat pushed its way through the troubled water.

"We're here. This is Kollumdijk. . . or, what used to be Kollumdijk."

The boatman's announcement roused Anneke from her thoughts. The night had closed in around them. Storm clouds still hung heavy in the sky, as though not satisfied with the damage they had caused.

She ought to be seeing the rooftops of Kollumdijk, the towers, steeples and especially its gates. But where was the beautiful water gate that greeted the villagers as they entered the town and the bridge that extended from it to welcome the people in? She remembered sailing through its open archway when she and Romke drifted away on their honeymoon, and how its twin towers seemed to gaze down on them in blessing. But the twin towers were no longer there to welcome her home.

Had the flood wiped out her village, too? She had to know. But she didn't have a boat like this man did. She didn't even have a compass to guide her. But, crazy or not, she'd come too far to leave now. Yet how would she get there?

The rescue boatman turned to Anneke. "I'm heading to Spakenburg. You'd better come with me."

"Thanks, but I want to keep on toward home."

"You won't find anything out there. You don't even have a boat."

"We've seen scores of them adrift. I'm sure we'll see more."

"Even if we do, you wouldn't be safe out here alone!"

Anneke caught the alarm in his voice.

He turned and faced her. "There's no point in continuing at this late hour. We can't see a thing out there. It'd be best to come to Spakenburg. Tomorrow morning we can seek help."

She was almost convinced—and yet, Zevendorp, her own village, lay just three kilometers inland. To be so close, and then abandon her family? Never! And if her family was in need, tomorrow might be too late. Surely, Zevendorp had escaped the worst of the flood. But how would she know for sure if she didn't go there and find out?

Something caught her eye as it bobbed on the water. "Look, there's a boat! It's mine, now."

Her companion peered through the darkness. "You're really determined, aren't you? Well, let's go get it then."

In no time, the young man had reached the deserted craft. "It appears to be in fairly good shape. Wait, it's damaged here on the side, but not leaking. Tell you what. You take my boat. I'll take this one."

"Are you sure?"

"Listen, I'm more concerned for your safety. I should get to Spakenburg before this one springs a leak. You think you'll be okay by yourself?"

"I'll be fine," said Anneke. "I've gotten this far; three more kilometers seems like nothing."

"There's a trunk under your seat with blankets and clothes and behind me a small ice box. Inside there's food and canteens of water. We even keep several baby bottles filled with milk." He chuckled. "I know you won't need that, but we always come prepared for any situation." He paused. "Both the trunk and ice box are bolted to the deck and sealed securely, so you won't lose them or their contents, even if the boat capsizes."

"Capsizes?" A shiver ran through Anneke. "But what about me. . . if I'm thrown out?"

He shrugged his shoulders. "That's the risk you're taking. If that should happen, cling to the boat and don't let go."

His words resounded in her ears, sending shivers through her body. Maybe she was making a terrible mistake in venturing out alone.

The boatman reached in his shirt pocket and pulled out his compass. "Here, take this. It'll keep you on course."

Anneke exhaled with relief as he placed it in her hand. "Thank you."

"And some rope. It may come in handy. If you get tired of floundering in the sea, you could secure the rowboat to something stable like a dormer window or a tree—if you find one, that is." He paused, a scowl deepening his forehead. "I don't know why you insist on going there. Nothing's out here. Everything's destroyed—the place is deserted. No rescue boat will come through here again. You're taking an awful risk."

She looked about. Only open sea stretched before her. Goosebumps rose on her arms. What dangers lay ahead of her? She tried to calm herself as she took the rope and turned it over in her hand. She winced at the feel of the coarse texture. It felt like a foreign object to her as her fingers wrapped around its thickness.

"Do you know how to make a secure knot?"

Anneke hesitated. "No, not really."

"Let me show you." He took the rope back, then reached for his lantern and lit it. The light cast an eerie glow around them, and the frothy waves seemed to come alive, ever moving toward them in an unearthly aura.

"The bowline knot is one of the easiest to make. It's also very strong." Step by step, he demonstrated the procedure. Anneke marveled at his skill while she watched his nimble fingers slide the working end of the rope through the loop, around the back and through the eye of the loop once more.

"For extra security, make a stopper knot, which is an extra half hitch, like this. There. You won't have to worry about this coming loose." As if by magic a perfect knot appeared in the rope. Then, just as quickly, he undid it and handed the rope back. "Now see if you can do it."

Uncertain, she took the rope and made a loop. How different this felt compared to the soft, thin, woolen thread she used for spinning. Her fingers felt clumsy as she pushed the end of the rope through the loop. She paused, twisting the end in her hand. "I'm not sure what to do next." Her face grew warm and she wished she had paid closer attention.

The young man half smiled and took back the rope. "There's a little story I learned as a kid which will help you remember. Think of the loop as a hole in the ground. The working end, which hangs down, is the rabbit. The rabbit comes up through the hole in the ground, around the tree, and back into its hole." Again he undid it and handed it back to her. "Now try it."

Anneke laughed. "Thanks. That makes it easy to remember." She completed the steps, even adding an extra half hitch. Last of all she pulled both ends of the rope to test its strength. It held fast.

"I did it! It really is simple." Anneke looked at the finished work in her hand. "I feel like a sailor now. Dank U wel. You'll never know what this means to me."

The young man's brows knit together as he shook his head from side to side. "I still think you're making a dreadful mistake."

"Don't worry about me," said Anneke. "I have a safe boat, food, rope and compass. That's everything I need, right?"

"I hope so. Just remember, if you find nothing left of your village, you can always come to Spakenburg. It's southwest of here, on the southern coast. Just use the compass— you'll find it."

Anneke stared at him. "But there's no coastline!"

"There will be in Spakenburg. They weren't hit by the flood."

Uncertainty washed over her again. She knew she'd never find it in the dark, compass or no compass. And she didn't have a lantern like he did. Maybe she should go with him after all. At least he knew what he was doing and could see where he was going. She tried to speak but found her jaw paralyzed. As if in a dream, she sat helpless, incapable of voicing her doubt and fear.

The young man climbed into the empty rowboat, taking his lantern with him. He sat down, set the lantern at his feet and looked up at Anneke. "Good luck." His face grew solemn as he waved good-bye.

Anneke broke from her spell and smiled bravely as she waved back. She had to know if her family survived. Grabbing an oar in each hand, she began to row. The light from the lantern faded as the young man sailed further away. Soon she found herself shrouded in darkness.

Was this actually where Kollumdijk had stood? There were no signs of proof that it was. Further on, something caught her eye. She strained to see through the blackness. As she drew closer, the tops of two conical-shaped towers rose above the water. The rest of the gate lay buried in the watery grave. "No!" Her heart wrenched. "The beautiful town of Kollumdijk—gone!"

Scraps of wood floated everywhere. A long plank, white like the bridge, surged past her. She shuddered. On she rowed, waiting for something still intact that looked familiar, but no landmarks remained. The flood had destroyed them all.

While she continued on, she strained her eyes to see. Would there be anything left of the town square—where since childhood, she'd followed the maze-like paths that wound their way through the marketplace? She searched through the darkness, but nothing remained. All trace of land had vanished, leaving nothing but surging waves on an endless sea. Kollumdijk no longer existed.

Fear turned to panic. Was it like this in Zevendorp, too?

By now, she should be in her own village. Frantically she tried to visualize where her home would be, but in a world of only water, it was impossible. In despair she took in the nightmarish scene. If nothing had remained in the town of Kollumdijk, of course, nothing would be left in her little village. Suddenly she screamed—screamed at the wind whipping her face, screamed at the waves threatening to scale the sides of her boat, screamed at the void surrounding her.

Time dragged on as she formed the endless circular motions. Before long her arms ached, but she couldn't stop now. She must go on until she reached her home—if she still had a home. The autumn wind grew stronger, thrashing the waves against her small vessel as it bounced on the restless sea. Now that she was alone on the troubled water, engulfed in darkness, fear, again, filled her heart. She rowed harder, ever pushing on for what seemed like hours. Would she never get there?

The closer she came, the greater her anxiety grew. Her family couldn't possibly have survived this.

An intense longing for her family seized her. "Vader—Moeder—Kea!" She screamed out their names, but only the waves replied as they slapped her boat. Reality hit her. She was *alone in the world—deserted, without hope.* The words rang in her ears. No, this couldn't be happening to her. It was Cobie who was alone, abandoned, with no hope.

How Anneke had dreaded seeing her. After all the misery and anguish Cobie had put her through, Anneke never wanted to cross paths with her again. And now, Cobie's warnings and taunts had become reality. How would she ever bear more ridicule from her? But Cobie was gone, too, along with Vader, Moeder, and Kea. "No!" She screamed back at the howling wind. It was too final.

Then her own plight loomed before her. What was left for her? Nothing—no home—no family—no village! She thought of the thousands who had drowned. Why should she be spared? Why not let the water take her too, as it had the rest of her people? She struggled with the idea. Confusion overwhelmed her. She could no longer distinguish the throbbing in her head from the pounding of the waves against her boat. In her torment she released her grip on the oars and, squeezing her head in her hands, struggled to gain control of her thoughts. Her boat thrashed on the angry sea, rolling from side to side, dipping, soaring, and finally dislodging the oars from their rings. Unknown to her, the oars slipped from the gunwales into the waiting jaws of the waterwolf.

In her urgency to steady the vessel, she reached for the oars; but they were gone. Desperation overpowered her as her fingers clutched the empty rings. She must recover the oars. Leaning over the edge, her hand searched the froth. For an instant her fingers touched the surface of an oar. If she stretched a little more, she would have it. She plunged her hand in deeper, lost her balance, and fell into the raging sea.

Anneke shivered as the icy water penetrated her clothes. She forced her head above the foam, scanning the area for her boat. She saw it rising and falling in the shadows. She reached out to grab it, but before her hands could grasp it, the current lifted it high, sending the vessel surging past her. In a frenzy, she followed, fighting to retrieve the boat. Then heavy fog swept in and hid it from view.

The waters stirred beneath her, then around her. Suddenly the waterwolf stretched its mighty paw above her, threatening to attack. In the wailing wind, she could almost hear Mrs. Tasman's words of doom. Horror struck her as she remembered the woman's bony finger pointing straight at her in the marketplace, the eerie sound of her hollow voice, her threatening words:

> *"Zevendorp will be destroyed,*
> . . . .
> . . . .*the waterwolf will reign."*

Tremors slithered up Anneke's spine. The blood-curdling cry that had followed Mrs. Tasman's warning seemed to hang in the air.

For a moment, the waterwolf's frothy claw hung suspended above Anneke, then rapidly it drew nearer. In fear, she made a swift turn, struggling to keep from its reach. Glancing over her shoulder, Anneke watched the giant paw sink in the Zuider Zee.

She no longer knew which direction her boat had gone. Turning this way and that in the turbulent sea, she only grew more disoriented. With nothing to cling to, Anneke floundered in the waves.

The waterwolf lifted his paw again. In panic, she watched it descend toward her. She trembled as its icy claws attacked her. Just in time, she pulled herself from its clutches. But again it lunged, its mouth gaping to swallow her. She felt its fangs pull her down—down to the fate of her people.

Chapter

34

Frantically Anneke kicked, struggling to bring her head above water. Her long hair, tangled and drenched, swirled around her on the waves—her pretty cap, gone forever, clutched in the waterwolf's claw. Her arms no longer did her bidding but beat against the tumultuous waves. Again the current pulled her down. Helplessly, she thrust her arms above her head, striking something hard. In the darkness, she grasped it. Was it the rescue boat? She ran her hand along the rim. No, too narrow, and the rim dipped and rose in a pattern, like waves. "Strange boat." Her heart sank.

Clinging to the object, she paddled with her feet, hoping to somehow find the rescue boat. The wind whipped her face, while the waves threatened to wash her under. Her hands grew stiff, her body weak. How much longer could she hold on? Her fingers slipped. She tried to tighten her grip on the smooth wood, but her hands were numb. What was the use of struggling any longer?

The scene of Romke holding the water lily came to her mind. She could almost hear his words. 'Without God, when troubles come, we will drift, wither, and die.'

Yes, she did need a Savior, and she needed Him now!

"Lord, I'm dying!" she cried. "Please save me! Save my soul... my life!"

A sudden noise made her stiffen. She listened, but only the roar of the wind and the crash of the waves filled her ears. She heard it again.

Holding her breath, she waited. A faint whimper broke the silence. It sounded human, like—a baby!

Was she clinging to a cradle? Could a baby be tossing about on these waves, the only survivor of this violent storm? The cries grew steady.

Yes, it was a cradle, with a precious little life inside it! Then she wasn't alone after all. New purpose surged through her. She must save this child.

"God, help me!" Anneke's urgent plea rose above the wail of the infant. As she looked toward heaven, the black clouds parted and the silvery moon shone down, revealing the church steeple extended above the flooded land. She thought back to when she and Romke had been married there. Her eyes stung with tears.

"Oh, Romke, why did it have to end this way?"

She kept her eyes on the shining steeple. It seemed to promise new hope as it stretched toward God, refusing to give in to the raging flood. Then the psalm from Sunday's sermon resounded in her ears: *'God is our refuge and strength, a very present help in trouble. Therefore we will not fear, though the earth be removed, and though the mountains be carried into the midst of the sea; though the waters thereof roar and be troubled.'*

The powerful words flowed over her soul. She fixed her eyes on the steeple while she repeated the words. *"God is our refuge and strength."* Now, could she claim that promise for her own? Was Christ really her Savior and she, God's child? With tears in her eyes, she searched the sky.

The baby's cries grew steadier.

"Oh, God, if you are truly my refuge and strength, please help me find my boat so I can save this little child. I desperately need your help."

She clung tighter to the cradle, refusing to let go, while she watched the moonlight glisten on the steeple. Then something else caught her eye, something bobbing on the waves far ahead.

"The rescue boat! Oh, Lord, please give me the strength to reach it in time."

Clinging to the rim of the cradle, she swam toward the distant vessel. If only she could reach it, she could use the rope to tie the cradle to her rowboat. Closer and closer she came, when suddenly the waterwolf, in its determination to conquer its tiny victim, wrapped its frothy arms around the cradle.

The infant cried louder as though sensing his doom.

"Oh, God! I need Your help, now! Only You are stronger than the sea!"

The waterwolf's claws loosened from the child. The winds died down, the waves lost their power—the waterwolf was held captive.

Anneke trembled at the realization. "Lord, you heard me. You answered my prayer! Forgive me for not knowing that you are a God of love. Oh, my Lord and my Savior, now I know I'm in Your hands."

She swam the last few meters to her boat. Her body shook uncontrollably as she grasped the gunwale. Holding the cradle firmly with one hand, she pulled the rope from her boat, and slipped one end through the cutout heart opening in the headboard of the cradle. Exhausted, she wrapped both ends of the rope several times around her wrist. She tried to steady her craft to climb inside, but her wrists pained from rope burns. Struggling to keep a grasp on the gunwale, she eased herself up and over, and drew in one leg. Her other leg followed easily. At last, she was safe inside.

Her drenched clothes clung to her skin. Cold drops of water slid in streams from her head, down her neck, and seeped through her clothing. Her body shook, and her teeth chattered, but she couldn't stop now. Kneeling, she unwound the rope from her wrist and strung that end through an empty oar ring on one side of her boat. She forced her stiff fingers to tie the bowline knot and make it fast with the stopper knot. With the cradle tied securely to her boat, Anneke could finally relax.

"Oh, Lord, my Savior—my God. Dank U, Dank U wel! You've protected this baby from the jaws of the waterwolf, and you've safely brought me here to rescue this little one." Tears of gratitude filled her eyes.

She remembered the trunk the rescue man had told her of. She opened the clasp and lifted the lid. Inside lay several blankets. She chose a large, thick gray one to wrap around herself and a soft, blue coverlet to replace the soaked one in the cradle. She set them down beside her and searched through the clothes. She found a baby gown and a pile of cloths that could be used for diapers. Next she opened the icebox and retrieved a baby bottle. Now it was her turn to chuckle. Neither she nor the boatman had known that she would indeed need this. She wrapped it in the thick blanket, hoping to lessen the chill of the bottle.

When Anneke raised her head, a beam of moonlight rested on the small form lying in the cradle. The baby kicked until his blanket broke loose. Letters embroidered in blue on the front of his gown spelled out the name *Hans.*

Love welled up in her heart as she bent over him. "So that's who you are, little one." She smiled at him. "Soon, you'll be all warm and dry, Hans." How sweet he looked even though he was crying. She reached over the gunwale, removed his wet blanket, and lifted the frightened infant from the cradle. His eyelids opened wide, and his round, blue eyes, sparkling with tears, rested on her face. His crying ceased, his body calmed, as if he sensed he was safe at last.

She covered her lap with the thick blanket and laid him on top. After removing his wet clothes and drying him off, she replaced his diaper with the clean cloths and dressed him in the fresh gown. How precious he was. She wrapped herself in the large, gray blanket and swaddled Hans in the soft, blue covering.

While cradling him in her arms, she planted a kiss on his chubby cheek, and then touched the nipple of the bottle to his lips. His mouth opened wide and he latched on, his tongue sucking desperately. As she gently rocked him in her arms, she marveled how God had provided everything she needed—a boat, a rope, blankets, clothes, and milk! But most of all, He had made her His child and kept little Hans safe in the palm of His hand. Through this dreadful experience, He had brought her to Himself. She bowed her head in a silent prayer of thanks.

While she sang a lullaby, she touched his tiny hand and watched his fingers curl instinctively around her own. Anneke felt a tug at her heart. She studied his features, and watched his chest rise and fall. How long had this dear baby gone without food? Probably two days, she surmised. He was so new in the world and to have already encountered such an experience. But he would never remember it. In perfect trust, his eyelids closed.

"Poor little child, left without a home and no parents to love and take care of you." Anneke caressed his head, and kissed him on the forehead. How tiny his mouth was, yet he could make his needs known, and God had heard his cries. Then a thought gripped her. Had God sent her here to care for this child—to give him a home—to be his mother?

And this little one, in turn, had kept her from drowning. In awe she realized God had brought them together, each to meet the needs of the other.

Already she loved Hans and felt responsible for him. Yes, God had surely given him to her. But how would she take care of him? She had no home. How would she feed him? She had no means. How would she ever get back to civilization?

Again, helplessness encompassed her. Anneke hugged Hans closer. If God had brought him into her life, wouldn't He also provide for him?

Turning the problem over to the Lord, she laid the thick, warm blanket on the bottom of the boat, then lay down with baby Hans and wrapped the warm, gray blanket over both of them. The steeple still shone in the moonlight, pointing toward God. Gradually the clouds drifted together, until all was dark once more. God's peace filled her heart while the soothing motion of the water lulled both her and the child to sleep.

Chapter

⊙ⱲⱲ⊙

35

Romke hoisted the sails, loosed the moorings, and then steered his boat southwesterly toward the Zuider Zee. When he entered the open sea, the wind surged, lifting his spirits as it carried his boeier along. Still, it would be hours before he reached Zevendorp.

He thought again of Anneke. What sort of vessel was she in, just a small craft being used for a lifeboat? He scanned the water. No other ships were in sight. Loneliness crept over him.

An hour later the water had risen drastically. Farmland lay in soaked fields. Another two hours had gone—and so had the beautiful farmlands, swallowed by the waterwolf, buried in the sea.

Ripe apples, torn from the trees, bobbed on the waves, while others, caught by breakers, were carried off into the deep, never to be relished by the farmers and their families. The waste made his heart ache for the people. Further on, the water rose higher, now leaping and slapping the windowpanes of the homes he passed, while one small cottage lay submerged in the flood. Finally the current grew stronger, pulling him faster, closer to Kollumdijk. Fears gnawed at his heart. Had the marketplace withstood the disaster? Would Zevendorp still be standing? Would he ever find Anneke?

Horror gripped him when he saw the devastation on every hand. Window shutters surged past him on the waves. A kitchen table, legs upturned, bounced about on the breakers. Everywhere, men's caps whirled and tossed on the water. He cringed. Was that all that remained of this beautiful land?

Dusk closed in on him while he sailed on. His hunger reminded him he had eaten nothing since the previous day. Romke reduced speed and reached for his knapsack, removed his canteen, then pulled out the bread and cheese. He remembered the first time he had offered Anneke his bread and cheese at their picnic by the river, and how much she loved it. But now she wasn't here to share it with him. His mouth grew dry. He couldn't eat.

A half hour later, he felt himself growing weak and knew he had better eat. If only she were here, eating with him. He wondered if Anneke had eaten anything today? He knew how much she loved his bread and cheese. He ate only a small portion and saved the rest for her. When he had finished eating, he felt renewed.

Hour after hour passed. The air grew colder and the waves more restless. Now the winds, coming from the stormy west, had picked up speed—whipping his face, flapping his sails, and pitching his boat. On and on the storm raged, hurling gales at his vessel, refusing to give in.

In the darkness, he fought the winds and battled the waves. After adjusting and tightening the sails, he began tacking, taking a zigzag course to defeat the wind by using its power to his benefit. Now he was master of the wind. He thought of the fisherman docked in the harbor at Oostenhaven, his boat virtually beyond repair. Would that happen to him, too, before he could reach Zevendorp?

The morning hour of five drew near but brought no light with it. He searched for the harbor of Kollumdijk, but only the breakers reigned on the horizon, rising and falling with ominous force, lifting the foam and water to cover the tombs of the villagers.

Up ahead the tops of the twin conical towers raised their heads above the waves. The rest of the water gate lay submerged in a tempestuous crypt. The watery graveyard surrounded him, while the eerie call of the wind echoed the cries of the absent villagers, filling him with dread.

An ominous silence settled over the water. Then in the distance, a wail shattered the stillness. A tremor ran up his spine. He held his breath and listened. In the dim light, a soft cry begged to be heard.

Could an infant be alone on the sea—a helpless victim of the raging flood? Now, only a whimper reached his ears, and then, no more. Urgency flooded him. He must reach this child before it was too late.

Another thought haunted him. What if he were too late to find Anneke! What if he never found her! He veered his boat in the direction he had heard the cries.

Then he saw it. A boat in the distance bobbed and thrashed on the sea. His hands clenched the tiller as he headed for the abandoned craft. If he could just reach it before it capsized. Drawing near, he hesitated. What if it were empty, or what if Anneke were...could she possibly be inside—alive? He drew up alongside the boat. Every muscle in his body tensed.

"Noooo! Oh, Anneke!" The agonizing cry tore from his lips. Inside, lay the body of a woman. He'd caught a glimpse of her dress. The same pattern as Anneke's—the one she wore when he first met her in the marketplace here. "No, no, oh, God, no!" His stomach churned.

He leaned over the gunwale and retched, then threw himself down in the boat. "Gone! Gone!" He remembered shouting that same word in his home when Beppie had asked where Anneke was. Then this trip had been in vain! But he knew he would never have been able to live with himself if he hadn't come and searched for her. His body crumpled, convulsed. He buried his head in his arms and wept.

Chapter

36

Romke sat up with a start. The fisherman's words sprang to his mind. "*A beautiful woman. Her eyes were the loveliest shade of blue, and her figure, unsurpassable. But she wasn't dressed like the women of Kollumdijk.*"

"She wasn't dressed like the women of Kollumdijk. Then this can't be her!" New hope filled his being. New strength replenished his body. He forced himself to look more closely at the figure lying in the boat.

He leaned near the corpse then gasped at the contorted face, its features permanently set, pleading silently for help. He could almost hear her screams of fear pulsating in his ears. Or was it just the wind? Wrinkles etched her graying skin, and the hair blown loose from her headpiece matched the dull brown leaves of autumn. Pity stirred in his heart for this unknown woman. Anneke might even have known her. A deep sigh escaped his lips.

But where was the baby? No infant lay in the boat! Had the child been washed overboard? Perhaps he had only imagined the cries. Maybe his nerves were reaching their limit.

An eerie feeling pervaded him. He had to move on. The longer he stayed, the deeper depression would weigh him down. He sailed off, drifting aimlessly, not knowing which direction to take.

Would he ever find Anneke—or had the same fate fallen on her that had happened to the older woman? No, Anneke was young, strong, determined. She would fight to the dea… He caught his breath and shuddered. No! That was not the right word.

He moved along on the lifeless sea. An object thrashed weightless on the water, surging, plummeting, and again, emerging. As it lurched upward, Romke snatched it from the waves with a pole. He sat paralyzed. There in his hand lay a woman's cap, blue with the pattern of delicate white snowflakes. Anneke's! Fear gripped his whole being. Had he come all this way to find only her cap? He remembered how her blue eyes glistened like sapphires when she wore it. Then she, too, had lost the battle with the waterwolf!

"Oh, Anneke!" His painful cry soared above the clamoring sea, only to be swallowed by the pounding waves. "Just when I thought there was hope! Now this! Lord, you promised to be my refuge and strength. If ever I needed you, it's now!"

He felt the Lord's arms encircling him, the comfort of God's peace enveloping him. He could go on—but to where? He scanned the area in all directions. It was useless. He could see nothing. He strained his ears for the slightest sound, but the wailing wind would not be silenced. Helplessness surged over him. "Oh, Lord, if Anneke's here, please help me find her—before it's too late."

The winds calmed. Only a gentle breeze lingered, flittering around his ears, like God whispering words of peace and assurance. On the horizon, the dark clouds parted and morning sunbeams shone through, lighting the church steeple in a soft, golden aura. Romke stared transfixed. It was as if God had turned on His holy light. He thought back to their wedding. Suddenly he felt as though Anneke were with him. Her presence seemed so real. She was here—somewhere. He knew she was.

Far off in the pale light, something rose and fell on the gentle waves. He steered his boeier toward the object. A boat! But would this one be deserted or worse—like all the others? "Oh, God, I just want to find her—alive!" He tried to constrain himself.

Closer and closer he came. Someone lay in the boat. "Lord, not again!" He could feel his stomach churn as he turned his face away. But he had to know for sure. Holding his breath, he drew up alongside the boat. The rising sun shone down on a young woman with long, blond hair. She lay asleep, a baby wrapped in blankets in her arms.

Were his eyes deceiving him or was this really her? He reached out and grabbed the gunwale, pulling the boat close to his.

"Anneke!"

ᑐᗑᗢ

A gentle touch on Anneke's cheek roused her. As she brushed it aside, something caught her hand in a warm clasp. She opened her eyes. There beside her in the boat knelt Romke, love and gratitude shining in his eyes. He leaned down and cradled her in his arms, smothering her with kisses. "Mijn lieveling!"

"Oh, Romke! Is it really you?" She laid the infant down beside her, then reached for Romke and held him tight. "I've wanted you so much. I'm so thankful you came." Her eyes teared as she breathed a silent prayer of thanks to God.

"Romke. . .my family." She choked on her words. "They're gone! All of them!" Sobs wracked her body.

He held her closer to him. "Oh, mijn lieveling, I'm so sorry."

Finding comfort in his arms, she let the tears fall. Moments later, she raised her head. "Romke, how did you ever find me?"

"You should know my dear wife couldn't run away from me that easily." Romke forced a smile, and then grew serious. "I'm just grateful to God that I found you. He heard my cries."

"Romke, can you ever forgive me for what I did to you? I don't deserve your love anymore."

Romke placed a tender kiss on her lips. "I was shocked and heartbroken when I found your note." He turned away and wiped his eyes, then met her gaze again. "I know it wasn't easy for you to stay after all my parents put you through, especially hearing through the closed door their demands for your banishment." He smoothed back her hair with his fingers. "I've come to take you back home, mijn lieveling."

"But your parents, Romke. They won't let me come back."

Romke gathered her closer in his arms. "You are my wife. You're my very life, Anneke. Wherever I live, you will live."

Anneke clung to him. "Will your parents agree to that?"

"They'll have to realize they can't separate us. We are one." He paused and swallowed. "You'll never know how much I regretted leaving for the fields without coming back to you, first. I will never let them send you away again—never. It won't be a perfect environment, and at times it'll still be difficult, but I'll always stand up to them, even if it is against our ways. Perhaps in time, we can build our own house further back on our land. And you'll be the queen of our cottage." He brushed his lips across her forehead.

Tears welled up in her eyes. "Oh, Romke, that would be wonderful." But even as she spoke, she wondered how early they could start construction. Winter was coming soon, so she knew it would have to wait at least until spring. That meant she was destined to live for endless months in the same house with the very ones who had driven her out. Was she ready to return to Lijdendorp and stay with her in-laws? But she no longer had to bear it in her own strength. God's strength would become hers.

"Darling, do you remember when you handed me the water lily and told me that I needed to be joined to the life-giving Stem? Last night I was grafted into that Stem. Christ became my Savior, and I became God's child."

Romke placed his lips on her neck. "Oh, Anneke, I knew He would answer my prayer. Tell me how it happened."

"In the most crucial hour of my life, I remembered the illustration."

Romke listened intently as she relayed her story.

"And then, since I experienced the beautiful truth of the water lily, I could claim God's wonderful promise."

Together they recited the words of comfort. "*God is our refuge and strength, a very present help in trouble. Therefore we will not fear, though the waters roar and be troubled...*"

Romke held her for several minutes in silence. Her neck grew moist as tear after tear fell from his eyes. How wonderful to be in his arms again. Thanking the Lord once more for bringing him back to her, she kissed him again and again. How much safer she felt with him by her side. Yes, she was willing to endure anything as long as Romke was with her.

"Darling, would you like to see this little one who saved my life?"

Romke released her long enough to peer at the sleeping infant. "So this is the little fellow." Romke grew quiet as he caressed the swaddled baby. His eyes misted. "I could never thank God enough for bringing this dear child to keep you from drowning. I'm so grateful, Anneke." He paused and swallowed hard. His voice deepened. "God's love is unfathomable. His ways, unsearchable."

"Yes, darling. And He brought me here to save this baby! Can we keep him—for our own?" Anneke waited for Romke to speak.

He watched the little form lying peacefully asleep, and then drew Anneke back into his arms. "You love him already, don't you, darling?"

"Yes. I could never part with him now."

Romke smiled at her tenderly. "He is our little son. A special gift from God."

"Yes, our own little son," said Anneke.

For the first time, she realized she'd seen this cradle before. An undulating pattern like the waves of the sea was carved around the rim of the cradle—the very cradle she had seen at Jorie's stand in the marketplace! She remembered how she had thought it looked like it belonged on the sea, rather than by a cozy hearth.

She turned to Romke. "This cradle has a story of its own." After sharing it with Romke, she chuckled. "So this cradle *was* destined to rock on the sea, but now it will rock by a hearth."

Romke clasped her hand in his. "Our hearth, mijn lieveling."

She smiled up at him.

A soft whimper broke the silence. Anneke bent over the infant and picked him up. Taking his little hand in hers, she turned toward Romke. "Meet Hans!"

Romke raised an eyebrow. "Hans? How do you know that's his name?"

She reached for his gown, spread out to dry on the icebox with the other wet clothes. "Look, his name's embroidered on his gown."

Romke grinned. "Why, so it is."

Hans began to cry. Anneke cuddled him and fed him the rest of his bottle. She watched Romke tie the rowboat securely to the back of his boeier. "What will we do with the rowboat?"

Romke checked the knot. "We'll return it to the Rescue Squad in Oostenhaven on our way home." After transferring Anneke's valise and Hans's damp clothes to the boeier, he untied the cradle and lifted it onto his boat.

When Hans finished his milk, Anneke placed him against her shoulder and patted his back. She held him close and ran her lips over his soft hair. "The sea couldn't have held a dearer treasure than you, little one." She kissed his forehead, and then handed him to Romke.

Anneke searched through the trunk until she found some sheets to replace the wet ones in the cradle and retrieved a handful of cloths to use for diapers. She remembered the compass and placed it on top of the items in the trunk. The icebox had several more baby bottles full of milk. She added them to the pile laid across her arm. After she found what she needed, Romke helped her into the boeier.

How thankful she was that Hans would have clean, dry sheets to lie on tonight. When she stripped the wet bedding from his cradle, something fell from the sheets. She picked up a pair of miniature wooden shoes dangling from a short leather strap. The *klompen* seemed to clap for joy as they jostled about.

"Romke, Hans has his own toy shoes." She jiggled the strap and the two little shoes clicked and clacked. "They make an interesting rattle, don't they?"

Romke ran his finger over their smooth surface. "They sure do. A real craftsman must have made these." He turned a shoe over. The name "Jorie" was painted in script across the bottom. "Jorie made these. No wonder they're crafted so well. Does the other shoe have Jorie's name on it, too?"

Anneke checked the other shoe and gasped. She moved slightly, letting the sunlight fall on the name. Yes, she had seen it right. The name "Cobie" was painted on the back. She shook it from her hands as though it were a poisonous snake.

She felt the old wounds flare up as Cobie's taunts pierced her heart anew. She wanted nothing more to do with her, but God had placed Cobie's child in her care! She looked at Hans in Romke's arms. He cooed as Romke tickled his ear. How could she refuse a helpless infant—this baby she'd grown to love in so short a time? But could she accept Cobie's child as her own?

She turned back to the cradle. While she smoothed the clean sheets over the mattress and tucked the corners underneath, her mother's words came back to her. "Cobie is a very troubled girl..." Anneke shivered, remembering her own battle just a few hours ago with fear, desertion, and loneliness. Is that how Cobie had felt her whole life—alone, insecure, with no one to turn to? Anneke could almost hear her moeder's voice—*"Forgive her, Anneke."*

Now Anneke could feel Cobie's pain. She thought of the love and mercy God had extended to her last night in the raging sea. How could she not forgive Cobie? Her eyes smarted with tears. If only she could have shared Christ's love with Cobie, but that would never be. A chill ran through her.

She looked up at Romke. He was watching her as though he were following her thoughts. Anneke reached out for Hans, and Romke placed him in her arms. Tears of regret fell on his fuzzy head as she hugged him close to her.

Romke gathered Anneke and Hans in a warm embrace. "What a comfort to know God guides us even through the most difficult times."

"Yes," she whispered. "Because God has led me through these troubled waters, now I can better understand Cobie's desolation." All the hatred she'd felt toward Cobie drifted away. Anneke leaned her head against Romke's chest. Her hand rested on the brooch pinned to her blouse—the brooch he had given her. At last she had found true peace in Christ, the life-giving Stem. She felt as serene as the water lily.

She looked up at Romke, tears of release now filling her eyes. "I've forgiven Cobie. Now, I can love her child as our very own."

The End

GLOSSARY of Dutch Words

Dutch Word	Pronunciation	Definition or Character
Albert Botterman	**Ul**-bert **Bo**-<u>tt</u>er-mahn Long 'o'; '**tt**' more accented	Beppie's brother in college
Anneke Haanstra	**Ah**-nuh-kuh Hahn-strah	The young girl in love with Romke
Anton Veenhuizen	**Ahn**-tone Vain-**how**-sun	Romke's younger brother who's handicapped.
appel taart	**Ah**-puhl-tahrt	apple tart
Ard	Art	The captain's son on the barge
Assepoester	Ah-seh-**post**-er	Cinderella
Beppie Botterman	**Bep**-pea Bo-<u>tt</u>er-mahn Long 'o'; '**tt**' more accented	Anneke's dear friend in Lijdendorp and Albert's sister
boeier	**boo**-yuhr	a small yacht
broeder	**broo**-der	brother
chocolade melk	sho-ko-**lah**-duh melk	chocolate milk
Cobie Tasman	**Ko**-bee **Tahs**-mahn	A troubled, jealous young girl in Anneke's village
Dank U	**Dahnk**-oo	Thank you
Dank U wel	**Dahnk**-oo-vel	Thank you very much (formal)

Dutch Word	Pronunciation	Definition or Character
Dionysius / Dion	Dee-o-**nis**-ee-us / **Dee**-on	Mrs. Tasman's missing husband
dorp	dorp	village
The "G" sound is gutteral / spoken from the throat		
Geertje	Gaar-chu	The tall, thin, and plain girl: friends with Beppie and Wietske
Gelderland	**Gel**-der-lunt	Anneke's province
guilder	**gil**-der	A Dutch coin
Hans	Hahns	Baby, found in the sea
Haanstra	**Hahn**-strah	Anneke's and Kea's last name
ja	yah	yes
Jaap	Yahp	College friend of Albert's, and in love with Beppie
Jorie	**Yor**-ee	Wooden-shoe maker in love with Cobie
Kea	**Kay**-ah	Anneke's feisty, younger sister
klets koekjes	**klets kook**-yuhs	splash cookies
Klompen	**klom**-puhn	wooden shoes
Kollumdijk	**Kol**-luhm-dike	Town with marketplace near Anneke's village
Kraplap	**Krahp**-lahp	A bib-like vest worn by the women
Lambertus	Lahm-**bair**-tuhs	Anneke and Kea's young mischievous cousin
Lijdendorp	**Lie**-duhn-dorp	Romke's village "Village of Sorrows"

Dutch Word	Pronunciation	Definition or Character
makronen	mah-**kro**-nuhn	macaroons
Mejuffrouw	muh-**yuh**-frouw	Miss / my young miss
Meneer	muh-**near**	Mr. / sir / gentleman
Mevrouw	muh-**frouw**	madam / my missus
mijn lieveling	mine **lee**-vuh-ling	my love
Moeder	**Moo**-duhr	Mother (Mrs. Haanstra) Anneke & Kea's mother
Mr. & Mrs. Haanstra	**Hahn**-strah	Anneke & Kea's loving parents
Mr. Tasman	**Tahs**-mahn	Cobie's missing father
Mrs. Tasman	**Tahs**-mahn	Cobie's mentally unbalanced mother
Mr. & Mrs. Veenhuizen	Vain-**houw**-sun	Romke's strict, cold, & mean spirited parents
nee	nay	no
Oostenhaven	**O**-stuhn-**Hah**-vuhn	East Haven
Oostelijk River	**O**-stuh-like ruh-**veer**	Eastern River
oorijzer	**Oar**-i-zer	Metal headpiece women wore beneath their cap
Overijssel	**O**-vuhr-**I**-suhl	Romke's province
Poffertjes	**Po**-ffer-ches	miniature pancakes
Romke Veenhuizen	**Rom**-kuh (R is trilled)	Young man in love with Anneke
Slagroomtaart	**Slahg**-rome-tart	Whipped cream tart
Stroop koekjes	**Strope Kook**-yuhs	Cookies made with molasses or fruit syrup
tule	**Tu**-luh	A thin, fine netting of silk, rayon, nylon, etc.

Dutch Word	Pronunciation	Definition or Character
Vader	**Vah**-duhr	Father (Anneke and Kea's father)
Waterwolf	**Waah**-ter-wolf	The raging sea
Wietske	**Veet-skuh**	A hostile, young girl in Lijdendorp who's interested in Romke
Zevendorp	**Zay**-vuhn--dorp	Anneke's village
Zuider Zee / Zuiderzee	**Zouw**-duhr-**Zay**	Southern Sea
Zwartland	**Zwart-l**ahnt	Black land